_____ Death and divorce have shattered the families of Bridget and her friend Dylan. The two teenagers move numbly through the wreckage of their once happy lives. Desperate to find a world in which others cannot hurt them, they finally run away—not to a big city, but to a mountain wilderness in northern California. There they plan to live peacefully off the land as the Indians once did.

But living off the land turns out to be incredibly difficult. Bridget and Dylan must learn to hunt and kill their own food—or else starve. And even in the wilderness other people still intrude. Like the last Indians who lived in the area, the two teenagers retreat farther and farther into the mountains, searching for a place where they can be alone.

Slowly, painfully, and sometimes humorously, Bridget and Dylan learn how to survive in the wild. And slowly they begin to come back to life emotionally . . . to confront their unhappy past and make new decisions about the future.

Dennis J. Reader has written a spellbinding novel that pulls us into the mountains with Bridget and Dylan and compels us to experience the beauty and terror of their days.

Coming Back Alive

Coming
Back
Alive

_____ **by Dennis J. Reader**

Random House 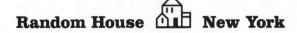 **New York**

Copyright © 1981 by Dennis J. Reader

All rights reserved under International and Pan-American Copyright Conventions.
Published in the United States by Random House, Inc., New York, and
simultaneously in Canada by Random House of Canada Limited, Toronto.

Library of Congress Cataloging in Publication Data:

Reader, Dennis J
    Coming back alive.
    SUMMARY: Two teenagers, both recently devastated by personal tragedy, abandon
civilization for the isolated mountains of northern California, where they hope
to survive on their own.
    [1. Survival—Fiction. 2. California—Fiction. 3. Friendship—Fiction]
I. Title.   PZ7.R23525Co   [Fic]   79–5147

ISBN: 0–394–84359–2 (trade); 0–394–94359–7 (lib. bdg.)
Manufactured in the United States of America   1   2   3   4   5   6   7   8   9   0

———————— *To* DALE AND MARGARET READER,
parents appreciated

CONTENTS

Coming Back
Alive

ONE

Us

i _____ Bridget is my name. I am a survivor.

Learning that particular job takes some doing, and for the education I thank my particular friend, my Dylan. (Dylan Lander. I envy that name. Too pretty to squander on a boy, isn't it?) I once saw Dylan's mother and father standing in a school corridor, nose-to-nose, temper-to-temper, hurling voice bombs at each other. It amounted to a very sick scene, and in fact they gave up the ghost of holy matrimony a few months later. There stood Dylan in the corridor, right by them, his scorched face fading to pale pink, paler pink, eventually to white—and I mean like paper white. But by that late date he had become war-wise, and Dylan never oozed a tear, and he didn't slump, didn't even hang his head. This was before I knew the bad times and the sad times myself, and how handy it could be to have some toughness put away in your pocket.

We both were born and raised brotherless and sisterless in SuperSuburbs, America, or in this case the sweet expensive foothills of the East Bay, across the water from San Francisco. His father wore a tie and made lots of money. My father wore a tie and made lots of money, maybe even more. His mother was copper-haired beautiful and *Vogue* sleek and my mother was

3

ebony-haired beautiful and *Vogue* sleek. I loved my folks, still
do, and I was happy—being happy came easy. Yessir, while I
had it, I really did have it. Dylan loved his folks, once. I
wouldn't wager big money, but I expect he loves them yet,
although when they went off the edge, of course he got pulled
over with them, and a *long* ways down. "I throw up about
twice a night," he matter-of-factly confessed to me one
peaceful July afternoon. Such news jolted me because, as I say,
this was before I myself had been hit by those cold winds that
can blow on you, freezing you down to nothing. Even the East
Bay foothills don't block out those winds.

And the two of us, I can see now, became just what our
parents hoped us to be. Clever rascals, for instance, top stuff at
school? You betcha, with a row of report-card A's and smiling
teachers trailing to infinity behind us, applauding. Handsome
young things, too? Well, why yes, since you ask—so
everybody said. Bridget: pure black hair combed to the waist,
toothpaste-ad teeth, tallish, a graceful walker. A regular
budding beauty, if you get the picture. Dylan: on the blocky
side, with a strong broad back, strong broad face, always
muscular for his age, but with Hollywood eyelashes so full of
curl that it seemed (like his Hollywood name) a shame some
girl didn't have them instead. You could argue whether his
hair was brown with red tints, or actually auburn.

Once upon a time, when he cared to, Dylan had been a slick
athlete, and earlier still, photographs testify, a model Boy
Scout in a tidy, yellow-kerchiefed uniform. I had my own
talents. Besides being promising at ballet, I considered myself
something of a poet. This condition was caused by early
contact with the great Henry David Thoreau, who infected me
with the pleasures of mixing nature and words, and which led
to my writing reams of nature description, even to this day.

Look back at the two of us, Dylan and me. A Boy Scout-athlete and a ballerina-poet! My god, that tells it all.

So what happened, what is it that sends the cold winds and aims the ice?

For Dylan, anyway, it went something like this: "Do your folks ever act like they still love each other?" He asked me that question after school once, and when I answered "Sure," he wanted to know, precisely, how I could say *sure*. "They tell it to each other," I gave as my proof, "and they kiss." "They do? No exaggeration, no bull now, they do?" "Sure they do," I said.

Later that same year, early in our summer vacation, during one of his almost daily visits to my house, Dylan asked me another question, about the worst things I could remember my mother and father calling one another. What I remembered didn't impress Dylan. He said, "How about 'bastard'? Or 'bitch'?" Naturally, that showed me what was happening in his family. A little later yet, when he passed along to me that news of his nightly vomiting, I asked him what was stirring up such trouble between his parents. Understand I wasn't being nosey, because I knew he came over to my place to get out of his, and I knew he wanted to talk with somebody, and besides, we had been closest friends and fellow-confessors since second grade. Everyone back then—the teachers, our parents, all the adults—thought it was "cute" for a boy and girl of our age to be buddies. You see, during the second grade, after a year or two of jostling to decide who would be crowned leader of our class, a tiny all-A's emperor or a tiny all-A's empress, we settled instead on the notion of an alliance. We discussed it, in our seven-year-old way. From that moment on we had a special friendship (for lack of a better word) and as time went by we just talked more and more and more. We began being the brother and sister that each of us never had. So I became the one who on a certain eventual afternoon heard about the throwing up, and I was the one who asked, "Why are they fighting like this?"

"Love fizzles out," Dylan said, "and I suppose when love stops, nothing's left but to start to fight. Could be they never had any love to begin with, really. Now my father has a girlfriend. That's right, can you believe it? A girlfriend, my father. Claims he loves *her* now."

Mr. Lander and a *girlfriend?* I was horrified/fascinated by the thought. "Are your folks getting a divorce, then?" I wondered aloud, but softly, afraid that saying it could be bad luck.

"My father wants to, but my mother's too mad. She won't let him have anything he wants even though she wants it herself."

"Maybe she does still love him."

"No," he said, very definite. "They just shout a lot. That's what they do." He repeated, "Bridget, they shout."

As grim as this spectacle sounded to me, his home life apparently took a nosedive from there, since late in the summer he mentioned the pills. "I actually had the things in my hand," he told me, "about two dozen. Pinkish small jobs."

Being the naïve Bridget that I was, I was confused at first. "Well, what were they for?"

"Tranquilizers—sleeping pills—my mother's."

"But two dozen?"

He looked at me, square on, his eyes showing a dull misery. His face seemed to be sagging with weariness or sudden old age. I wanted to swallow, except there was nothing wet in my mouth. Glancing down, I saw that my fingers had a white-knuckle clamp on his arm, the nails gouging his skin. It must have hurt, although he never flinched. "I wanted to know," he said, "how I would feel with the pills in the palm of my hand. I had no plans after that, Bridget. But for the first time in my life I said to myself, 'Hey, you can remove Dylan. End him. How about it?' It wasn't a pretend question."

When I recovered my voice, I dug my nails in deeper and made him swear never to raise that question again. I was scared and unashamed to beg. "Please, promise. Don't do this to me, Dylan, please." He did promise, and I sighed with relief, because Dylan is a strict Puritan with his promises. After I settled down some more, I had to ask, "What the heck did your father and mother do to you?"

"Not to me, so much," he said. "To each other, god, yes."

"What? What?"

An unusual hesitation stalled him. Finally he answered, "I've heard of shooting with guns, but not of sending bullets with your own bodies."

A riddle. And I couldn't interpret then what he meant—his parents were maybe punching with fists now instead of words? I understood, however, that there was some mystery, something so bad, bleak, that Dylan was keeping it from me, or couldn't say it, and either way that was rare between us. His sadness is what sliced into me. While I did feel sorry for Dylan's parents—after all, I had spent lots of hours with them—their troubles seemed unreal, like I was watching a soap opera. Dylan, though, was and always will be flesh and blood to me. I'll admit to you my own secret, one I mostly kept from him: in those years since second grade Dylan had become something more to me than my buddy.

At the finish of that long summer, Dylan disappeared for a spell. When I saw him again, about school time, he was carrying himself inside a special shell, which you could practically see glinting around him like a hard layer of transparent plastic. Call it protection. Toughness. He was braced for *any*thing. Prepared, for instance, to stand in a busy school hallway while his mother shouted that his father stunk, and his father broadcasted that his mother didn't deserve to hold on to her son.

Anyway, if tough shells were in, at least pills were out. That's how the story went for Dylan.

ii _____ What exactly aims those icy winds at us? Believe me, that question has chewed me hollow. I think the answer is that sometimes there's no answer. A lot of different bits, nothings, simply roll together, willy-nilly-silly, and cause something big to happen.

For example, imagine a late March day. Let us suppose it's the twenty-sixth of March, during the spring that Dylan's folks finally got their divorce. The usual California sun comes up that morning, warm without any of summer's heat. At the back of an East Bay house, and over along a ridge, the eucalyptus and oaks idly stir their stiff leaves, the way they always have. A few thin clouds sit glued, stuck, in one far corner of the blue sky. The day looks like March 25th was and like March 27th is going to be. Hours drowse contentedly by, even inside stuffy classrooms. Eventually, as expected, shadows point themselves eastward, the blue sky gracefully purples—a little like this prose.

Okay. At this moment—on this same March 26th—a man in Richmond, California, with initials F. W. (let us suppose) steps from his apartment and gets into his mustard-colored Dodge pickup. Back inside on the kitchen table, let us *suppose*, stands a freshly emptied pint of Jim Beam, 80 proof. He fumbles the pickup keys and starts the engine no sooner or later than he does. He backs out, turns left, then right, not right then left. He stops at one red light and goes through two green, not two red and one green or three red or three green or any other sequence. He slows here. He speeds up there. He takes the highway down the bay to Berkeley. Twilight dwindles closer to night, but his headlights don't come on, let us *suppose.* At El Capitan Avenue he exits the highway, winds through town, gets stalled now and then (not then and now) in the evening traffic, pulls onto the four lanes of Foothill Parkway, heads toward Bridget's suburb. He accelerates along the passing lane, facing car after car from the opposite direction, dozens and dozens of cars, and then, just past a giant floodlighted sign that advertises a Reno hotel, just at 7:17 P.M., just with the speedometer at 70, he crosses the divider line and kills himself and the two occupants of a late-model Buick Electra, license RMJ 638. Let us suppose.

Ridiculous, right?

iii _____ I'm too tired, too frazzled, to explain any more of this.

All right, okay. I can finish it. Besides, now you already know the rest. You can see another tale of an adolescent's woe coming, possibly more woeful than usual.

When the black-and-white patrol car pulled up into our driveway that night, I peered out the window more curious than concerned. Although the clock showed almost nine, my folks weren't late, and I had enough calm to bookmark my Fitzgerald novel before answering the door. Page 86. My memory refuses to dump the strangest details.

The highway patrolman, poor man, hardly expected to find only a girl in the house. Nervously, he shifted his bluish bulk from foot to foot. Were there other children in the family? No. Any relatives who lived here? No. Nearby? No. Nobody? No.

A coldness began at the ends of my body—toes, feet, fingers, hands, ears, face—and it moved colder and faster into my arms, legs, back. *Cold, cold.* "What—" I tried to ask, but my tongue garbled that, and quit altogether. The air froze in my lungs. My entire body was freezing away, numb, faint, even sleepy. I began shivering.

The patrolman opened his mouth, slowly, slowly, taking minutes just to separate his lips, and out came the polar wind that my shivering skin already knew about. It was loose in the room. My eyes asked, Please, stop, I'm not old enough or strong enough for this cold—please stop. His eyes pleaded back for forgiveness. He held himself up by his uniform, half-strangled himself, and spoke his duty. The wind stormed.

The highway patrolman must have fetched our—now *my?*—next-door neighbors and later someone's minister came wandering through, and after midnight they finally called my mother's sister in Santa Barbara, who departed the same night to drive up and stay with the new orphan. Despite memorizing page number 86 and tons of other trivia, I can't recall any exact expression from those faces—except they were all uncomfortable—or any exact word of the pity, the sympathy that they used in an attempt to rescue me. How can anyone thaw and save a completely frozen ballerina?

Their faces, their words, I didn't want inside our home. They didn't belong, with everything about them sounding or poking up out of place, and I shut them off, WHAM. You realize my feelings. You know who I wanted to hear and see. This house, this actual breathing life of mine, had been made, *made,* by two who weren't here, but who had always been here before. I didn't believe that this house or my life could go on without my parents. And if I could somehow go on, it would be shameful. My head was so scrambled, I couldn't pick out even a little end of mental thread to unravel and begin thinking. There existed no up or down or right or left, no direction. It's a scary feeling, because no place is no place to be.

My mind panicked. It tried to find its balance: spinning, spinning, looking for a horizon, a path, a sign, an anything. I went to my bed, turned out the light, abandoning the neighbors downstairs where they could gossip in peace about what would become of pathetic Bridget. But when my head finally stopped spinning, it damned me. The only focus it managed to find was in making movies of our Buick, which I had been inside only that afternoon. The car moved down a highway (I knew none of the true specifics yet) when, zoom, a gigantic long-snouted semi came looming up, a snorting mechanical monster, and bashed our familiar grill and hood backward into the engine, with the whole mess a clenched fist being punched into the front seat.

Then the car reconstructed itself and began another trip, another version. This time the truck, breathing dragon smoke from its diesel pipes, pulverized the car from the side, shooting out a spray of shiny glass chunks. My Buick put itself together again, like those scattered gay pieces of a kaleidoscope that fall back into a shape. Now on another run the car was hit, flipped twice, landed on its top, got crushed so flat that the doors and windows winked shut and vanished. Next there I sat inside the car myself, with the usual upholstery smells and humming motor. A red/white/blue schoolbook titled *Cavalcade of U.S. History* had been left on the rear seat (ultimately the car's sole survivor). Here sped the monster truck once more, after jumping up from nowhere like a terror, its immense chrome front coming right through the windshield, jolting to a vicious halt all motion and light. Still again, on another ride, I found myself tossed over in the air, inside the car, hearing metal and bone snap. I invented a total of fifteen or twenty versions. And then my head, which had been substituting driblets of detail in place of total accuracy, grasped that I wasn't by myself in the car.

I couldn't stop my mind: the movies of my mother and father switched on and I stared.

Do you have the steel stomach for this? She was wearing her lemon-yellow linen dress, while he had on the smooth charcoal blazer, a favorite of his and mine. On impact those immaculate clothes twisted like throwaway rags. (Christ. I had to ask myself, where were the clothes now—on or off their bodies? If off, would the hospital or mortuary ever send them back here, wadded up in a plastic bag?) Blotches of blood soaked through the charcoal and lemon. I watched my parents' necks, arms, legs break when the car got hit, as it whirled and whipped them around in their seats and seatbelts, its tires squealing. I watched their faces slashed by glass, skin pared away like apple peelings. I watched my mother's black shimmering hair and her pearl-toned complexion—the source of my own black hair and white skin—film over with a solid sheet of red. I watched my father's large dark eyes in his slender face—my own face and eyes—get squeezed pulpy.

Ugly, I know, I know, but I couldn't turn it off—my own mind. I saw my mother and father being broken into parts, gushing blood, mutilated, their heads cut clean away. Stumps. Dangling arteries and veins. Mangled meat. I saw them so torn and smashed they were not recognizable, hardly human. In point of fact, I never would truly see my folks again, not even at the funeral, since the coffins were kept closed. What I saw in my head must have been mainly right.

The peculiar part is I *wanted* to see all that ugly gore. The uglier the better, because I wanted to punish my own hurt. Have you ever done that to yourself, or seen some run-over animal bite itself, crazy with fear and agony? I wanted those bloody scenes to bring their bloody whip down on Bridget, split open her flesh clear to her skeleton—her punishment for being alive. Oh, I wanted more than anything else, and I begged, to die in that crash, for the Magic Man to rewind his tape machine and let me leap into the car before he sent it forward again. I wanted to bleed away and have our family slate wiped perfectly blank. If that wish failed, then I wanted the pain never to stop and the night never, never to end.

But outside, dawn had started to seep into the sky. March 27th. A new horror slammed down on me: the sun was coming. The normal business was going to keep on, the sun, the people, as if nothing much had changed, except it damn well had changed, with my parents obliterated and me here waiting alone for this day and for every future day. Alone. I had gotten left behind. As I looked out at the brightening dawn, a sick surge forced upward in my gullet, and while I expected to splash vomit against my bedroom window, I shook instead with hot, bitter, empty retches.

"I throw up about twice a night": so Dylan had said. I remembered that, and him. I remembered and at last I *heard*, absolutely, his meaning. For now I knew, World, what the bad times were, because the bad times were here. And Bridget could find no toughness down in her pocket. And Bridget cried.

TWO
House and Home

i ———————————— Houses can talk, I soon found. Every word ever spoken inside had gotten soaked up by the walls and furniture, by the drapes and carpets, and all I had to do was meander through the house and the voices would call out again. Every conversation my mother and father ever had, together or with me, waited its turn to be heard. The entire house murmured and buzzed as if wasps were swarming behind the woodwork.

I listened. Sure, I realized there were no bodies to go with the voices, and I knew the voices would only make me sit down and blubber. Still I needed to listen. Those voices and that house were the sum total of Bridget and must not be let go of, or I would get subtracted down to zero, zilch, nothing. So I made my pilgrimage from room to room, from the living room, where we always put up a fancy Christmas tree and where I could still hear Christmas carols being sung joyfully off-key, to the kitchen, where in recent years we had jointly made breakfast and discussed our various plans for the coming day amid the smells of toast and coffee.

The real killer was my parents' bedroom, and I suppose I went there the most. Throughout my life I had gone to that bedroom, the way a kid will do when she's skitterish at night or when she wants to wake everybody up on a Sunday morning or when she wants to enter her folks' private realm for a private talk herself, or maybe just wants to sneak in and try on her mother's jewelry, especially the matched-pearl necklace. All of it was there yet, each piece, including the necklace, including their bed unruffled and untouched— waiting for sleepers. I fingered through the closets, because the clothes were waiting too (it struck me) for their owners to hurry and wear them. Touching those dresses and coats and shirts was almost like . . . well, you know. The rows of shoes, with toes warping, made the most forlorn appearance. A shoe without a foot, getting dusty in a closet, is a lonesome critter.

I sat down a lot and I blubbered a lot. Then I shuffled softly through the rooms of my dear shrine, before sitting down and blubbering some more. One week had gone by since the funeral and I had yet to take another step outside the door. No fooling. And I had no intention of stepping outside the door again whatsoever, one week or one year in the future. Outside there were only people who would either waltz merrily by, innocent of Bridget's suffering, or who would whisper and stare: "She's the one. Did you hear?" "Look, there, that girl. Did you read?" "No, *really?*" "Yes, indeed, oh indeed." "Terrible." "Horrible." "My-my-my." "Can you imagine?" Mumble, mumble. And as for returning to school, that would be like swallowing broken light bulbs. Impossible. Impossible for me, anyway. The notion of sitting in a classroom now and studying the sex habits of trees, or why England blew it in America . . . how *paralyzing*. Why pretend that such stuff could matter to me anymore. Impossible, don't you see? Hey kids, Bridget La Freaka—over there—returns. Notice how she dreams off into space, and yesterday, when asked in class about cross-pollination, she actually blubbered.

I could figure no purpose in making my old friends uncomfortable, and in making me the school leper, spreading gloom and gossip wherever I passed. They were better off without Bridget, Bridget without them. It came out an even trade: I wouldn't step on their fun; they wouldn't step on my misery. A fair exchange. Some other time they could learn about icy winds themselves. Meanwhile my proper place was inside my house.

Of course I didn't live by myself in the house, because my aunt Charlene had arrived from Santa Barbara the day after the accident, and she stayed with me, my solitary relative and—it would develop—my legal guardian. She had Bridget whether she wanted Bridget or not. Plop, directly into her middle-aged lap.

On March 27th Charlene had come wobbling through the front door, banging it with her suitcase, and she had the nerve to be blubbering herself, which irked me, I don't mind telling you. She only saw my mother about once a year.

"We mustn't cry, we mustn't, my Dear, oh my Dear," she said immediately, guaranteeing that I would.

My earliest memories of Charlene all centered around candy. She always smelled like a candy store, and it therefore followed that she might be worth a sample bite. Shortly after taking the sample I learned the difference between candy and perfume. Here she was again, hugging me inside the same tasty aroma, exquisitely dressed (she had a sharp eye for fashion) and still an attractive woman, despite a new borderline case of the chubbies. Certainly she had the looks, and even the money—courtesy of my grandfather, who exited life before I was born—to have been married fifty times over. She never had been, I suspect because being married to someone would represent endless bother, years full of discussions and decisions, and a battle to keep the house neat. I consider neatness a virtue of my own, and I once had renown for brushed hair and smudgeless school papers. But with Charlene I'm talking *neatness*. For her, passion meant a room ready to be photographed for the cover of *House Wonderful*. Dust becomes important when you don't have people around to worry about.

Now Charlene found herself with plenty to fret over, bet on it, and that could partly explain why she came in crying and half in shock. Here she had her life laid out in neat stepping-stones ahead of her when—*bingo!*—she wins the prize and gets to be mother and father and spiritual leader to a broken-down teenage kid. Bad bargain, I'll admit. I'll also admit that Bridget never welcomed her with open arms, or with closed arms. Charlene's looks may have somewhat resembled her sister's, my mother, but Bridget desired no substitutes and absolutely no imitations, thank you.

She did come prepared to give it the good try. Each day, early, she worked at parenting with the same energy and concentration that she used when applying furniture wax to my father's walnut desk. Each evening, relentless, she pressed onward until Bridget was shoehorned safely into bed. Busyness itself seemed to be a key stratagem of hers. "Dear," she would say, "would you vacuum the carpets today?" The carpets were already so clean they squeaked. Or, "I wish you would help me with the grocery list. You don't eat anything I fix, my Baby." She knew why I lacked an appetite. Her plan behind this full schedule of activities was clear:

Keep a girl busy, every single day,
And dead parents might be forgotten that way.

Charlene, you miss the whole point, I felt like informing her. Bridget needs to remember and to hang on, not to let go. To let go is to become lost. To forget is sacrilege.

Charlene pushed onward with her good intentions, too far along in her life and manners ever to become spontaneous at her mothering and fathering. She found herself, abruptly, at the controls of a 727 jet airliner, the pilots dead, and while in desperation she flipped pages in the flight manual, she smiled bravely at the one bug-eyed passenger, saying, "Sweep out the cabin, would you, my Baby?"

Along with my chores I received the benefit of little lectures and big clichés. Rise and shine. Early bird gets the worm. (Excellent excuse for staying in bed, no?) Food is fuel—fill up, fill up. Study, my Dear, that's the ticket: your mother was such a wonderful, wonderful student, like you, and how proud we were of her, Phi Beta Kappa, you know: you look so like her, with your hair that way: I'll expect Bridget, my Baby, to be Phi Beta Kappa one day herself, and it'll come true if you stick with your studies: smart, and attractive on top of that, my, how fortunate you are when we stop to think about it, really.

Apparently down in Santa Barbara Charlene never received the news that I had some more birthdays after my seventh one, and she forever called me "Baby" or "Dear," which I couldn't muster the strength to protest, or to discourage with a scowl. We did cross purposes, however, after that first week, when she got unsettled over my violent disinterest in school and, to boot, my showing no signs of ever intending to open the front door and step out.

"Today we go shopping," she announced hopefully one morning.

I simply shook my head—a no-nonsense shake.

Charlene clucked her tongue, fussing at length in her uncluttered purse. Later, she was chatting about the virtues of spring sunshine and asked in the same breath, "School on Monday?"

Another shake of my head.

"Is Monday a holiday, then?" she asked, all innocence.

"No."

"But my Dear . . ."

She waited for an explanation. We both waited.

Finally I said, "My own home is where I belong."

ii _____ Late the next week the doorbell rang, and Charlene let in a stranger, a tall woman who smiled solemnly at me. I unsmiled in return.

"Bridget," began Charlene, "this is Mrs. Pace, from school. I spoke with her on the telephone and she felt that . . . that it might be a good idea if she had a talk . . . a conversation with you . . . and she kindly . . . sit there on the sofa please, Mrs. Pace. Well. I'll tend to fixing lunch while you two . . . go ahead."

With that Charlene weaseled out of the room. Thank you, Charlene. Bless you.

Mrs. Pace smiled again, solemnly again. "I'm a psychologist, Bridget, a counselor at the school. My, but you have a marvelous academic record—I read through your files yesterday. Marvelous."

I sat as upright as a ballerina can possibly sit, which is ramrod straight, believe me.

Mrs. Pace sighed comfortingly and smiled a very solemn, very friendly, very intimate, very professional smile. "We've had some sad times lately, haven't we," she said. "I understand how you feel, Bridget. You have my complete sympathy, my complete understanding."

I felt myself coming unglued at the edges. How I wanted, needed, some toughness to hold me together, to keep sitting straight, and say: *We've* had sad times? *You* understand how *I* feel? You claim that to my face? Lady, did a highway patrolman come to your door when you were a kid?

"Your aunt has gotten quite, quite concerned about you, Bridget. She might not have let you see that concern, but she has it, feels it, as we all do. We all care about you and what happens to you." Mrs. Pace tilted toward me, across the sofa. Around her eyes and mouth sprouted permanent patches of worry lines, combat scars from the counseling business, no doubt. I heard her stomach rumble. She said, "Your aunt tells me that you haven't once left the house, other than for the funeral. Is that correct, Bridget?"

Bridget was dissolving.

"She tells me that you mope here and cry and cry."

Yes, lady, that's right. She told you right.

"You make *her* want to cry, Bridget, just watching you this way. We know how you're suffering, sweetie, and we both wish very much to help you, and the first step, listen sweetie, is to spend part of your day outside with other people. Your classmates and your friends miss you. Here's what we'll do. Listen carefully. Now on Monday you get yourself dressed in your prettiest clothes and go to your regular classes. Try to make it a normal day. Don't bother about make-up work. I've already spoken to your teachers and they will see that your return is as easy for you as can be managed. Now, listen, sweetie, instead of going to your physical education class you'll come to my office—take this slip of paper with the room number on it. Come every day. I intend for us to become friends, too. We need to have lots of long talks together, to get all the turmoil you have bottled inside brought up and thrown out, out, out and away." She made a little baseball pitch. "You're a bright girl, and you comprehend what I'm saying. I have some books for you to read that candidly, openly, cover the subject of death, and I believe, Bridget, they can give you a hand in adjusting back. Now then. The two of us together, and your aunt, can pull you through these bad times, but you're the most important one. You have to start forgetting. Today."

Bridget, sorry to say, was blubbering.

They had me walking the pirate's plank, and Monday morning, in my prettiest, I slipped out into the naked sunlight, blinking and inching my way downhill toward the bus stop. Trees, house windows, mailboxes, flying birds, all gawked at me. The early sky opened wide with surprise at my appearance. Here she comes, World!

At the bottom of the hill, I could look on down the curving street and see a knot of kids waiting in the distance. The same old crew at the same corner: Timothy Hardle, who one Halloween had put a lighted jack-o'-lantern atop our roof; Bobby Meyers, known crudely behind his back as "Zits"; Tami Thompson, famous for reaching puberty when the rest of us girls were still struggling to master cursive writing; Marla Smolt, who had a severe interest in Timothy Hardle; Mark Irving, who had a severe interest in Marla Smolt, and who customarily gave her M&M candy handouts, hopeful that she would make the Mark&Marla connection.

As usual, they were scuffling around, horsing off—typical All-American teenage stuff. My feet slowed from slow to slower. I heard the roar of the approaching bus and asked myself for mercy. While the bus halted, picked up the kids, and continued on its route, Bridget skulked behind a clump of oleanders. Sorry, Charlene. Apologies, Mrs. Pace.

The street quieted for the moment. Where to, what to, now? If I couldn't go back, still there was no going ahead.

"This is a first for you, isn't it?" came a deep voice from immediately behind me.

I jumped, and landed facing the other direction—almost, anyhow. There sat Dylan, on a stack of school books, peering up at me.

"How long have you been there?" I demanded, touchy at being caught skulking, or at being out-skulked.

"Long enough to see the whole show." He rapidly blinked those Hollywood eyelashes, but the eyes and his wide face remained expressionless. "I wanted to find out whether you would or wouldn't get on the bus. My money was on would. So already today you've cost me cold cash, plus the shame of failure."

"Failure builds character," I said, sitting on my own books.

"It *is* a first for you, isn't it? Your first gen-u-wyne cut?"

"You know it is." I suffered an instinctive pang of guilt.

"An act of truancy, an act of treason, practically," Dylan said with suitable melodrama. "This is a historical day for you, Bridget. Historical."

We had played these needling games often, although we never called them games, and they really weren't, come to think about it, not regular play at least. It was a special method we had for dealing with a sticky subject. I said, "Bridget finally becomes a sinner."

"Don't belittle this, Bridget," he said, "until you learn the consequences. Remember my uncle from Florida? No? He was a hard-working guy, conscientious and honest—like you —but one morning he showed up five minutes late at his job."

"Oh-oh. Here comes Parable Time."

Dylan possesses a fantastic storehouse of pithy stories and parables and, I swear, he can cook one up while crossing the street or tying his shoe. Maybe he lies awake nights getting them ready. Whenever he took a certain full breath and raised his eyes, I'd say: "Parable Time." Sure enough, out would come a zinger. He has an impressive talent for it.

"So what kind of job did this uncle have?" I asked.

"No matter what kind. He just showed up five minutes late, and that surprised him, you better believe. He'd never been late before, not once for one minute."

"What a coincidence. Like me all right."

"He didn't get too upset. One time out of an entire lifetime was darn good. But then the next morning—guess what?—he shows up five minutes late again. Now while once in a lifetime is respectable, two times late is getting worse, which suggested to him that he had gotten trapped on the downhill road to plain *bad,* period. Well, the following morning he gobbles breakfast, doesn't even brush his teeth, another first for him, and still, doggone it, arrives late. His boss squints at him. Squint. A what's-going-on-here-Herman sort of squint. Herman was my uncle's name. He began realizing how hard it can be to scramble back to your old self."

"The first slip leads to the big fall."

"Almost my uncle's own words. And as much as he tried, never again did he make it to work on time. Never—not even when he took to getting up out of bed in the middle of the night. Not even when he didn't go to bed at all. The only thing he eventually got to, early, was his grave."

I said, "My hunch is, first, that you don't have an uncle in Florida. Second, that you probably don't have this uncle anywhere."

"I don't?"

"But your message to Bridget is to hurry herself right down to school before she slips into the big bad fall," I said, slumping over under the heavy weight of more good advice. Add Dylan to the pile already on my back.

"Nope," he said.

"Nope? That's not the message?"

"Nope, it's not, because you don't know the rest of the story."

Dylan, be advised, can be considerably interesting with these parables of his, and I now had considerable interest. I corrected my slump.

"It seems," he continued thoughtfully, "that while Uncle Herman believed he was five minutes late every morning, instead his boss had been setting the office clock another five minutes ahead each evening before. Finally, at the end, when my uncle imagined he was going to work on a Monday, actually it was Friday. With luck, that boss could have squeezed a free extra month out of Herman's paychecks."

"Uncle Herman is not only made up, he's made up and crazy, but I feel sorry for him anyhow."

"Feel sorry?" Dylan's jaw muscles tightened down and twitched. "Damn no," he said, a handy remark, and one of his favorites. "Herman was too dumb to think his boss might be suckering him. A nice fellow, Herman, they tell me, except he died of congenital dumbness."

"End of your uncle. Now what'll I tell my aunt, Charlene?"

"Tell her you were on time"—he stood up—"but the bus

was five minutes early. Let's walk somewhere."

We started down the street, in the general direction of the local shopping center. The traffic became busier.

"Your uncle . . ." I began.

"What about him?"

"Is he why *you* stayed off the bus today?"

At that, Dylan would have laughed once, but I hadn't seen him laugh since about a year ago, back before last summer, and I suppose he had abandoned the custom. During the past year he had grown grimmer and sourer with every month, more cynical, until he got convinced that only two kinds of people populated the earth, the beat-up ones and their beaters. In other words, Herman and his boss. Dylan didn't want to be a beater, but not a Herman, either: he judged he had already been Herman long enough. That left him without any choices and without any laughs.

Dylan was a walking diagram of differences and discarded customs, when you compared him with last year or before. He outdid those Before and After photos of bust-builders and body-builders that you find in back of certain magazines, which is no slight feat, and he got no help from sucking in the belly, the way they do. For instance, his attendance record had once been as spotless as mine, but this day was not the first or his twenty-first cut from school. Anybody on the verge of dropping out of the human race is naturally also at the brink of dropping school. In fact, he told me, he had been promoted to the school's number-one rescue project: Star Student Fallen on Bad Times. He had considered his premier ranking untouchable for the season, until a latecomer named Bridget entered the contest. Yes, he knew Mrs. Pace intimately (Mrs. Pacemaker, he called her) since they had logged numerous hours together in her office, where she leaned across her desk—instead of across my sofa—and spoke earnestly to him about the tribulations of a broken home, and the responsibilities he must now shoulder. Be a big boy, Dylan.

I could visualize his face across from hers, with his high, broad cheekbones—a solid rectangle that stared through Mrs. Pace's individual molecules, while never unbending its own corners. Tough. His style of fury nowadays was to harden into stone.

"Let's talk about your inner turmoil," she might say, coaxingly. "Dylan?"

Fat chance.

Even the other students watched Dylan very carefully, from a safe distance, as though circling around a friendly neighborhood dog who had lately taken to acting odd, growling instead of wagging its tail, and who might have picked up rabies. Semisurly, he could frequently be observed off by himself reading, usually some book about Indians or mountain men or woodsmanship. (More on that later.)

To me he still talked: the single exception, although I saw less of him, too, because of his cuts and disappearances. But there was our old brother-sister bond. We had developed a ritual over the years—sharing confessions, debates, stories —and that ritual never quite got broken, despite other things around us that came apart.

We reached the shopping center, fooled around, wandered through the stores, tried to act older. Dylan spoke the most because his voice had already changed—he could pass for an adult on the telephone.

At noon we ate hamburgers and shakes in the noise and litter of an establishment personally responsible for murdering millions of steers.

"School tomorrow?" Dylan asked, on our return walk.

A good question.

He said, "So, I'll have to wait and find out."

I gave a sidelong look. "Are you taking bets again?"

"Hey, sure. You're making school interesting again for me."

"What side is the smart money on this time, she will or she won't?"

"Listen, I'm not tipping *you* off. I lost today, remember, and you know how I am about not losing."

"Coward."

"Winning, I don't care much about. But losing, I do."

Before I went inside my house he touched my shoulder. I understood what he meant by it—his way of telling me more than words could—and I realized he had deliberately not mentioned my parents all morning. He knew better, just as he had known not to call and push in on me the whole time I stayed at home. A practicing cynic, maybe, but Dylan will never forget how to treat a fellow beat-up comrade.

iii _____ Charlene was thoroughly in what some people call a dizzy tizzy, brought on because Mrs. Pace had phoned promptly to report my nonappearance. While Dylan and I were walking and talking, Charlene had been walking herself, in little circles by the telephone, wondering whether to notify the police, the hospitals, no doubt the governor in Sacramento if necessary. She settled for two more calls to Mrs. Pace, who advised her to wait for the lost lamb to find its way home.

After performing a reenactment of the panic I had caused, Charlene asked me for the details of my misadventure. For an instant, a bare instant, I considered trying Dylan's early-bus story on her. But I had already made her life difficult enough. She required a simple answer, and I gave it: Bridget just did a wrong thing. Bridget and Uncle Herman were late.

That evening, Charlene took a firm grip on her quaking guardianship and bravely sat down with me to "thrash this business out." Would you—she wanted to know—please go to school in the morning? Yes, I answered.

"Would you make that a promise?" she asked, raising her hand like a Brownie den mother leading the troop in a solemn pledge. All together: A good Brownie is obedient.

I didn't raise my hand, but I did promise.

Charlene seemed much relieved at that, and settled herself comfortably into some of the reminiscences she fondly told, especially about my mother. She always made my mom sound far away and gone. Either reminiscing was her own therapy, or entertainment, and she couldn't help the talking out loud, or for some reason she believed I enjoyed hearing about her version of the dead past of a dead mother. Do I enjoy slivers shoved up under my fingernails? I escaped to my parents' bedroom, where there were solid, live objects that I could see and feel, and live voices to hear.

Later, as I got ready for sleeping, she eased in for one more shot at me. She was in a syrupy, sentimental mood.

"My Baby," she said, sitting on my bed, "one day you'll know how lucky you were, to have the parents you did. My, yes. It's not important now, of course, but you should know that when you reach the legal adult age, then, Dear, you will be a well-to-do young lady. Your parents have quite a sizable estate, including what your grandfather left your mother. You're fortunate for that, my Dear."

When I continued my hundred brushstrokes through

my—and my mother's—black hair, failing to comment, she added, "It's another reason to do right by your mother and father. They wouldn't want you to be missing school, after all." She moved behind me and took over brushing my hair, the way my mother had, many times.

"My Dear," Charlene said, "I can imagine how hard it is at school. No one your age likes to be singled out as different. Gosh, I wouldn't like it either. Do your best to finish this term, and next fall it'll be so much easier to begin at a new school."

"New school?"

Charlene brushed vigorously, finding a trouble spot far down my back.

"What new school?" I repeated, smelling a secret.

"Why, a new school," she said lightly, flailing away.

"But where?"

"Why, Santa Barbara."

Santa Barbara. Santa Barbara.

"But how can I be in Santa Barbara?" I asked. How dense I was.

"Why, we move there."

She had her stroke count revved up so fast my hair snapped, crackled, and popped—enough electricity to run a light bulb.

"How can I move there?" I asked blankly. "I'll be here in this house."

Snap, crackle, pop.

"Why, this house will be sold."

The hairbrush clattered to the floor, flipped there when I swirled around.

"Now, my Baby, my Baby," said Charlene, unnerved by my eyes.

I swear I could have destroyed her right then. "You can't sell our house!" came crying out from me. "It's Mom's and Dad's house! It's *always* been our house!"

Charlene flinched and tried rapid-fire to explain: I had become her full responsibility, and she lived in Santa Barbara, so now I must live in Santa Barbara, because this house was too big for a young girl, or even for the two of us, since my life was with her now, and we would be together in Santa Barbara, and we were the new family, and besides, Mrs. Pace agreed.

"Mrs. Pace?"

"She agrees that you should make a fresh beginning in a new place, away from here . . . this house . . . these reminders of . . . bad things. . . ."

Charlene looked around, almost with a shudder, and I saw that—for her—my dear shrine was a haunted mausoleum. For her this house was repulsive. That offended me, sickened me.

I pleaded, "Give me my money now . . . and I'll *buy back* the house—"

"Bridget, please—"

"I'll buy it back anyhow, now or later—"

"Please . . . listen. . . ."

Bridget was through listening, and she got no sleep in her shrine that night.

THREE

World, Goodby

i ———————————— Still dark outside. Nothing else to do, so I decided to get dressed. I forget whether or not it was in my prettiest.

Charlene carried on with a cheery air at breakfast, and I departed fast, reaching my stand at the oleander clump one heck of a lot earlier than five minutes before bus time. Uncle Herman again. Eventually the other kids drifted in, while I kept out of sight. No sign anywhere of Dylan. Then came the bus. It rumbled into view but I couldn't budge . . . my legs couldn't go. Despite promises, Brownie vows, Mrs. Paces, sizable estates, the legs were stuck.

By myself, I retraced yesterday's trail toward the shopping center. For the first time in public, outside the house, I felt myself weakening, close to blubbering. Here I was walking, helpless, without any idea of where I should go or what I should do whenever I got there. Alone and lonesome. I turned a corner in a teary half-mist and there sat Dylan waiting on the curb, reading a book.

"What took so long," he said.

Whoosh. I love that Dylan with his surprises. A smart-alecky, grateful answer to him—about losers who win bets—started up my throat but hit a lumpy barricade. I dragged in a deep breath, to clear the passage, and he flashed a

31

look over my face, reading it intently, like his books. We walked on, without talking, the fingers of our inside hands hooked together.

After a morning of dragging around, and over lunch at the same hamburger factory, I began telling Dylan about the night before. In the middle of all those milkshakes and littered papers I got the sniffles, thinking again of leaving my folks, our house, and Dylan, and living with Charlene off in Santa Barbara. That was a bleak future for me, without what few leftovers of myself I could claim as worth saving. Using a napkin I dabbed at my nose and eyes, certain I had sent Dylan slinking down in his seat, since he preferred death to being caught with his own emotions on display. But he appeared not to notice, or to care if our neighbors were peering between sesame-seed buns at my weeping.

"What would you want to do now?" he asked calmly.

"What *can* I do."

"No, what do you *want?*"

Another of Dylan's good questions. I had an automatic answer for this one: "Escape," I announced, "desert, leave the entire mess behind me. Get away."

His long lashes squeezed down, forming narrow slits. "To where?" he asked, calmer than any real calm would be.

"Anywhere away. Anywhere."

"When?"

"When? I don't know." I blotted my eyes again. The answer was sometime, anytime, before last March 26th, that's *when.* "Tomorrow," I said to him. "Today. Yesterday."

Dylan understood, nodded carefully, and began to chew a pale French fry with elaborate concentration. "You don't have a plan, do you," he said.

I, obviously, was no longer capable of making plans. Plans

demanded purpose, direction, order, future, desire. Those
words didn't belong to Bridget.

Dylan finished all his fries and his cola drink—carbonated
ink, he described it—and then focused directly on my damp
eyes. "I want to ask if you mean it. About the escaping, the
getting away."

I meant it so much that my sniffling broke out anew.

"You do then," he said.

"I do."

"All right." Dylan leaned over on his elbows, his face next
to mine. "Hey, Bridget. I can make a plan. I can make it
happen." At my wide-eyed reaction he almost laughed,
looking very bright and boyish, for Dylan. He handed me
another napkin. "We can do it, Bridget, and let's really by god
do it."

I was weak, tired, while he had energy. I grabbed hold of
his toughness. Yes—I told him, without knowing exactly
what it meant—I would go, because I needed to go. "But,
Dylan," I said, "why you?"

He pulled his face back from mine, sitting up. "Bridget,
you ask that?" Deliberately, he removed his gold wristwatch, a
gorgeously expensive thing, a birthday gift from better days,
inscribed: *To Our Dylan with Our Love . . . Mom & Dad.*

He stated bluntly: "I will now smash this watch on this
table top." His arm rose.

Panic. "Don't, please," I said, reaching out, more afraid of
this smashing of living parents than of causing a scene.
Whether he actually wanted to or not, I can't say, but he
would have plastered the watch, I do know. I said to reassure
him, "You have your mother at home. You two. Your mother,
you can't leave her."

He blinked, and another of those strange hesitations set in, the way one had last summer, so that I thought maybe I would hear about the big mystery, the really awful thing he was keeping from me. But his news was new. "Three's a crowd," he said. "Two's company, but three's a crowd, the saying goes."

"The three of us?"

"No, at my house." To clear up my confusion he added, "A man at my house." Since I was still slow on the draw he said, spelling it out, "My mother has someone who sleeps over. You know, man/woman stuff. So the son makes three, makes a crowd, and there I stand like a fool while those two carry on and I pretend not to notice. Besides, I can't bear the guy. He walks in like he owns the house, and owns my mother. I dream about one hard punch to his smirky face." He paused, expressionless, yet acting out of breath. "My mother. She minces around, pleased with herself, looking like an over-the-hill whore."

"Dylan!"

"It's true. If only my father could see them. Well, no, I guess he wouldn't care, would he. Damn no."

Under the table, out of public notice, our feet pressed together in private understanding.

"Your dad can't help?"

Dylan snorted, or sighed, or in between. "The last I heard from him was . . . four, five weeks ago, a postcard mailed from Flagstaff, Arizona. He and Miss Susie Sweetheart were headed back east to his new job. He's supposed to marry her, I guess."

Dylan's father had grabbed his girlfriend and vanished into a new life. Dylan's mother had a new boyfriend parading around in his father's old place. Musical chairs and Dylan gets left without a seat. No wonder that he latched onto my wish to take off, and no wonder, as I soon learned, he had already worked out a plan.

"I have you," Dylan said. "You're it."

"I have you," I said. "You're it."

"Our own little family. You and me. Salt and pepper."

"Salt and pepper."

Dylan bent close to me again. "Let's make a pledge, a pact, here in this crappy hamburger place, to dump this crappy world. Call it a renunciation pact. Do we renounce?"

"We renounce." Hallelujah, yes.

More napkin dabbing.

"What happens next?" I asked, not having much of an idea myself. Buy tickets to London? No, that took passports, and serious money.

"Next," said Dylan, "is 'Brer Fox, he lay low.'"

"Not another Parable Time, please."

"We act normal. No calling attention to ourselves. Let everybody relax and take their eyes off us, so we can get ready without raising eyebrows. Because we have to work on our plan in peace—collect cash, buy gear, hide it. The trouble is, now, both of us are being studied like a couple of ticking packages about to explode."

"What does acting normal mean, exactly?"

"Going to school."

"Oh no."

"Giving Mrs. Pacemaker a friendly embrace. Then seeing The Light with her."

"But, Dylan, that woman wants to brainwash me, make me forget my mother and father."

"You dole her out a few inner turmoils, and I'll slip her some inner tensions. We'll reform together, then split together."

"School . . . is impossible for me," I said with fervor. "My body won't go."

Dylan said, "It will, or you stay stuck forever, you and your body both." His tone got a little frosty: "You go home this minute, hang your head, smother your aunt from top to toe with remorse, swear an oath of good behavior, and tomorrow morning put your rear in gear and go to school. Just keep telling yourself, 'Brer Fox, he lay low.'"

"It's torture," I mumbled bitterly, "*torture.*"

"That's the title of the book."

ii _____ You can believe I didn't care much for showing up at that school. Grim. I gritted my teeth and went through my act, according to Dylan's instructions. Mrs. Pace and I had our "healthy" discussions: we became "friends," and she was "exceptionally pleased" with my "progress." Dylan, too, attended school faithfully, producing a "wonderful breakthrough" and an "encouraging adjustment" of his own. We seldom spoke to each other at school anymore, in order to keep people from joining the two pieces of the puzzle together, Dylan said.

After school, when carrying out our plan, Dylan positively glowed like a lantern, relieved to be in action at last. He was tickled by the idea of intrigue, of pulling the rug on everybody around us. We slunk hither and thither like a pair of secret agents, with a schedule of rendezvous locales and drop points that would humble the CIA or KGB. For instance, Dylan had asked for my father's hunting knife. The arranged drop point was Number 5, which meant at the biggest eucalyptus tree on the ridge, and so one evening I sauntered over there, casual as can be, and buried it under some leaves by the trunk. Lord only knows when Dylan dug it up. Probably in the middle of a moonless night, the way a good spy should. But he did get it. I asked him why I couldn't just hand him the goodies, instead of digging holes all through Alameda and Contra Costa counties, where some stranger could break a leg before we finished. That didn't tickle his funny bone. No, he insisted, any other method was too chancy. Tom Sawyer, I called him, because his shenanigans reminded me of Tom Sawyer's.

That didn't slow Dylan down. He cooked up a system of code words for telephone messages in case my aunt answered first, which she usually did, being jumpy about ringing telephones.

"Who was that?" I would ask Charlene.

"Wrong number, Dear."

"Who were they after?"

"A Mr. Greenfield, Dear."

Or: "Who was it?"

"Wrong number, Dear."

"Who did they want?"

"The Greenbergs, Dear."

Green was the code word for *urgently need money,* and hardly a day went by without Dylan being urgent for money. He used cash by the handfuls to buy . . . whatever he was buying and storing in the attic at his house. (He would show me soon, he said.) When Dylan started to run dry on names with green in them, I told him not to call anymore with green since I was bringing him money as fast as legally possible anyway.

Yellow was the code word for *cancel rendezvous,* and a rough one to drop into a name. Dylan once tried "Yellowfin," which is a type of tuna, I think. *Red* stood for *extreme emergency—call him.* That one, thank goodness, we had never used. At last Charlene complained in strong language to Pacific Bell

Telephone about all the wrong numbers she was receiving, and
Dylan reduced our telephone code to only *red.*

Not long after our renunciation pact, during a Saturday
rendezvous at a distant picnic table, Dylan unfolded a big map
of California. He placed a forefinger on a blank green area up
in the northwest corner, labeled TRINITY NATIONAL FOREST in
a sweep of dark letters. An irregular section sprawling inside
was marked Primitive Area.

"That's the spot," he said.

Squinting, I could discover no red road lines, no black road
lines, no road lines at all, just blue wiggly lines for rivers and
creeks and contour lines tracing mountaintops. The highest
mountains were labeled Trinity Alps. "How can that be the
spot," I said, "when there's no town."

"That's why it *is* the spot."

"Because there's no town? I don't get it."

"Wait," Dylan said. "Ask yourself what makes a town."

"Uh, buildings."

"No."

"No?"

"People do. People make a town."

"All right," I agreed, "people do. But I still don't get it."

"Bridget, getting *out* equals getting *away* from people.
People do the things to you. People chop you up. People cause
the problems, yes?"

Brrr, what a voice he had when he talked that way. But I
got the message. Our taking off was going to let Dylan put his
new self-reliance doctrine into actual practice. When we had
renounced the World, he *did* intend for us to be away by
ourselves, nothing less, no fooling. We truly were saying
goodby. His plan was awe-inspiring, and I suppose unreal to

me at the time. I could only dumbly ask, pointing at the map, "How do we get there without roads?"

"On our own."

He meant walking, one foot moving in front of the other, which seemed to me a huge bite for us to chew. But he was the ex-Boy Scout, and if I expected to transport myself away it would only be by clamping a tight grip on Dylan's shirttail. I was foggy yet about where the shirttail would lead me. "When we're there, what? Won't we need jobs?"

"No jobs." Dylan returned to the map, and dreamed down at the Trinity National Forest, a block of placid green paper. He had never been there before, except he *had* been there, many times, in his mind, if you catch my drift. Months ago he had already escaped to these Trinity mountains, by day-dreaming a better life there, by losing himself in his wilderness books, and, I bet, by relocating there his happy memories of the backcountry camping trips he had taken every summer with his father. Boy, he used to love telling me about those trips.

"No jobs," Dylan repeated, "at least no usual jobs. We work at living, just the two of us."

Now I saw for certain that Dylan counted on turning his theories about independence into hard fact. Well, he was the one who had memorized stacks of wilderness survival hand-books, and that beat me. My Thoreau and my other naturalist poets gave me strictly armchair adventures. Dylan had, I discovered, read every book in every library around on the subject of Indians and Indian lore. I asked him if he hadn't caught Indian fever a bit late, at his age. "I'm not *playing* Indian," was the reply. His mind was hooked, really hooked, on comparing himself to Indians. To illustrate, he gave me a parable that sounded suspiciously like the Trail of Tears, in which, you remember, the Cherokee were invited to leave their homes in Georgia and take a forced march to Oklahoma. He classified himself as some special breed of white Indian . . . a white Last of the Mohicans.

I'll testify—from first to last—that regardless of what happened later, Dylan never forgot what he had read about his woodlore or his Indians. On his report card, put another A after Reading.

At my home, meanwhile, Charlene gratefully found that Bridget, her ward, now seemed normal: went promptly to school, hadn't plummeted into drugs or a mental breakdown, apparently would return to being a regulation girl after all. Charlene began getting bubbly about Santa Barbara. The fun it would be for me there. What a team we would make. Where we would go, what we would do. It made me squirm to hear that, and to make back encouraging noises, while meantime I was plotting—and *wanting*—to leave her flat.

Anyhow, it put Charlene in a mood to fork over money. Food money. Book money. School money. Purse money. Browsing money. Amusement money. Borrowed money. Allowance money. Clothes money, lots of it. Charlene never knew which outfits in my closets were new or old. Religiously I passed the money on to Dylan.

When Dylan's mother expected to be gone one afternoon, a rendezvous was finally scheduled for his own house, to let me examine and appreciate what our money had bought and what Dylan had laboriously sneaked into his attic. After sidestreeting and backdooring we were at last in his house, pulling down the attached ladder that led up through the garage ceiling.

"Get yourself prepared for this," he said, shutting the trapdoor behind us.

"I can't see."

"You will in a minute."

Through the dim attic, pencil shafts of sunlight poked at a sharp angle. Dust motes, floating in the warm air, traveled lazily up and across the shafts. My eyes adjusted.

"Here it all is," said Dylan, with satisfaction, prodding me toward a mound heaped up in a corner.

It was an impressive pile, braced on the sides by two aluminum-tubed pack frames with nylon packs and rolled sleeping bags already cinched into place. On top of the pile sat two pairs of hiking boots.

"Fifty bucks a pair, on sale," said Dylan, taking down the boots. I tried mine on. They fit, but each boot weighed like a boxcar. "Call these over a hundred dollars," Dylan went on, handing me my pack and sleeping bag. Next he folded together a bundle of clothes for me—wool and cotton shirts, trousers, socks. "Just your size," he pointed out, "so it's not necessary to strip and try them on here."

"If you insist."

"You bring your own underwear. Three extra sets."

"Three sets." I already marveled at his attention to detail. My underwear.

Now Dylan put together a small hill of different dried foods, packaged in separate plastic bags, along with a lightweight nested cooking set, some eating utensils, and a tiny folding propane stove about the size of a man's hand.

"That's amazing," I said. "Does it actually work?"

"The best that money can buy. Swiss import."

He laid in a row: a sheathed hatchet, my father's hunting

knife also in its sheath, a whetstone, fishing line with a collection of hooks, twine, a light tarp, piano wire for animal snares. I felt the thin, flexible steel wire. "Does it choke or cut?"

"Both. Go on, look through the compartments in your pack."

Inside my backpack I found a compass, a sewing kit, insect repellent, waterproof matches, flint, hand soap, a first-aid kit, toothbrush and toothpaste, a collapsible plastic water jug, a comb, more bags of dried food, and down in a bottom compartment three boxes of tampons. That startled me. Can you imagine? Later, and not much later, I would uncover an ancient rule: when privacy and practicality fight it out, practicality wins, and a good thing. Otherwise, bye-bye.

Dylan said, "The best for last," and brought forth his prize, two prime northern goose-down jackets, plush and puffy, with parka hoods.

"Luscious," I said, squeezing the cotton-candy soft, airy down.

"And a miracle in the cold. Even in the mountains"—he rattled his ever-present map of the Trinity Alps—"even on the blessed mountain*tops,* we're safe."

"And they're expensive, I'll bet."

"Very expensive. But guess what. The two of us have been crackerjack fund raisers." He lifted a roll of bills from his pocket. "Nearly a hundred and fifty dollars left. Who says that affluence doesn't provide important advantages to children?"

"I wrung money out of my aunt that we didn't need?"

"We'll need it, Bridget, to buy more food up north, at the last town."

"Ahhh, that kind of talk makes me nervous. What happens

after the hundred and fifty dollars are spent and eaten?"

"Then the children turn water into milk and rock into bread."

"Parable Time?"

"By then we have our own food supply."

I didn't press that because, remember, he had the survival manuals and the fishhooks and piano wire. Anyway, I wanted to trust him, and nobody before ever went far wrong in trusting Dylan.

"Hatchets, snares, flint, food," I said. "I get now why you kept calling this pile our *cache*. I thought you just snatched that word from a *Jim Bridger—Mountain Man* book. But this—"

"*Listen.*"

Dylan lurched forward, grabbing my arm, as a car drove into the garage under us. The motor shut off, the door opened, packages rustled, the door closed, heels clicked across concrete.

Your mother? I mouthed soundlessly.

He nodded, saying very low, "Back early. We'll wait, then get you down fast, and around behind the house."

We sat, leaning back against our rolled sleeping bags. We waited. The shafts of sunlight changed their angle. Already we might have been on the road, fugitives, or anyhow doing a dress rehearsal with a live audience, and it caused odd, mixed feelings, sweet and sour. I was beginning to suspect that nothing would ever be simple again.

Down below, silence. Dylan made a motion. We rustled across the attic and he lifted the trapdoor—all clear. As we scrambled down the ladder (which we had left in plain view, directly in front of the just-parked car), our thumping feet made each rung vibrate and sing out, and hurrying through the garage I kicked a lawn rake. Dylan waved me on and turned to stroll in the opposite direction, decoy-fashion. I scurried home with a dry mouth.

iii _____ That same night, while I flopped on the living room sofa, still recovering from my unexpected flight, the telephone jangled.

"Sorry, no," answered Charlene, and hung up. She said to me, "At least that's our first wrong number in a while."

"Who did they want?"

"Some Mr. Reddington."

A legitimate wrong number. I stretched out again on the sofa, replaying the scene in Dylan's warm attic when his mother drove into the garage. Click/click/click went those sharp heels again, matching my sharp heartbeats. How on earth had Dylan slipped all our paraphernalia in unnoticed?

Reddington.

"Was that a man or woman who just phoned?" I asked Charlene.

"A man, my Dear. Why?"

"I know that name, I think," I lied.

Reddington. *Red*dington. Could it be? If so, *why*—what emergency? *Red*dington. Something about that name sounded like an alarm bell. *Rrr*reddington. I had to risk making a call, and I went to my bedroom.

Dylan picked up the telephone immediately.

"Bridget?"

"Yes—"

"Let me do the talking"—he spoke swiftly—"while I have the chance." His voice was edgy, a little excited, but the

volume remained carefully normal. "We leave tonight. Eleven
o'clock at your house, beside the garage. My mother has been
showing signs she . . . could know . . . about our cache.
Eleven o'clock—you understand? And don't get seen by
anyone, and don't accidentally tip off your aunt."

Holy, holy. Leaving?

"Wear jeans and a sweater," said Dylan, "and I'll bring the
jackets. I'll bring everything from the attic. For Christ's sake
don't forget to leave a note behind . . . the way we planned,
okay?"

Just like that. In the middle of the night.

I suggested through code double-talk that we might wait
until tomorrow, to find out for sure about his mother.

"Damn no," Dylan said bluntly. "Too risky. Tonight's the
night, or we could find ourselves fenced in here for certain,
with an attic full of useless toys." I could see his eyes,
smoking, when he said *toys*. I knew Dylan, and Dylan was
stoked and charged. And me? I gulped, shut my eyes, and
took a tighter hold on his shirttail.

"Right," I murmured.

"Eleven?"

"Right."

"Until then, ballerina."

Down went the receiver.

I looked at the clock: two hours, twenty minutes to go. For
a first step, I informed Charlene that I was going to bed early,
and she glanced up from watching television and smiled. It
always pleased her when someone went to bed early—one
more thing properly in its place, and ahead of time, for a
bonus. I turned back a moment to examine her in front of the
television set. A comic waved his arms and joked about being
drunk. Charlene cocked her well-groomed head and laughed,

unaware of naughty Bridget's plans. And of Bridget's life, I thought, because I understood, and any person who remembered last March understood, that drunks weren't funny.

I went slowly down the hallway of my shrine, trailing my hand along the wall. Yes, I went into my folks' bedroom, and sat on the bed. I opened their closet. Yes, I touched their clothes again. And, red-eyed, you know what else I did . . . hard.

Next I took a hot, hot shower, not only to get clean and to erase my streaked face, but because it is a ritual of mine before any big outing or event. My mother and father had named it my "purification" ritual. Inside my own bedroom, wearing a bathrobe, I remembered to stuff three sets of underwear into a pair of jeans, and to compose my farewell note to the world:

> Dear Charlene:
>
> This house will soon be someone else's home, and I must now go away for a time, perhaps far away and perhaps for a long time. Honestly, it is best for both of us.
>
> Do not be fearful—I will be somewhere safe and in good hands. Please make no attempt to find me since I am doing what I wish to do.
>
> If you can, sell the house to people with children. That is also my wish.
>
> Your niece,
> Bridget

There: the perfect stiffish tone of formality, just enough hint of self-righteousness, and the full quota of brave words.

At least Charlene would realize I hadn't been kidnapped, as would Dylan's mother after reading his note. Placing the paper under my jeans, I switched off the light and slid under the bed's top cover. On the nightstand a clock pointed its luminescent hands at me.

Eventually, Charlene paused outside my closed door and called, "Good night, my Baby."

I didn't respond, partly because Bridget, she lay low, like Brer Fox, and partly because I lacked the heart for it.

Her footsteps went on. I listened to my house, a final listening. Above, in the darkness, was the ceiling that had protected me over all my years. Around me, the only bedroom I ever had. Around me, the only house Bridget ever lived in. The only parents. Silent voices came talking to me again, gathering in the corners of the dark rooms, flowing out through cracks under doors, forming a collection, an eddying, seeking stream. It, they, found Bridget.

Then the clock showed the hour. I eased from bed, from my bathrobe, caught a last pale-skinned portrait of my bare body in the mirror, and pulled on my jeans and sweater. I straightened the bedcover, the dresser, the entire room. No use making it any harder on Charlene than it already would be. Gently, I walked down the carpeting to the brick floor of the dining room, where I placed my note center stage on the big table. All was dimmed and still, my voices gone. The stillness weighed like sadness, and at the front door I had to look back. I waited, and waited, and I think the voices were returning, but I stepped out and shut the door.

Dylan's words came from the shadows before I could see his shape: "The note?"

I nodded, and he handed me my backpack as we went down the hill, keeping to the black patches.

"Everything go fine?"

I nodded.

At the bend in the roadway I halted and faced back up toward my house, before it would disappear behind us. The roof carved familiar lines—as familiar as my life—against the starry sky.

"Dylan."

"I know."

Trembling, despite my prime northern goose-down jacket, I asked, "Why do we have to go in the middle of the night?"

"Because, starting now, we're illegal. Come on," he prodded, a velvet prod, "we have a midnight bus to catch."

FOUR

The Road to Away

i _____ Curving down from our span-
gled foothills, the local bus rolled on its way to the Greyhound
depot in Oakland, its wide rear seat populated only by two
peculiar travelers and their bulky packs. Night and the lights
flowed by outside the windows. We didn't say much. Dylan:
expressionless, stoic as ever. Bridget: paler than ever.

Reaching Foothill Parkway the bus put on speed, and I
steadied myself for what was coming up soon. The spot. Put
that in bloody capitals: THE SPOT. By now I had acquired all
the morbid, gruesome details and I fastened my eyes on the
road ahead, anticipating, tense. Sure enough, a brilliant
billboard rose out of the sky, rushed at us, proudly displayed a
colorful picture of a Reno hotel, receded. I got a good look.
The pavement, of course, was washed clean and peaceful, with
no red X, no broken glass piled up for a monument. This
bareness of the spot tried to mock me, but I wasn't fooled. I
heard the tires scream. I heard metal demolish metal. I saw
glass scatter like somebody flinging buckets of beads. I saw
two limp-necked heads behind a blasted windshield. I heard, I
saw. And—scary—I felt that piece of pavement just jump up
and follow me, tagging along, no matter how hard the bus was
trying to leave it back there.

More billboards, more lights, then we were in the glare and

between the buildings of downtown Oakland. We hauled our packs into the Greyhound depot and after Dylan bought tickets to Sacramento we sank into some worn chairs off at the side. The chairs, the whole waiting room, had soaked up the smoke of a million cigarettes. Ugh. I'd never waited in a bus station before. Never had to. Never want to again. The faces seemed drooping, tuckered out, with soldiers and sailors in uniform scattered around the battlefield, an old man tipped sideways, asleep, and a small child curled in a ball like a kitten. Nobody paid attention to anybody else, except we drew a few stares.

"Why are we worth looking at?" I said to Dylan.

"For one thing, we hardly pass for brother and sister."

"Meaning?"

"You know. Boy and girl off together. Romeo Montague and Juliet Capulet."

There was an idea. Romeo and Juliet, Dylan and Bridget.

"But why would they think that?"

"Because of the second thing," said Dylan, tapping his pack. "What would cross *your* mind if you saw two kids with backpacks in a bus depot . . . at midnight . . . during the school year. These packs are like flashing Runaway Badges."

I glanced around me, feeling the urge to flip on my jacket hood and hide. Dumb, I know, yet I never quite considered myself running away, only *going* away, escaping. When Dylan had said we were "illegal," he meant it. Bridget was now a lawbreaker for more than hooky.

I wondered, "Will they tell the police?"

"These people?"

"No—"

"Your aunt and my mother? Good god." Dylan showed his

teeth. "Tomorrow, before the rooster crows."

"Tomorrow sharp," I agreed, "my aunt will be on the telephone, demanding an All Points Bulletin for her Baby. An APB—I remember that from the police shows. Dylan, this is getting creepy."

He reassured me, or made an attempt, explaining that his plan arranged for this. We would go unreported tonight, and tomorrow morning would find us "underground," to repeat his term. Still, when our Sacramento bus arrived, I hustled aboard, and I noticed Dylan didn't drag his feet either.

From inside the darkened bus we watched the sparkle of Oakland, then Berkeley, and the mellower lights of houses on the low hills, as they glided by us. Living jewelry, I always thought. I had seen this dozens of times when riding with my folks. These patterns, and the glitter on the bay, and the silver mound of San Francisco across the water were the old, old sights of home. Only after the bus crossed the Carquinez Bridge, left the bay, and headed inland, did we feel the cutting loose. Next to me, Dylan stirred, relaxing in his seat.

"Well," he said, as if releasing a breath he'd been holding.

"Well."

"Yeah."

"Yeah."

We shifted the packs at our feet to get comfortable, while around us the other passengers already dozed. But we couldn't sleep, no deal, because we sensed the electricity, a tingly charge along the skin, of finally being on the way. Where, really? Mainly to someplace different, to some change. My friend, you appreciate our need for that.

Dylan became talkative, his head turned so the words tumbled out by my ear, that nice rich voice of his which I'll listen to any night or day. "It's us, now," he explained. "Instead of things only happening *to* us, we *do* some of our own, and we take care of each other." Then he put together a parable about the Oregon Trail. The guy was in great form.

Bus wheels hummed—dimness inside, few lights outside —as we traveled into the flat, spreading reaches of the Sacramento Valley. Escape it is, Bridget: you wanted, you got.

ii _____ In the predawn murk we slipped from the Sacramento bus station, through the city and its rambling outskirts, and holed up among a grove of towering cottonwoods on the river bank. The daybreak sky appeared, brushed by a faint russet, and when Dylan, checking his wristwatch, said, "Past seven," we knew word was out that Bridget and Dylan and the cat were out of the bag.

After a while, Dylan hiked to a grocery store, returning with bananas, crackers, cheese, peanuts, doughnuts, and two quarts of orange juice. We made breakfast from that collection. And lunch. Later, it would happen, dinner too. But after breakfast we decided to rest there, with sunlight passing between cottonwood leaves to dapple the grass, with the big Sacramento burbling and rippling by, muscling its waters on toward the same bay we had deserted last night. Understandably we were tired, and Dylan fell asleep first, on his back, his goose-down jacket under him. I'd never seen Dylan sleeping before and it caused me an uneasy tug, like accidental peeking, to find him unprotected from prying eyes, mine included. He's six feet tall, with thick shoulders and thighs that make him seem stocky—more a man's body than a kid's. And yet, sleeping, his face looked younger, much closer to his age, especially when his girl's lashes covered his greyish eyes—they could be plenty hard grey eyes—and when his rounded lips were parted. Usually he kept those lips pressed into a line. His cheeks and chin showed a slight glint of copper stubble. Whatever color you would call his hair, his beard definitely qualified as auburn.

That afternoon after school hours (to be less noticeable), we donned our packs and walked toward Interstate 5, to start hitchhiking north. This hitchhiking, we intended, would keep us away from public transportation terminals—and the police—and save money. While new to me, Dylan had hitched around home. A girl along made it a snap, he claimed, since it was common knowledge that girls never tolerated any crime or meanness.

"Sugar 'n' Spice 'n' Everything Nice?" I suggested.

"In at least one case," he said, bowing to me, making a compliment into a joke, or the reverse.

And we hadn't gone far before a man and woman did pick us up. "You see, Sugar," said Dylan, as the car pulled over.

"Destination?" asked the man, friendly, and driving again.

"Going north," said Dylan.

"We live just up in the bitty town of Yolo," apologized the woman, "no more than twenty miles from here."

"Fine. That'll take us away from this commuter traffic," said Dylan, professionally. "That'll be fine, ma'am."

"Where you young folks from?" asked the man, and I commenced squirming.

Dylan, smoothly, allowed his grown-up voice to resonate: "Canada. Vancouver. We've been on school vacation, my cousin and I, but we're glad to be getting home."

"My, so far," the woman said, glancing back at me.

I smiled weakly. Neither of us had ever been to Canada. And, when confronted, I never could carry off a direct, flat-on-the-table lie. Fizzle, every time.

"Don't your parents worry?" she inquired next, obviously a prime worried-mother type herself. "I mean, don't they wonder what's happening? I mean, I do know how parents can worry."

That knotted my tongue.

"Not with kind Americans like you to help us," said Dylan, neatly filling my blank space. "Besides, we keep in constant touch by telephone." Dylan then turned on the charm. He can do it, the rascal, when he wants to, or more likely when he has to. Before he finished they were urging us to spend the night with them in Yolo. They were, really, a decent couple, and their nosiness was only their instinct to protect all kids.

We declined their offer, anxious to make miles and avoid questions, but it was an invitation we should have accepted. Indeed. For we had been walking again just five minutes when a punched-out old Ford van, a faded corn color, squealed to a standstill and we climbed in, cheery over our good fortune.

An adventure unfolded.

The van reeked of pot—a miracle the thing didn't float off the highway—and the van's occupants already were floating, and from harder stuff than grass, judging by the pinched looks on the faces. Yeah, a girl from the East Bay foothills recognizes such looks. Those faces are available everywhere and I well knew we were surrounded by four dopeheads.

Dylan and I exchanged a quick understanding. We were by ourselves in the second seat, sitting on our jackets, the backpacks by the door. Two guys, counting the driver, sat in the front seat, and two more sprawled on the van's cargo floor

in back—all about the same age, twenty or thereabouts.
Nobody spoke . . . one of those cloudy, sinister silences.
They didn't bother to ask where we were headed and Dylan
didn't bother to say. Immediately, the four of them and the
two of us were enemies, squared off and testing the scent. Bad.

The van rattled.

Right in front of me the driver, woolly haired and wearing
glasses with inch-thick lenses, studied us in the rear-view
mirror. He seemed to be the leader because after a while the
other one in the front seat, who sported a rakish Pancho Villa
mustache, turned to him, sort of inquiring.

But no words. The van went rattling on.

Dylan, reaching over, fiddled with his pack, altering the
mood enough so that the driver broke our silence. "Runaways," the driver bluntly declared.

"That's right," said Dylan immediately, to my immense
surprise.

Now the two from the rear leaned forward, against our seat,
like groggy mutts called up to the porch for foodscraps.
"Where you running from?" asked the one behind me.

"Sacramento," said Dylan.

"Haven't got far, have you," said the one behind Dylan.

"Not yet," said Dylan.

Pancho Villa gestured at our packs. "Fancy goods."

"Should be," Dylan said, "we stole the best on the market."

Rapidly, the driver squinted into the mirror at us.

The creep behind Dylan said, "Say, we could use gear like
that, you know?"

"Man, sure could," said the one behind me, and his fingers
teased at my hair. Gathering the hair, he let it dangle behind
the seat, on his side. "Looky," he called out, delighted, "her
hair touches 'bout down to the floor."

Pancho Villa asked the driver, "How much you think that camping gear's worth?"

The driver twitched a shoulder.

"I got us an idea," said Dylan's creep. "We'll leave this young pair off somewheres, and for payment we keep the gear, to settle our expenses. Fair?"

"I got us another idea," said my creep. "We leave the feller off and keep the gear *and* the girl. Better?"

Pancho Villa covered me with his eyes. "Hummm. She's an ice cream cone, vanilla skin, no question."

My creep walked his fingers up through my hair and then kept going, across my front anatomy. I jumped, believe me. Dylan didn't spring to my rescue, didn't show any particular interest even. Automatically—a Bridget reflex—my elbow swung around and cracked my creep flush against his muzzle.

That amused Pancho Villa, and his mustache winged up over a big grin. "An ice cream cone," he repeated. "Very nice. A tender one, vanilla skin and vanilla pure."

Rubbing his nose, my creep said, in stupid fascination, "But looky at that coal-black hair color." For once I wished my hair was chopped short, to the scalp.

"You're running off," Pancho Villa reminded me, "so why not run with us? There'd be good times with us."

Dylan's creep said, "Just as good as anywheres."

My creep agreed, and began playing again with the ends of my hair.

Dylan himself, after fiddling some more with his pack, spoke up in a clear but unexcited voice. "I'm sure hoping I don't get you guys in any trouble."

A loud pause, with everybody puzzled. Trouble? Wasn't trouble on the other foot?

Dylan said, full of earnestness, "Heck, I sure hope you can stay free of it."

He had everybody's attention, mine included.

"What does that mean?" asked the driver, sounding awfully touchy.

Fussing again with his pack, Dylan talked with serious deliberation, to all appearances trying his darnedest to help us solve a mutual problem. "Well, it's plain you're tempted," he said, "by these packs and by the girl here. And I told you before, they're hot as a pistol, straight out of Sacramento, down the road. The girl is stolen, too, you might say. She's fresh news, fresh police bulletins." Dylan sat up, concluding, "That's my trouble, and easy enough it could get to be yours."

"Let's take 'em to a canyon," said Dylan's creep. "We just do whatever we want there."

"Sure, and we can party there," my creep said.

"Shut up," ordered Pancho Villa.

The driver chomped at Dylan: "Okay, wisemouth, what do you suggest?"

How could that Dylan act so calm? He answered, "The safest deal, for you, is to dump us out, fast, here."

"Just like that?" protested my creep, to the whole van and then directly to the driver—"Just like that?"

"Shut up," Pancho Villa said. "He knows we won't stop. He's bluffing." Pancho Villa addressed Dylan: "Was that your only suggestion, hero?"

Dylan gave a calculated sigh, and produced his wallet. "You guys want money, anyway, not backpacks."

The driver's eyes, magnified behind his glasses, snapped to the mirror.

"How much money you talking?" asked Pancho Villa.

Dylan bunched the money into a fat fistful and held it up, bills sticking through his fingers. "Seventy bucks. All we have."

The other half, I knew, was in Dylan's pack.

"Hand it over," said the driver, impressed.

"Listen," Dylan said, "we need part to live on. We have to eat somehow. Let's split it."

Deadly, the driver said, "I'm telling, not asking. Hand it over."

All of Dylan's strategies had been dry wells, it looked to me, and instead of dreaming dreams about the Trinity Mountains, I was living nightmares in the Sacramento Valley.

"It's getting stuffy," complained Dylan, rolling down his window. Then he jabbed his fistful of money far outside the window, with the bills flapping and popping in the wind.

The van swerved, wobbled from lane to lane. "What the Christ!" the driver shrieked. "What you doing, man!"

Now Dylan was *not* calm, his grey eyes changing to shiny hate. "*You stop,*" he forced out between clenched teeth, "or I let this money blow goodby across the state of California." He also swore. Wow.

Pancho Villa got convinced pronto. "He means it. He'll do it."

"Jesus, don't let any slip," pleaded Dylan's creep.

"Easy, easy," said the driver, soothingly, lowering his voice. "I'll find a side road . . . the first side road. You hang on to that bread."

Dylan's no fool, and he demanded, "Right here, on the highway—and right *now.*"

"Why, man, I can't stop on a highway—" began the driver.

"You have until *ten,* clown," interrupted Dylan. "One, two, three—"

Brakes wailed. Dylan hitched sideways, and I saw tucked under his thigh my father's hunting knife, somehow worked out of the pack and out of its scabbard. He had no intention of giving our money to anyone. I wanted to tell him, no, don't get hurt, give up the lousy money, run . . . except to speak would reveal the knife, and besides the van was already rolling along the shoulder, slowing.

Before the van even halted Dylan banged open the door, kicked out our packs, grabbed my arm—down to the bone—and pulled us both flying off the seat. I landed skidding on my hands and knees, losing skin across the pavement.

"Run," Dylan called, thumping me painfully with his foot. I did. I hauled myself up and hooked on my pack and ran, although it felt like slow motion, frantic slow motion.

Gasping, I wheeled around to see Dylan juggling his pack, the money, the knife, and backpedaling from the four dopeheads. Too awkward. Dylan, Dylan, run, I begged silently, searching desperately for a heavy rock or stick, afraid to leave Dylan, yet afraid to go back. If only Bridget weighed 220 tough pounds instead of her measly 120! What use is a ballerina in a fight?

Dylan held out the knife, swinging it back and forth, and the dopeheads closed in very cautiously, because no one wants to mess with Dylan, knife or not. Like a smart pack of dogs, the two creeps circled behind. Pancho Villa made the first move—rushing Dylan—but sent up a yowl when the knife took a bite. By then the others were on Dylan, and he had no choice, and scattered the money, bolting away, sprinting toward me.

While the dopeheads scrambled for the bills, we ran together . . . off the highway, over a fence, across an alfalfa field. With every jarring step Dylan panted, "Those—those —those—bastards."

iii _____ After we had been walking for a time, Dylan groaned.

"We still have some money left," I said to encourage him.

"No, our *jackets*." He pressed his hands to his head, sinking down and kneeling on the ground.

Dylan's prize jackets, warm enough for the mountaintops. They were in that van.

"Bridget, we needed those."

He was furious, with himself and the dopeheads both. I asked, "Buy new ones?" but he said we only had sixty or seventy dollars, too little, and anyway we had to save that for food.

We went onward, very glum, Dylan scuffing the dirt. He took it hard and I nursed my own burning scrapes, those raw patches on my knees and hands. When dark came, an unfriendly wind also came up, reminding us about the goose-down jackets. The best shelter we could find was an empty irrigation ditch in the middle of some farmer's land. Fumbling in the dark, we unrolled our sleeping bags and crawled halfway inside before eating our gritty cheese and sandy crackers, with a few peanuts. Nothing to drink. I wanted to brush my teeth. I wanted a shower—my nightly habit. I wanted a shower that night not only to get my vanilla skin spotless, but to wash off the whole greasy day and make me altogether clean.

The wind jerked at the weeds, at our packs, at the sleeping bags, at our faces and hair, as we huddled awake, thinking back over what happened. Here was our first evening. Here, in

a ditch in a farm field, spending a cold, miserable, disappointed night. We were supposed to be in the Trinities by now,
snug in our jackets and cozied up to a campfire. Instead, this?

Dylan read my mind, or it was his mind, too. "We're not
away yet," he explained in soft tones, "and it's the same old
problem. We won't be safe until we get clear."

Clear of people.

A little louder he said, "The knife's right under my bag.
From now on that baby stays in close reach. Don't worry."

"Be careful. We don't want to be part of . . . anything
gory."

Bitterly: "Us or them made gory?"

"You know."

"What leaves us alone, I'll leave alone."

Then I tried to thank him, or praise him, for what he had
done in the van, since, believe me, I was grateful. But he
wasn't interested, and he cut in, "Think about a world with
freaks like those in it."

I did think—about what might have happened to us, what
almost really happened. They were low thoughts, lower even
than our ditch. In a windy, dim ditch, thinking about
dopeheads' hands in your hair, you can miss terribly your
house and your parents. You can sob. Without Dylan—the
rock—what would become of me? Say, my friend, but did I
ever need his rock to cling to. For me, Dylan was the complete
ball of string: my blood-oath brother, my substitute father,
my future.

Later, barely audible, Dylan asked, "Asleep, Bridget?"

"No."

"I . . . forgot to tell you: good night, ballerina."

And he went into a sleep, although not much of a restful
one. Dimly, only a yard away, I could see his shape inside his

sleeping bag, and it twitched and sometimes shuddered, like somebody under the heel of a fever. Maybe in his sleep Dylan finally lets himself be scared.

In the morning, we chewed dried fruit from our packs, and taking the devious byways and dusty backways started hiking north toward the next town. Actually, we hadn't decided what to do from there, whether hitchhike again (help!) or risk a bus. We had about 150 miles yet, Dylan figured, before reaching the Trinities, most of those miles directly ahead through the Sacramento Valley's huge open tableland. We could see mountains strung along on either side of us: on the right the distant mass of the Sierra Nevadas, on the far left the bluish Coastal Ranges, where eventually we would plant ourselves. In between, the day's heat was trapped, held in the valley by the embracing mountain chains, and Dylan and I soon became hot and thirsty. Our last drink had been the orange juice, yesterday. We trudged and slinked and searched for water. No water. To make it worse, there were few trees, little shade. My raw hands and knees from yesterday had meantime gotten stiff and darn tender.

Near the end of the afternoon we spotted a town off in the distance, signaled by a surrounding cluster of inviting greenery. When we at last arrived, I stayed with the packs while Dylan rustled up two cold cans of carbonated ink. Ah, that poison pop never tasted better. Then we rested four tired feet, waiting for Darkness, our protector Darkness, the patron saint of criminals everywhere. What we would do in this little out-of-the-way town, we determined, was eat a cooked meal in a little out-of-the-way café, keep innocent faces, keep to the shadows, check the bus schedule.

To look more respectable we brushed our clothes and combed out our tangled hair. We stowed our packs in a hidden culvert. Darkness settled around us. All systems being perfect, we put on our innocent faces and approached the town.

"I'm starved," I said, dizzy from hunger.

"I'm twice starved."

A car passed. My hunger vanished.

"Dylan, did you see?" It had been a county sheriff's car.

"No problem," Dylan said. "He went right on by. Relax."

In a minute car lights came back up the street toward us.

Dylan cussed. "I can't believe this. Aren't we allowed any luck?"

"Let's run."

"No, wait. He might not stop, but he sure will if we take off."

The car stopped anyway. Rolling down his window, the deputy said "Howdy" with a generous smile.

We returned "Howdy" with cheer and enthusiasm.

"You folks aren't local kids, are you." Not a question.

No, we admitted, with less enthusiasm.

"You see, I recognize all the kids hereabouts. That's why I wondered how you two come to be out here by yourselves." That *was* a question.

End of the line for Bridget. I told you I'm a loser as a point-blank liar, even to save my own scraped skin.

Dylan had already introduced a story about Canada: how we were on a school holiday, how our car had blown a water pump over on the highway, how we had walked here—warm today, wasn't it?—for help, how everything would be fine now, and thank you, Officer.

The deputy nodded agreeably. "Why not show me some identification, please," he said. "Your Canadian driver's license, for instance."

"Will do," said Dylan, digging into a hip pocket before he

slapped a thigh and turned to me. "Helen, is my wallet in the car, in the glove compartment?"

I gurgled.

The deputy pushed up his cap—displaying a pleasant, fortyish face. He leveled his words directly at Dylan: "Do that girl's parents know she's off with you?"

Dylan leveled back: "I should say so, Officer. They're my aunt and uncle."

The deputy's features got less pleasant and more official, more full of business. "What I want now is for you two to get in with me. Just routine. This door over here."

"Will do, Officer," Dylan said, leading me forward.

One, two steps, then—*pop*—my arm was yanked from its socket and we were on the run.

"Through there," breathed Dylan, and we raced across a lawn and between two houses. Behind us, wheels shrilled, a prolonged rubbery squeal, as the deputy's chasing car spun a half-circle. We charged across more lawns, trying to avoid street lights, house lights, all lights, zigging over gardens and zagging over flower beds. While we zigged and zagged, the deputy's car roared up and down—fortunately missing connections with us—and it ended up slowly patrolling the streets: the deputy hoping, I guess, to flush us out like a covey of spooked quail.

And we ended up inside the culvert, joining our backpacks, eating sticky mouthfuls of dried apricots. The black place suited our black mood. Sure, we were living on our survival food all right, but crammed into a tube of corrugated steel, not in the mountains. Discouraged? Yesterday and now today were enough to crack the soul of Hercules. Like two blind moles we curled under the ground and wondered if we could ever surface again. We talked. We couldn't see our faces, but we talked anyhow, quietly, voices amplified by a dull metallic echo. Both of us were certain: running away from people we had planned on at home, and running away from people we had actually been doing, and running away from people would be our future. Every human creature had to be assumed an enemy. Our renunciation pact had proved itself a prophecy.

Around midnight—a favorite hour for us lately—we crawled from the culvert. We were going to keep moving, Dylan said, even if it meant walking every inch to the Trinities. He had himself pumped up and set on edge once again, ready for battle and with a new plan. This time we would skirt the town and search out the nearest truck stop, to pay for a ride. Suspicious backpacks or runaways—no matter, because money closes eyes, the saying is. How much money would close them could be a snag, since half our funds were in the pockets (or bloodstreams) of the dopeheads. Still we plodded ahead on sore feet, exhausted from already walking during the day, yet jumpy, too, and hair-triggered to sprint from any wrong noise in the night. We were a far piece from the jolly sport of telephoning with code words and burying knives under eucalyptus trees.

On the town's other side we warily entered a truck stop: a café and service station ringed by a dozen diesel rigs. In the shadowy spaces between the trucks—most of them with motors left running—Dylan raised his voice and made his pitch. The first man was traveling south. The second and third and fourth just didn't buy. I felt like we were lurking in an alley trying to sell dirty postcards, and not very good dirty postcards.

Then we found our man.

"Going north?" called Dylan.

He checked us over, a lanky fellow in cowboy boots and cowboy hat, fresh from a meal and sucking a toothpick.

"Yup."

"Redding?"

"Yup. But my company has a no-riders policy, and they'd stick my fanny if I broke it and got caught."

"We'll pay," Dylan said, and the cowboy, who went by the name of Spud, perked up his greed. "Five dollars," Dylan offered.

Spud snortled, which is part snort and part chortle, neither one too positive. "Big spender, huh?"

"There's not enough to spend, is the truth, to be big spenders. We're skimping by on what little we have. Ten bucks would hit us hard . . . but . . . it's yours."

Spud wagged his head, soberly, and shifted the toothpick from cleaning his teeth to cleaning his fingernails. "Son, it's purely illegal for me to take riders, and bejesus, you all being so young, and a girl there. . . ."

He settled for fifteen.

Next Dylan asked him to buy us two sandwiches from the café. "Say, you done something serious?" he questioned us, curiosity aroused, and Dylan answered, "Not so you'd notice." We swallowed those sandwiches like wolves auditioning for a television pet-food commercial.

As we climbed into the cab, cowboy Spud said to Dylan, "There's a way to save your fifteen dollars."

Surprise. Dylan asked him how.

Spud dumped our packs behind the seat on his sleeper bunk, with a bounce. Using his eyes he drew a line from me back to the bunk.

Dylan said, "Don't bring that up again. Understand?"

"No offense . . . other couples pay for their travels that way."

"Don't bring it up again."

"It's your money you was complaining about," said big-hearted Spud, and away we went, winding higher through endless gears, deafened by the rapping bellow of twin-smokestack exhausts.

It's not every day that a girl hears her market value quoted, and learns what she's worth.

Out on Interstate 5 the truck reached cruising speed, the diesel engine settling down into a deep burbling gargle. At last miles were being put behind us again. From the dark cab we saw shiny lane reflectors vacuumed in under the truck, flashing beneath, bip-bip-bip-bip, each marking another quick step ahead. Telephone poles glided past. It was drowsy and peaceful, being gently rocked by the ride, lulled by the monotonous diesel and the faint dash lights, watching the night and the Sacramento Valley slide by, interrupted only by an occasional fuzzy, sputtering voice on the CB radio.

To make conversation, Spud asked once, "What are you, runaway lovebirds?"

To unmake conversation, Dylan merely grunted—an affirmative grunt. No more quizzing.

No more talk, until Spud announced, "Here comes Redding," the name penetrating for the first time, informing me where Dylan had gotten his Mr. *Red*dington code word, and why. From here, we would exit the concreted Interstate, turn a sharp left—aiming west—and head for the forested Trinities.

Naturally, we weren't eager to wander the streets of Redding, so Dylan asked Spud to arrange over the CB for our next ride, a lift, if possible, directly to microscopic Trinity Village. He was willing but doubtful: not much traffic going up there through the mountains late at night, he advised.

"The Idaho Spud here, rolling north. Got me a cargo of lovebirds here, looking for a haul on 299 to past Weaverville. A ten's in it for somebody. Any takers?"

No mention had been made about money, but Spud knew what it took to get cargo hauled, and praise be, a calm electronic drawl came back: "Roger. Ah'm five minutes from leavin' for the coast and Eureka." When that trucker left for Eureka we left with him, letting Spud go on alone with only our fifteen dollars for company. Well, if he got lonesome for Bridget, he probably had a wife and six kids waiting in a Pocatello potato patch.

FIVE

Mountains, Mountains, Mountains

i_____ The clustered lights of Redding dropped behind and *below* us while we began rising out of the Sacramento Valley. The truck shifted down a gear, then another gear down, while we went up, up, upward, in elevation and spirits both. As we put more and more distance behind us, deputy sheriffs and dopeheads and the East Bay were plucked off us and held back by a wonderful reverse gravity.

Hurrah. Getting away, getting safer, without having arrived anywhere new yet to worry about, is a royal treat.

The road looped with curves, tight curves, the truck laboring upgrade, topping one pass, coasting down and around, laboring up to top another pass, down, crossing a river. "That's the Trinity," Dylan said to me. "Water flows the other direction now, away from the Sacramento."

A river called Trinity, and running westward. We were close, but still we had a restless time of more curves, more gear shifting, sitting, leaning, waiting. Weaverville passed. Big Bar and Junction flitted by—blink twice and you might miss them. We followed the Trinity's snaky gorge, *feeling* the invisible mountain hulks looming around us. Soon now.

There: a few points of light ahead, almost swallowed up and snuffed out by the crushing blackness.

Few points or not, we took no chances and stopped the truck before it quite entered Trinity Village, and we skittered off the road to dodge any passing traffic and snoopy observers. Our truck throttled away again, loud and rackety, trailing behind a long wavery streamer of fainter and fainter sound, until silence made more noise than the truck did. We had arrived, ready for our walk into oblivion.

If in theory we were willing to walk, the practical fact was we couldn't see three steps in the night, particularly with our groggy fatigue. Time for good children to nap, said Dylan, and hoisting the packs, we fumbled and stumbled into a roadside thicket where we sat hunched in our sleeping bags, dozing shoulder-to-shoulder, or trying to doze. It was already the wee hours, thank goodness, and when the sunrise gave enough glow, we found a flatter, softer spot of ground and burrowed inside those bags to sleep like pooped rabbits.

At noon we unburrowed, smoked out by the sun's heat even in our thicket. We stretched, chewed some of those apricots from our packs, and viewed through the branches an infrequent car or truck zooming past. Then the good children did take an old-fashioned midday nap. We woke up thirsty, teased by the undertones of distant water running in the canyons. Dylan said we would be down in one of those canyons ourselves before much longer. As we sat there we stared at the mountains—the way you might stare, during the first meeting, at some newcomer your family is going to adopt or some pen pal you've agreed to marry.

Dylan consulted his wristwatch: Zero Hour. Combed and dusted, cash in pocket, we emerged from the thicket and sidled into the village, trying to be any ordinary two kids strolling home after school, ordinary kids materializing out of the brush, wearing backpacks, buying thirty dollars' worth of imperishable food. Just ordinary kids.

The toy town, perched on benchland above the river, had several legitimate houses it could claim, plus ten or so teetering cabins, a nest of trailers, two service stations, a matchbox café/bar, and, forming the civic center, the main attraction—an elongated one-room grocery/hardware/sporting goods/clothing/variety store and post office. Apparently loggers and hunters and tourists all found themselves at Trinity Village in their respective seasons. But which were we? None of those, to guess by the proprietor of the emporium, whose red fleshy face squeezed into a squint. An older man carrying a sizable beer paunch, he was a scowler, a hippie-hater, except we made that thirty-dollar purchase and even scruffy teenage drifters are tolerable when they have money to spend.

Our packs were fatter, lumpier, and a lot heavier when we departed the village, but we hustled faster than ever, trotting almost, anxious to shuck off this final outpost of civilization before it snatched us around the ankles at the very last moment. Come back Bridget and Dylan! You two are not *allowed* to go away! Downward, half-sliding, we went into a broad canyon where a big northern tributary rushed powerfully to meet the Trinity. North up this canyon we hustled ourselves, along its river bank, stepping on boulders and circling willow groves, hurrying, getting splashed and scratched. We must have covered most of a mile.

It came to me presently that the village was out of sight, long since out of sight. I slowed up. All villages and all towns and all cities were out of sight. We couldn't see them and they couldn't see us . . . couldn't hear us either. Around us were plain trees and rocks and water. Water: I knelt and gulped a gallon of it. Ahh, colder, sweeter, than Dylan's sugary carbonated ink.

My loud whistle caught up to Dylan, who was still charging forward. It got his attention, and extra, and he reversed his charge, jogging back to me, shushing me, saying, "*Any*body could be behind those trees. Who knows?"

"Indians?"

I untied and pulled off my street shoes. My feet were already bruised from constantly stomping on objects either too hard or too jagged, usually both, and now I got the message why hiking boots had to be thick and heavy.

Dylan relaxed some, taking probably his first full look around. "You forget that the Indians are us," he corrected me, but slipped off his pack, sat, scooped up a drink.

I put on my double socks—cotton, then wool—laced my fifty-dollar sale boots, combed my hair again, and brushed my teeth for ten solid minutes since it felt so doggone good. Oh, for a bath. Dylan bubbled his face in the water to cool down. He ended by shoving his whole head under and then letting his hair drip for the evaporation effect. With a flourish he buckled on the knife and hatchet, which hung sheathed from his belt in a defiant declaration of our independence. "When in the course of human events it becomes necessary for one people to dissolve the political bands which have connected them with another . . ." I had memorized that in my better days. Our "self-evident truth" was the Trinity National Forest —here, right here, surrounding us—no more an abstract, flat design on a worn map.

After Dylan reshuffled and balanced the pack loads, we

continued up the river at a more measured pace. This was the real thing, the real start, the real place. The real Trinities: mountains rising by us, higher mountains behind those mountains, higher mountains behind those mountains, ridge after ridge, until somewhere back there, not even in view yet, were the Trinity Alps and a 9,000-footer. Steep slopes ruled the terrain. Once out of the canyons, you plodded panting up or slithering down—too slow one direction, too fast the other—and little choice in between. Mountains shot up wherever you turned, mountains all over, and all over the mountains marched waves of trees, especially the ramrod firs, each tree a green spire alongside another green spire. Here and there were rocky outcroppings, too sheer to hold the trees but sprouting chaparral, while up near the ridges jutted some barren cliffs too vertical for soil to hang on to. Lower on the slopes appeared occasional open spots, gashes in the green mantle where slides during the rainy season had cleared the ground and jumbled trees.

And cutting through these real mountains ran a real tumbling river, wide and rough with the spring runoff. It smacked and frothed over massive boulders, some the size of limousines, tugging and sucking at logs and tree roots and even standing trees, impatient with anything stationary, anxious to take earth and wood and leaves along for the free ride into the Trinity, then into the Klamath, then into the Pacific, a day's distance. The water showed white excitement when it hit rocks or branches, or when it fell, spraying, and there were cascading sections of the river beaten almost entirely into whiteness. When the river became flatter or deeper, it showed not white, not blue, not clear, but a color like pallid iron. And talk about the real sound of a real river.

We heard it where we were, behind us where we had been, and coming from ahead, where we were going.

Henry David Thoreau would have loved these mountains and this river. If he had ever seen them, his famous *Walden* would be called *Trinities* instead, and be a thousand pages longer.

Twice when our route was blocked we (*very* cautiously) had to cross the river, using giant granite blocks and fallen timber that formed bridges. Then we skirted the water's edge, climbing logs, thrashing through underbrush, heading upstream to . . . some tiny nook in the Trinities that we would recognize as the perfect nook for us. Dylan had once said, "When we see it, we know it." How, I wondered, could Canyon X be much different from Canyon Y? I wondered because Bridget was sagging under the growing pain of her backpack, twice as heavy since its being stuffed with cans of vegetables and meat. Those cans weighed like cannonballs —no joke. But Dylan surged onward—lugging the weight of cannonballs plus the cannon—and Bridget, grinding her toothpaste-ad teeth, followed, although it hurt, it hurt.

When we quit, we were forced to quit: dusk and a fork in the river. In the morning we could decide which branch to take. We dropped our packs the way you throw off cruel and unusual punishment, flopping ourselves on the grass that bordered where the rivers joined. This would be our first genuine night in the mountains, in the open, with cooking and without hiding. Even if our business in the mountains was to stay secluded, still that wasn't like being bottled up in a culvert.

Dylan got his midget stove unfolded and fired up, no bigger than the can of chili it tried to heat, cute as a button, but the can never warmed through and we served piping cold Mexican chili. We were too hungry and too tired to care. For dessert we gobbled Hershey bars, the kind with almonds. Then—slam —night came down fast, while we were cleaning dishes at the river, and we had to unroll our sleeping bags by starlight.

Dark. Lord, how dark it gets in the mountains, not only with no direct lights—not even a single candle—but no particle of metal or glass to glimmer, no nearby city lights to reflect against the night sky. The two rivers mashed noisily together, filling the dark with loud reminders of their sleepless motions. I welcomed the loudness, because, cowardly Bridget, it screened away any other sounds that might be rustling in the darkness. Out of hearing, out of mind. Well, almost out of mind. Didn't bears come to grassy river banks during the night?

I asked sleeping-bagged Dylan about bears.

Mumble.

"Dylan?"

"Mmhuh."

"Is that yes?"

"Just black bears. I hung the food out of reach."

We weren't out of reach, and I about woke Dylan again to enlighten him. Instead, well, you remember how when you were little you pulled the blankets over your head? It works the same with a sleeping bag. Except, since it was nearly as dark outside the bag as inside, and the air considerably fresher, I eventually resurfaced. Bear, if you intend to get Bridget, come and get her, but be prepared for a screaming objection.

Falling asleep, I thought of Charlene, and what she could be doing this very night, this very minute. Watching television? Probably. Thinking about selling the house? Probably. Thinking about me? Yes, she was.

I also thought of how I once camped at Yosemite with my

parents, with a cot in a snug tent, a kerosene lamp on the picnic table, and crackling flames in the cement firepit, long ago.

ii _____ Right or left, northeast or stay straight north? The two rivers seemed identical, but upstream one fork might be friendly to us and the other nasty.

I told Dylan, "I'm not putting on this torture pack until you absolutely make up your mind." He'd been choosing since breakfast.

"If only we had a local topo map," Dylan regretted, for the sixth or seventh time.

His agonizing was sort of pointless, to my way of thinking. We couldn't peek ahead up those streams, through the granite, or divine by magic what waited up there, so we would just be taking our chances, qué sera. I said, "Do you realize what your so-called choice actually is? Your choice is, one, no choice, and two, no choice but only pretending you have a choice. Either number one or number two, we go up a canyon not knowing what the devil you chose."

He transferred his attention from the rivers to me. "Two rivers. We have to pick one. Isn't that a real choice?"

"That's my objection. Not knowing what will happen —what you picked—means you have nothing to choose between."

"A pick is a pick."

"But picking between chance and chance, is that a choice?"

"I should have brought a topo map. I could kick myself." He did kick.

"Eeny, meeny, miny, mo—"

"Hold it. No eenies or meenies. Let's search around, look harder."

Stubborn, stubborn. Look harder, or try harder, or get tougher, was always Dylan's final answer to himself when the questions asked were impossible.

Northward, he decided. We hitched on the backpacks and walked away from the fork, across an open field in morning sunlight, entering the speckled shade of cedars and firs.

I gave Dylan's bulging pack a poke. "Okay, why this canyon?"

He raised his voice instead of turning. "North."

"North, yeah?"

"Keep north and . . ."

"And?"

". . . Santa Claus."

We traveled out of the trees again and over a bare level stretch strewn with chunks of granite blocks.

"It's the wrong season," I called.

"How's that?"

"For Christmas."

Out of the open and into more trees.

"We can wait."

Now, there was an infant idea, to nourish and grow. Where would Bridget and Dylan be at Christmastide?

As we went onward it got warmer . . . another hot afternoon coming. By noon we noticed the canyon walls had pushed in closer, steeper, squeezing us against the river without leaving room to maneuver. When we stopped to eat the canyon was no longer a canyon but a gorge. We had almost undone our packs when we glanced at each other, hearing a new presence in the air.

"A wind?" Dylan suggested.

It might have been a wind, a powerful blast gathering in the treetops—but no wind ever arrived. And the noise remained at a distance, the same, like angry thunder trapped in a nearby cave, threatening, giving out deep groans. Then we both knew what it must be and without another word scrambled and raced on, the noise swelling angrier and angrier, very angry, until we clawed around a bend and met what we officially titled the Notch.

Dylan did some swearing.

I saw, clearly, we had come up the wrong river. Now, clearly, we would return to the fork and start over again tomorrow. Clearly.

Whitewater forced itself between narrow, nasty granite cliffs, roiling and boiling in a violent spew that shot through the V-slot so abruptly it hung for an instant suspended in air, before bouncing and shattering on the boulders below. We walked closer, until the walking had to end. All that rushing, battering energy made my soles prickle: slip, and you got ground into humanburger . . . after mercifully drowning. No possible path existed on either side of the river, as pure water shoved high up on pure granite, and the granite was naked except for a few stunted bushes in the cracks. Here the water noise was explosive—speaking meant shouting.

I shouted first: "Back!"

Dylan said No with his face. "Eat! Let's eat a snack!"

"For god's sake, here?"

He nodded, vigorously.

"Why?"

"To look for a route past!"

He wasn't laughing, but then, remember, Dylan never

laughed, even when he joked.

"Funny!"

"Let's take a bite!"

"Are you serious, Dylan?"

"I think there's a way! Let's eat, then try!"

Can you believe him? "You maniac! What way?"

"Those ledges!"

He pointed. There were ledges, kind of, maybe, on the cliff face—about three inches wide, it appeared.

"Let's eat, then try!"

"You maniac! Eat then die, you mean! I'm not eating here!"

"Let's climb up just a little! See what's beyond! We need to find out or waste a whole day!"

So we climbed, bellying over slabs of rock, above the river to the cliff face. Dylan motioned, pleased, and I was sorry to discover that the canyon widened again after the Notch —inviting us. Between our perch and our future journey was a hundred-foot-plus span of granite sidewall with puny ledges, although admittedly closer to foot-wide ledges, not three-inch. So near . . . so far . . . so tempting to Dylan.

"Ready?" he shouted.

Dylan, Dylan, is this toughness or craziness?

"Don't look down, don't!"

I looked down, anyway, to confirm that it would be as bad as I suspected, and it was.

We positioned ourselves facing the cliff, our packs sticking backward into space, our hands pressing greedily against the granite for friction, our boots edging, creeping sideways, along the ledge. Dylan led out into no-man's land. It was impossible to look down now, or the packs would topple us off. I fastened my eyes to the tiny fissures and crystal speckles on the granite in front of my nose. My total fanatical attention I fastened to my balance and my very gingerish steps, taken as if feeling with bare feet on broken glass.

"Careful!" shouted Dylan. "Rocksontheledge!"

I couldn't unscramble that over the bellowing water and my adrenalin-hyped, thumping heart, but soon my boots were teetering on bits of gravel and rock debris—big as boulders when out on that ledge. Worse, the ledge became wet. With spray misting all around us, the boots lost traction and I knew, *knew,* I could never make it across. I looked up the granite wall, hoping the sky would help. The wall rose on and on and I saw no sky. Instead, little circles dilated and contracted, tangling in my eyelashes. The deafening water confused me, made me dizzy, and made me want to sit down. My pack tugged. My body wanted to float . . . fly.

Dylan's voice I heard coming nearer, louder. He slithered, swayed, and grabbed granite wall. I swayed and grabbed granite wall and Dylan. "Back!" he fired into my ear, which helped to clear my faintheadedness. His hand stayed tight on my upper arm, keeping me pressured upright, propelling us back along the ledge and, at last, back down the boulders. We continued downriver until the Notch was safely out of view.

We did eat, or anyhow seemed to chew and swallow our food.

And are you prepared for this? While we sat there, still chewing and trembling, Dylan said we were going upriver again, through the Notch. My reaction? I was flabbergasted into a state of awe, and Bridget listened to Dylan's explanation without any hysterics. To go out on that ledge once, was madness. To go twice, therefore, must be sanity.

His new method, agreed, was uncomplicated and possibly

practical: cross the ledge with the awkward packs off our backs and the slippery boots off our feet. But what could his motive be? I asked him, as much fascinated as frightened, "Why do it? Why not go down to the other fork?"

Dylan had his own habits, and he took a certain breath, made that skyward examination, and right there in the middle of a national forest, in the middle of almost throwing our bodies to the watery wolves, he offered up one of his parables. I admit to being impressed. This Parable Time was like insisting on afternoon Tea Time during the London blitz in World War II, with fire still smoldering in the rug from last night's bombing raid. Stiff upper lip, very.

According to Dylan, a small boy once set out to visit his sick old grandfather, carrying a basket of food and medicine. No, he wasn't wearing a red hood. "When the boy got halfway there, going down his regular road, he saw the local bully blocking the path. The boy told himself, 'Small Boy, leave that bully standing there where bullies like to stand. Switch to the sawmill road. It's longer, but it goes by Grandfather's house, too.'"

"Smart kid."

"Very sensible. But pretty soon in the middle of the sawmill road he meets a snake, stretched across. Snakes can be dangerous. Better switch to the bridge road. It was even longer, but it went by Grandfather's house, too. Pretty soon, down the bridge road he meets a wolf."

Grandfather's house must have been a busy place, because four more roads passed by there, each one longer than before and each one with something awful stuck in the middle of it. "All right," I interrupted. "What happened? That boy's going to eat those sandwiches himself and graduate from college before you get him to the house."

"He did eat those sandwiches."

"Oh?"

He forgot where he was headed, and why, and he got hungry."

"But the sandwiches belonged to the grandfather." That sick grandfather had me worried, you see.

"No matter, he'd already died. The kid learned about it later from the woodcutter."

Dylan *would* have to go and kill off the grandfather. I said, "Are you trying to tell me that the other river fork has a notch like this one here? Like this monster?"

He only lifted an eyebrow, letting my feeble skepticism hang itself in the silence. I did in fact believe his parable: the Notch would be waiting on the other river fork, sure enough, or somewhere else in these mountains, even if the Notch went by another name. Getting to Grandfather's house took getting there, the doing it.

We walked toward the noise.

Before my life ended in a few minutes I elected to set history straight. "Hey, Dylan. This morning. I was the one, me, who said which fork we picked didn't matter. *You* were the one who diddled around, trying to decide, saying it made a difference. Remember? And *you* were trying to choose the easiest road to Grandfather's house. *Remember?*"

We rounded the bend, so that the Notch roared into sight, more frightening than ever. Dylan scrutinized the Notch and then scrutinized me.

"You misunderstood," he said. "I wasn't trying to pick the easy road. Why no, Bridget. The opposite. I wanted the fork that had the bully, the snake, the wolf, the bear, rolled together into a single spot, and I found it"—he waved at our monster. He was wiggling off the hook, and playing our teasing game, yet also being serious. "Listen," he continued, altogether solemn now, "would you cross those ledges unless you were being chased? Even if you were doing the chasing?"

"Not on this earth."

"Exactly. We need to go where other people are afraid to go. Get it? Their fear is our protection."

"What about *our* fear?"

Dylan nodded to himself, convinced. "If we go through there we lock shut a door, our door."

We walked on, and began climbing the rocks again. I swear. Dylan never planned for the Notch to happen—he never really picked this river to meet any bullies and bears, but by god I think if he *had* foreseen the Notch, and how it formed such a hairy-scary barrier to outsiders, we would be precisely where we were at that moment: rumps suspended over vicious water, risking our new lives to lock our old lives behind.

Our boots, the socks stuffed inside, were lashed to our packs, and edging sideways as before we scooted the packs along the ledge with us, in one hand like a prop. Push the backpack a step. Steady it. Take a step. Push, steady, step. Other hand, and the nose, pressed up against the granite wall. Push, steady, step. The scraping backpacks sent loose bits of rock tumbling from the ledge into the water—you could only feel that, not hear it, because the noise of the water smothered everything. That noise tried to break our concentration, shake us off, and then, above the wildest part, the spray and mist also smothered us, in a miniature rain. But our bare feet did the trick by suctioning to the wet shelf. I managed better while crossing the first half, because I accepted the worst, a fall, and had abandoned myself to disaster. Only when from the corner of an eye I saw the other end of the ledge beckoning safety to me, did I feel a gush of panic and want to dash across this rotten bridge before it collapsed. My former enemy, my pack, forced me to remain under control. Push, steady, step. Push, steady, step: a hundred times.

Success. We gawked back at where we had just been, disbelieving. Either the ground, or my legs, wouldn't keep from shaking. An earthquake? We laced up our boots and Dylan said, "Welcome to Grandfather's house."

And on we went, during the remainder of the afternoon. My back was numb, my feet sore from the new boots and too many rocks, my bones weary from too many miles, but how much better to complain about feet and bones instead of lethal ledges.

After a while the canyon opened into almost a valley, with acres of flat ground on both sides of the river. Then we met a ghost forest—black naked trees, standing but dead, where a fire had swept. Eerie . . . an evergreen forest without a speck of green, except for some underbrush making a comeback. Wind could get lost in all those empty branches. Even those dead branches were falling off into shattered junk heaps, turning the tall straight trunks into charred poles, and plodding through that shadeless forest made us glad to reach living trees again. Later the river formed a low marshy area—lots of grass—and we paused to get refreshed.

More plodding and the afternoon, growing advanced, was mixing with twilight shadows when we approached a lateral canyon, on the eastern side, where its creek joined the river. As we walked nearer I noticed Dylan eyeing the branch canyon.

"Know what I like about that little side canyon?" he asked.

I had an idea: "The logjam." A jumble of uprooted trees and

branches clogged the canyon mouth, and the creek had to exit by spilling between the logs. "Another barricade."

"True . . . and something else." He narrowed his eyes at the side canyon, an artist sizing up his subject. "We have to leave this river and the main canyon," he explained. "Too exposed here for a permanent camp. Too much a main highway through these mountains. Where would you say that branch canyon goes?"

"I would say probably to nowhere at all."

"Is that how it strikes you, too?"

Obscurity. Since that was our destination, we scrambled over the drenched logs—easy deal after the Notch—and once beyond that wooden maze we entered our private canyon. A deer trail wound among the boulders beside the creek and we forged upward, mindful of the increasing shadows, the path slowly gaining altitude. Alongside, the creek skipped through a series of riffles and pools, gurgling and gentle compared to the river below. We stayed by the stream: up, level, up, level, up. My body had sunk beyond fatigue, the legs moving by miracle alone, aided by frequent jolts of sweet talk from Dylan.

The canyon leveled, the creek leveled . . . and they kept level. A large meadow filled most of the canyon, with the creek widening into an enormous shallow pool, nearly a pond. No discussion necessary—we shucked off the backpacks.

"Home," I breathed, collapsing on the meadow grass.

A vista of the westward mountains spread before us, seen back down through the canyon. The sun had already set and so the black mountains were featureless, silhouettes, but across the sky glowing light still reflected, with brilliant cloud ribbons. We watched the spectacle as blue turned to violet and violet to smudgy grey, the oranges and scarlets to pale rose.

Above the last darkening clouds loomed one high tower of mellow gold. Beautiful. "Look," I told Dylan, "our mountain in the sky."

He was looking, head tilted, the stubble outlined around his chin and squared jaw. "It's fading," he observed.

When he said that, in his blunt way, it reminded me of when I once went running over a field and suddenly stepped in a hole and twisted my ankle. Bridget fell again, with that final light, when she hadn't expected to, and hurt herself. I was feeling puny, I guess, in a giant place with night coming down. I guess I had been counting on a gold mountain or a gold beacon to flash me a hopeful sign, even in the dark, especially in the dark.

Dylan, clearing his throat, patted the grass. "Bridget," he said, voice bouncing across the meadow, "this can't fade." He spat, not too artfully, a dribble christening his knee. "Not this here mountain, damn no."

I love that Dylan when he sets his eyes, sets his jaw, and swears "Damn no." Really, it's his way of wanting YesYesYes and then I want it, too, and believe it. I believe the YesYesYes more than he does himself, but his wanting it so much is what gets me hungry and believing. Someday I'm going to tell him, "Dylan, you're starving to death, man. Break the window. Reach in. Eat." I hope he does.

Warrior and Maiden

i _____ Bridget, Bird Lady of the Trinities, is what Dylan sometimes called me. With juicy grass and lots of water and space and sunlight, surrounded by all those trees and bushes and berries and seeds, the meadow was a gigantic aviary, and the birds and I got along great. Many an hour I studied them and they studied me back. They were as curious about the new neighbor as the new neighbor was about the neighborhood, and we introduced ourselves, rubbed elbows, became friendly. I fancied myself the first example of Homo sapiens of their acquaintance—maybe true—so I tried to make a good impression, to be a credit to my species, you could say. Some birds I got to eat crumbs within a hand's reach. Of course that ended when Dylan and I discovered we had better save every crumb for our own beaks.

The birds preferred me to Dylan because, besides sharing those crumbs of mine, I stayed in the meadow more and became a more familiar figure. But the birds were more familiar to Dylan, or at least their names were. When I brought to his attention a yellow and black and red bird—the glamor champion of the meadow—Dylan informed me: "Western tanager." When a large bulky bird startled us by shooting from its cover on booming wings, he said, "Blue grouse. If we ever get ahold of one, we'll have us a dandy dinner." After a while, I asked him if he made up some of those names, pygmy nuthatch, for instance. He shook his head, a little disappointed in my suspicions. "Straight from *California Birds,* the Mountain Forest section," he told me.

Dylan's crash course on escaping to the Trinities had included studying its flora and fauna (in particular anything digestible) and he also had—this took some prying out—an ancient Boy Scout merit badge in birdwatching. Therefore I, too, courtesy of Dylan, got to know most of my birds properly and formally. Besides the shy blue grouse, there was a resident covey of mountain quail, also potential menu fare according to Dylan, if you can imagine killing those sleek things with their delicate colors, seemingly applied by a Japanese painter's thin brush. Tribes of fox sparrows, white-crowned sparrows, and juncos foraged across limbs and the ground, a stir of flitting action. There were tree-pounding woodpeckers; tree-climbing brown creepers; airborne, careening swallows. The only birds that insisted on resenting our arrival were a pair of Steller's jays, who for several weeks screeched and shook their topknots at us, not from fear but for the sheer devilment of being loud. You know how jays are, everywhere. Later on we couldn't chase these blue bandits away, as they hopped over our camp thieving for food. Too bad they failed to qualify for our own menu. Opposite from the jays were the petite chickadees: tidy, trusting, calling "sic-a-dee-dee" in squeaky good cheer. The chickadees hunted for bugs by hanging under branches and leaves. Now that's a secret to learn—happiness even while seeing the world upside down.

The meadow. It was pear-shaped, with the upstream end the widest, then skinnying down toward the downstream end. To put the measurements in approximate numbers, the length, say, would be nearly a hundred yards, with the fattest cross point, the pear's bulge, about seventy or eighty yards wide. Crowding around the edges—and up and down our canyon, and the mountainsides—were different firs and a mix of pine, spruce, and cedar trees. In the meadow stood occasional Douglas firs and hemlocks, while in the wetter pockets grew brushy willows and some alders with their quivering leaves. Rocks of various sizes lay scattered throughout. The outlying meadow grass had begun browning, but closer to the water it was spring green, and heavenly soft to the cheek. During the flood season apparently the entire meadow could be covered by spillover, since a high-water channel had been gouged out on each side of the main stream bed, and all three channels were broad and shallow rather than deep.

The creek itself came churning into the meadow, hit flat ground, dug its biggest, coolest pool (where the biggest trout hid), and then with nowhere else much to go it calmed down and leisurely spread out to take in some sun. It ambled here and about, until at the meadow's other end it got restless, began to ripple, and dashed off again. When we first arrived, the creek kept fresh water in sections of both overflow channels, but barely. A little time after, the creek lowered enough to cut off the overflow channels, isolating them, so that Dylan and I scooped from there our first mess of fish, before the raccoons beat us to it.

We did our best to convert the meadow into our domestic domain, an eternal labor that eternally fell a tad shy of success, although I could easily boast about certain achievements and I will. And our clumsiest, most blushable failures did come the earliest, which counts as an excuse of some sort. Our number-one, first-off project was to build a shelter, because what is a home without a house? The perfect location for the shelter we spotted immediately: a cluster of tall trees at the lower end of the meadow, twenty strides from the creek, on the north (sunny) side.

Dylan spent a complete morning hacking down and hauling armloads of willows. He used willows, he said, because the hatchet cut their green branches in one swing and because they were whippity enough to be shaped every which way. Inside the cluster of trees was a hollow circle that I cleared of stones and lumps and scraped smooth. Sprinkled on top of this went an hour's worth of pulled dry grass, making a nicely cushioned bedroom floor. Over the floor Dylan started to bend his willow branches, like weaving a huge upside-down basket or putting together a wood rat's nest. When the last piece was twisted and intertwined into the mound, we stood back to admire this splendid hunk of brush.

"Snug as a bug until the rainy season," appraised Dylan. "And notice that we did it without any center support to clutter up the inside."

We stowed our gear in and unrolled the sleeping bags. That night the willow odor was tremendous, but the sleeping comfortable. The next night a wind whipped through the canyon, the way it sometimes does in the evenings—and we heard rustling in the treetops first, then groaning up there. Our rat's nest shuddered . . . and *bong,* one or two of those willow wands came unsprung . . . and *poof,* the entire she-bang, all 400 willow rods, came tumbling down around our ears, and around our everything.

While we were lying under a pile of willow trash, thinking it over, I said, "Parable Time. Once upon a time three little pigs decided to leave home. The first little pig was a jerk—let's forget about him. The second little—"

Dylan gave a moan, shaking the brush feebly. "Stop it, stop it, I beg you."

"The second little piggy met a man selling sticks. 'Do you want to buy some fine sticks,' asked the man, 'to build your fine house?' And this little nincompoop—"

"—said 'Only if they're willow sticks.' Now, do you want me to huff and puff too?"

"Too late, Dylan. That part's already over."

"Hey. I know what we should do now." He struggled upright and we surfaced, parting the debris. "Read a book. Guess which one."

"No guess."

"Come on. Here's a hint: a childhood favorite."

I sealed my lips.

"Well?" he prodded me.

"If you think you can get me to say *The Wind in the Willows* out loud, you *are* a nincompoop."

We did put those willow sticks to use, as fire kindling.

Our next shelter we constructed of stout evergreen branches, butt ends placed vertically in a circle and tied together at the top with twine, teepee fashion. They worked better than the willows, smelled better than the willows—and we did use the teepee for days—but after the branches dried out we would lie in there at night and feel shreds of bark and prickly fir needles rain down into our hair and teeth. Eventually we figured that no quick way beats the slow right way, and Dylan hiked the canyon and mountainsides, lugging back small trees that he had already de-branched and chopped into exact log sections. I could hear him off in the distance, *whack, crack*. In camp, he peeled away the bark and notched the ends log-cabin style. All this required many hours.

When it was finished . . . strictly class, the best building in the canyon. It had close-fitting log walls that reached five spacious feet high, a log roof, notched-in like the sides, and even a framed doorway. Architecturally, it resembled Very Early Pioneer: primitive yet still roomy enough for our needs, and solid, keeping out everything except a little wind, a few little spiders, or a big bear, but more on that later. And our cabin (as we called it) had portability. We could dismantle it later in the year and reassemble the thing on higher ground, with the tarp added to shed rain.

Our second project was to domesticate our cooking and eating area, particularly since Dylan's magical miniature stove proved to be a full-sized dud. One evening as we waited for it to cook something, anything, Dylan tossed his shiny beauty against a tree trunk, "to find out how well made it is." Not a break or bend. Very well made. "There, you see," said Dylan, "I told you it was expensive." The cooker got retired to the cabin and we built a firepit, midway to the creek, digging out and squaring the hole, lining the bottom and sides with flat rocks, erecting a rock windbreak with crossrods to hold the pots and the aluminum baking sheet. At a standing arm's reach above the firepit Dylan put up a wooden canopy, or glare screen, supported by poles, to scatter the smoke and camouflage the view from any aircraft overhead, which might be spotting for forest fires or searching for runaway kids. We also had a (hollow log) kitchen cupboard, a (log) table, (log) benches, (log) chairs with a (log) ottoman. A bunch of ordinary logs to any fliers-by, but up close they did their duty for us.

Down by our cabin and firepit the creek flowed swifter, making for Grade-A fresh drinking and cooking water. Because too many trips mire a creek bank, muddying the stream, we set down a platform of timbers where we could kneel or sit to fill our plastic jug or clean the pans or do the laundry. And while the firepit was being dug we dug two more pits, much deeper, one for Dylan and one for me, in the trees at opposite ends of the meadow, in accordance with the separate-but-equal doctrine. Boy, that ground makes hard digging. We also had separate bathing hours at the old swimming hole, or, in other words, the big pool in the upper meadow. Boy, that water makes cold skinny-dipping.

So, after a spell, we had managed some order and some routine in the meadow, although it took weeks and weeks until the mountains seemed what you might call the *normal* place to be, and which at first I never believed they ever could be. For one thing, we had to get used to living with those animals who weren't as open and cheery as my chickadees, or maybe as petite. For example. You could be traipsing down to the platform by the creek, to wash out one of those pairs of underwear, skipping and soaking up the morning sunshine, and who's already there on the platform to assist you with your underwear? A slinky three-foot gopher snake, and it looks a lot like a rattler until you check over the head or tail. And for example. You could be tiptoeing to the swimming hole, the notion of snakes in the back of your mind from yesterday, tiptoeing across the meadow when—zzzip—some creature scurries from under your tipped toe. What? Why, it's only Peter Cottontail, or a ground squirrel, or a fuzzy mouse, or a bitty blue-belly lizard, but just try to tell your pulse count that. And for example. You could be, you *very* well could be, lying in your sleeping bag at night . . . black as a tar bucket inside the cabin . . . Dylan asleep, breathing gently . . . when . . . *scrape, scrape* comes tapping, comes tapping at your cabin door, or rustles in the leaves outside the wall, fifteen inches from your head. What is it? Heaven knows. You wait, blinking at the dark. Then off away in the woods a bobcat squalls and you lurch sideways, and Dylan mumbles, automatically, "Mmmbopkolt," which means "It's only a bobcat," which means "Go to sleep." Or maybe an owl screeches or a frog plops like a dropped stone into the creek or a fish plops jumping out or a fox yips or a raccoon barks. Then comes *scrape, scrape* again, all night long probably, except finally, although you swear your ears still listen, sleep has sneaked in and switched them off.

For example. Ah, for example, our most famous acquaintance.

On one of those dark tar-bucket nights in the cabin one of those *scrape, scrape* sounds started up. The rustling in the leaves got heavier this time, not the usual mice feet. I heard: SNUFFLE. SNUFFLE, SNUFFLE, SNUFFLE, SNUFFLE.

"Dylan," I whispered, giving him a shove. This, I had a strong conviction, was worth waking him.

"Mmmkilkolt."

"Dylan . . . it's *not* a coyote."

"Mmm—"

SNUFFLE. *SNORT.*

"*Wake up,* Dylan." I threw a punch into his sleeping bag.

We listened together to the snuffling and snorting.

"Is that a bear?" I asked in my tiniest whisper, pretty sure of the answer.

Dylan whispered back, "It wants our food."

We had the food stored inside the cabin with us, away from sharp mice teeth and clever raccoon hands. Instead, bear teeth and bear claws were our problem now, and we continued whispering, hoping to make up our minds what to do before the bear did.

I said, "Let's throw it some food."

"No, we need it too much ourselves. Besides, the bear will just want more, and come in to get it."

I recalled, unhappily, that our door consisted of a hanging blanket, folded double.

"Do we have any pots or pans in here?" Dylan asked. "We can try making a racket—scare it off."

The pots and pans were in their hollow-log cupboard, by the firepit.

"Then we yell," said Dylan.

"Yell what?"

"Scream, Bridget. No lyrics. Just scream and clap your hands. On the count of three. Get set. One, two, *three*."

I screamed all right. My heart was in it. When we stopped, it was quiet outside, for sure. Even the frogs were quiet, no brupping over by the creek. The bear had evidently departed, but we stayed awake most of the night, to check on the situation.

The following night—SNUFFLE—both of us were already wide-eyed, noisemakers by our sides. We banged the pans and shouted and gave the meadow quite another shock. During the day we sat, groggy, and wondered how we would ever manage another lost night. Dylan wrapped up every bite of our food into the packs, including the cooked leftovers, and strung them up in a tree, although he was still afraid that raccoons—and the bear—could climb anywhere he dangled our nylon rope.

The third night the bear returned for his prowl and snorted around our cabin anyway, besides climbing the tree. When Dylan heard those claws dig into bark he took his pans and flew into a passion: food had become very serious business for us, you have to understand. Despite all this, all our scare tactics which so far were successful, that bear continued its visits, until we were its nightly custom. Worse, the bear seemed less and less concerned about our noises, apparently thinking that while the log box in the meadow erupted into an odd racket, now and then, the box would never amount to anything. Before long, our shouting might not do the job anymore.

When the bear began dropping by two or three times in the same night, Dylan got his Dylan glint in his Dylan eye. Stand back, World. Stand back, bear . . . Bridget has seen that glint before. Dylan fingered his hatchet and I said, "No, no, this Indian maiden has no intention of losing her warrior."

"Bridget," he said, musing, reviewing a lesson to himself, "let me tell you a fact about our friend, that bear. You won't believe it, but that bear is more frightened of us than the reverse. A fact."

"Does the bear know that fact? Could be it forgot to read the same book you did."

"It needs a little reminding."

"Dylan. What are you planning? *Dylan*."

"I'm still thinking."

That night I was edgy because Dylan had been too untalkative when we ate dinner and when we later settled into the cabin. None of our normal side-by-side chat in the darkness. I could feel him tensed over there, waiting. In about an hour, on schedule, came the deep-chested grunting and whuffing outside—like somebody coughing into a barrel —and immediately Dylan popped one of those waterproof matches he carried. I could see he had been atop his sleeping bag, boots on.

"What are you doing?" I asked, whispering as usual.

"Protecting our food."

"Please . . . nothing foolish . . . please." I had a flash—a fear—of Dylan's mauled body, of blood, of a car wreck.

"We take care of ourselves here," he whuffed in his own bear's voice. "We take charge here." Of all things, he was igniting his portable cooker, turning up the flame full throttle. In the wavering light his reddish beard seemed part of the fire and he had an eye winked shut, an old trick to preserve night vision.

"I'm going to burn a bear," he said, wielding the cooker in one hand and grabbing the doorway blanket with the other, crouching like a sprinter at the starting line, head cocked, locating the bear's sounds.

I didn't believe it. I thought he would shake the stove out the door, shout some, maybe. But Dylan had a fact to test, and probably himself. Flap went the blanket, and Dylan bolted out the doorway, and I followed—taking a big gulp. What I heard from the bear: not snuffle, not snort, grunt, whuff, but *squeal*, exactly what a burnt bear would say. What I saw of the bear: a low black ball humping it across the meadow.

"Dylan?"

He held up the flaming, flickering cooker, a statue of liberty. Victory: send Dylan your tired, your poor, your huddled masses. Tired, we were.

"Well, well," he said, extinguishing his handy-dandy imported pocket stove, "we got our money's worth out of this contraption after all."

And we did, because that terminated the great bear affair, and someday I may write a book on How to Discourage a Pushy Bear, Grizzlies Excepted. Later I learned the bear affair hadn't particularly been the bear's fault. It just didn't realize how we really felt about our food—and in the mountains you have to make such matters obvious. Later I learned that wild animals cause a heap less trouble than tame people and I got comfortable with all of them, not only the birds. When you consider it, the suspicions I had about the animals were mutual, since they'd never confronted a Bridget before, either. Why trust a Bridget that comes rustling through the grass?

We had busy, busy days, but the evenings were slower, more thoughtful. After cooking, eating, cleaning up, brushing teeth, we would return to sit by the firepit, dusk blurring the meadow around us. Cock quail called, gathering in the covey to roost. Trout broke the surface, *shlup,* striking at gnat swarms. An owl glided from one tree to disappear mysteriously inside another. As the sky darkened, we would add fresh wood to the fire, and by nightfall it was fully stoked.

Looking into a campfire is constant entertainment: shadows and shapes, glare and glow, surrounded by black. Stare and you can find faces and a story in there. When the flames die to embers, then the stars are another endless entertainment, more endless than the fire or Dylan and Bridget. Clouds and clouds of stars. You should see the summer Milky Way through the pure mountain air.

Between us, we knew some of the main stars and constellations. Of course, the Big Dipper in the Great Bear constellation, and the Little Dipper and Pole Star in the Little Bear. Boötes was a man chasing both the bears with a stick, like Dylan and his burning cooker. Leo the lion roared—and thank goodness no lions lurked in our woods, at least not the African variety. Mighty Hercules seemed to be holding a bow, which Dylan wished we could borrow for our own hunting. We made up tales about these starry characters, such as how they got there, what they were doing, where they were going, and sometimes we made up brand-new pictures out of other stars. There, over to the east, stars formed a tall fir with its top knocked off by lightning. There was a bending river. There was its waterfall. There was a Pacemaker, searching. There was Bridget. There was Dylan.

We sat on the logs and watched stars slowly track across the sky, or we lay on the meadow grass, backs down, so that the stars were silver raindrops falling toward our faces. When the night chill arrived, we turned from heaven to earth, raked the coals together under some ashes to last until breakfast, went into the cabin for our sleep. Our busy days meant rising with the sun.

Inside, by the sleeping bags, we had placed log benches, hewn flat. The walls were covered top-to-bottom with cubbyholes and hooks, whittled from limbs. We had memorized what got stored where and even in the blackness we crawled into those warm sleeping bags in seconds. Outside, strumming, could be heard the background songs of the creek and the wind. Dylan and I held our most important talks in the cabin at night. We talked on until our tiredness undid us, our conversation breaking up into longer and longer blank spaces. Some nights I stayed awake despite the tiredness, thinking of a certain curved driveway, a certain flagstone patio, a sloping yard with sunken redwood rounds for steps, a mowed lawn, a border of ground-hugging junipers, and roses, rhododendrons, irises, a young girl uncovering a turquoise Easter egg. Hands. Faces. Smiles. But no voices—silence, as our cabin was silent.

Some nights I sniffled. I couldn't lick it. I struggled to hold it back, burying my head in the sleeping bag so not to bother Dylan. Well, I knew he heard me anyway, and one night I had to speak up and say, "Sorry, Dylan."

He answered from in the dark, "Don't be."

"I hate to keep you awake with this sobbing racket."

"You don't."

"Sure I do. Who you kidding? How can you sleep with somebody crying in your ear."

"I mean, I wouldn't want to be asleep if you're feeling sad."

That's my Dylan. Soothed, I said, "At least you don't cry at night. One crier per cabin is enough."

After a pause, he said, "Oh, I've cried at night."

"So did we all, at age four."

There came another delay, but this one was different, longer, reminding me of his mystery pause way back last year, and I had a sensation that he was finally going to tell me about it. "No," he said, "not age four. Recent history."

I held my tongue.

"Remember once I told you about my parents, how they had fired bullets at each other with their bodies. Do you remember my saying something like that?"

You bet I did.

"I couldn't bring myself to give you the messy details then. Now, after what you went through, it's easier to explain, and you'll understand. Last summer, when my parents were really sinking into the pits, they had a helluva big blow-up. Hollering, swearing. They both stormed off in the afternoon, leaving me alone in the house. That night my father came back with his girlfriend, who I'd never even seen before, and pretty soon here comes my mother with some man on her arm. I think she just scrounged around the bars and picked him up to prove her point. The guy must have wondered a little what this kinky business was, coming to a house with the husband there. Christ, what a sight. Nobody said anything. Me neither. My father and his girlfriend went to his bedroom and spent the night. My mother and her man went to her bedroom and spent the night. I went to my bedroom."

For a moment we had only our black cabin—without speech—before Dylan's bodiless voice finished: "I would have kept you awake with noise that night."

More black cabin.

I asked, "But now. Would you cry over them again?"

"Never."

ii ———————————— Out of all our talks, one topic began ballooning bigger and bigger, interrupting us during the day, even shoving into our night cabin-talks, until it got to be the giant subject of discussion. Food.

How much is left? We were two misers fretting over a dwindling bank account: How poor are we today? How much is left?

How much powdered milk and powdered eggs? How much flour mix? How many packets of dried apples and apricots? How many cans of tuna? Of stew? Of hash? Of peas? Of corn? How much rice? How many bouillon packages? How many dehydrated potato packages? How many stroganoff packages? How much dehydrated soup? How much dehydrated meat?

Our bank account dwindled. The question switched from how many *kinds* of food left to how many *meals* left. We asked ourselves: How much *time* left, before bankruptcy and poverty?

"We ought to have killed that bear," Dylan said, not entirely in jest.

"Bear steaks?"

"Bear steaks. Bear everything. Burgers, bacon, chops, ribs, roasts."

"It would've objected, I think. Besides, bear meat is

supposed to be like old automobile tires."

"Bridget," he sighed, "if it's not poison, we swallow it and smile."

That became our daily script—find our daily bread, find anything we could swallow that wouldn't come back up or poison us. We spent precious little time, now, fixing or fancying the cabin or camp, and loads of hours scouring for food. Along the creek we dug for plants that grew any sort of tuber, no matter how puny. These got boiled, turning out decent in every case, with more flavor than blah canned peas according to my taste buds. In fact, grab any juicy plant, even fresh grass, throw it in a pot for a quick boil, add salt, and it turns out decent. Better than automobile tires, for certain. Also along the edges of the creek, in the shady spots, we found a floating water cress, which we ate uncooked and fresh, bringing it cool and dripping directly from creek to dinner table. And, while they lasted, we stole the early berries from my birds. Look up *omnivorous* in the dictionary.

Give thanks to the fish of the world, especially the trout in the Trinities, who were our best food supply at the beginning, right from when we shoveled out those glittery charmers trapped in the creek's overflow channels. Dylan and I began fishing every day, far up and far down the creek, doing pretty well, too, even without a license, until too many of the fish ended up in our stomachs and the ones still uncaught got cagy.

When the fishing began playing out, and the edible plants in our meadow got munched short, Dylan had to risk the trip back to the river canyon, where he could fish the river and gather greens from its marshy section, down toward the forest-fire trees. Dylan went alone in order to be less visible. Neither of us liked his leaving our own canyon. Sometimes he was gone the whole day, missing our lunch together, while I rattled around by myself in the meadow, doing a few chores and grubbing for roots or trying to outwit one of the granddaddies lurking at the bottom of the big pool. Like an anxious squaw, I waited to see if my hunter, first, would return uncaptured, and second, would return with food. On a few days he had a plastic sack crammed with fish, enough to last us for extra meals. Other days it carried a slim load. Once in a while the plastic sack came back folded up in his pocket. "No luck," Dylan would apologize, sinking on the log bench. "What about you?"

One day he returned early.

"Welcome back," I said, frisky, because now I had company and because an early return meant Dylan had brought food. "And so soon. Did you catch them in the creek, or what?"

"No fish. I saw tracks."

I chewed a fingernail.

"They looked like bootprints to me, and not mine. I decided to come straight back. They were near where our creek goes into the river."

"Who could it be?"

"A fisherman? I don't know who."

"But what about the Notch? How? You said that nobody but us would be crazy enough to cross the Notch."

"Maybe somebody else is crazy, after all. Maybe they came downriver, from up north."

That night we were fidgety, but the next morning, and the next mornings, Dylan went to the river again without seeing anyone. Our routine continued as before, except the fishing in the river got spottier along the stretch within Dylan's walking range. He began straggling in after dark, after hiking farther away to new fishing holes. Back at camp I began foraging higher and higher up the mountainsides.

In the cabin one night Dylan said, "We'll have to lay off the
trout awhile. They need a rest. Let's try the rabbits and
ground squirrels."

"Not in the meadow, though," I cautioned. No neighbors,
please.

Dylan set his snares. He took small logs and propped up
deadfalls, triggered to crush. He dug pit traps, covered with a
veil of leaves and grass. He whittled bows, strung with twine;
whittled arrows, fletched with paper strips wedged into slots.
He carved spears. Dylan dredged up every lethal device from
all those books he had read on How to Kill a Small Animal and
Stay Alive When Lost in the Mountains and Starving.

The snares got tripped, but their rigging lacked the finesse
necessary to noose the critters. Not a single deadfall even got
tripped, ever. The pit traps caught a good haul of sow bugs
and stink bugs—down in the bottom of the pits spinning
their teeny legs, trying to climb the walls. The bows and
arrows . . . forget them. It could have been funny if our
bellies weren't so solemn about the subject of being full. Dylan
experimented with six different kinds of wood for the
bows—each one either too stiff or too brittle or too rubbery
—and we concluded that for archery handicrafts you should
move to the Sherwood Forest. A spear? Deadly, if your animal
will stay asleep while you walk up and poke it. None ever
cooperated.

Dylan readjusted and reset the snares, transferring them to
the meadow where the rabbits ran thick. I saw his logic.
Meanwhile, he performed our first kills, clumsy as they were.
He sat on a low tree limb holding a chunk of log. On the
ground underneath was sprinkled some of our valuable rice.
Dylan had to sit there motionless for awful periods of time,
watching the birds steal the rice. What he finally squashed—I

hate to say it—was two quail. Their family cooled toward us considerably, afterward, avoiding us like the traitors we were. I hated it, I say, but you'll do what you hate, to eat. Bridget did.

The next strange event in the meadow was a baby's scream.

Dylan and I had been kneeling around the firepit, late in the afternoon, readying the fire for cooking. *EEeeeEEeeee:* a sharp, wailing shriek. A baby! In terrible pain! My mouth opened to ask "What—?" but Dylan had already said "It worked," as if amazed, and I could only run after him across the clearing, splashing through the creek, to where a mottled grey rabbit dangled from a wire noose. That wire was so thin the fur had to be parted to find it. The rabbit's neck was all bent into a kink, with its eyes bulging up white, and its legs still kicked now and then, treading air.

"Reflex," said Dylan. "It's dead." Then, in schoolroom fashion, he proceeded to explain how he had at last found a successful combination with the snares: how he located a rabbit run, how he put blocks on each side of the run, and between the blocks the noose—large enough for the head but too small for the body—how a slight push on the noose dislodged the trigger wedge, which released the arched spring stick, which hanged the rabbit. "Tomorrow, you can reset this one," he ended.

In the meadow the birds, quiet since the scream, tried to squeeze in half-hearted twitters before the light faded. Dylan skinned, gutted, quartered the rabbit—or hacked it into bloody pieces, really, its useful hide winding up in shreds, tossed into a hole with the innards. Later we would get much more accomplished at using my father's hunting knife as a butcher knife, both of us. That first rabbit we carried in a beeline to the firepit, since the hour was right and the fire was right. We barbecued the bunny sizzling on a spit and gobbled everything except the bones, forgetting somehow about the baby's scream and the sight of a membrane bag full of purple and green guts.

Our boldest food venture had to be the *grand* scheme we labeled Project Fishery. The idea occurred to us when we observed how near the creek's water level stayed to the overflow channels. Why not build a permanent pond, our own fish farm?

"Why not?"

"Why not."

So . . . on both sides of the creek we dug trenches to the overflow channels, wide ditches, slanted in the direction of the water's flow. Then we toted rocks—lots—to make a loose dam across the creek. It was the type of dam that backed up the water but still let some through, keeping the water fresh enough for trout yet preventing the dam from being knocked completely apart in the winter. The more boulders we toted the higher the water crept—until the edges of the stream reached the critical mark, broke away, and began sluicing into our trenches, into the overflow channels, into the meadow.

I said, "It's the Hoover Dam all over again. What hath mankind wrought?" And the spreading water actually was exciting, except for a while, as night came, we wondered whether we should dismantle part of the dam in case the entire meadow might flood. We went to sleep with visions that before morning the cabin would be floated off us by the tide. Glub.

But in the morning we saw that the water had stabilized, forming a pond just the proper size for our intentions. We added some boulders to the dam and started two rock piers, one for each side. The heartbreaker was stocking the pond:

catching the wily fish and then, after transporting them in a *cooking* pot, letting them go again. Once in the pond the rascals seemed to guess they were protected, the Chosen Few selected to populate a new ocean. It pained us to see those tasty meals lazily swimming under our noses, practically beside our blessed dinner table. Old-fashioned discipline is what it took and a belief that we would be repaid in the future for our sacrifice. Which naturally signaled the one sticking point to Project Fishery: splendid feat, but it would produce no fried fish before next year and the next generation of fingerlings.

iii _____ During the following days we limped along, snaring a rabbit here, catching a couple of trout there—splitting the fish between the pond and our stomachs. The food packs fell very flat and floppy, more pack than food.

I told Dylan I expected we would be making a trip to spend our last money. It had been on his mind, I knew. I told him, "Well, let's get it over with. We have the money, anyway, and let's spend the stuff."

He swore under his breath. We lay in the cabin at night, blanketed by the darkness, talking.

"I'd hoped we would never set foot in that village again," he said with conviction.

"Not ever?"

"Not ever." He sighed, and thrashed in his sleeping bag. In the dark, sounds like that say as much as expressions on a face do in broad daylight. "But you're right about the money."

"No sense in letting the mice chew it for nest padding, the way they have every other piece of paper around here."

"Jesus, have they yet?"

"No—I checked yesterday."

"How much is there? About twenty, isn't it?"

"About twenty."

He did more turning, twisting, sighing.

"Food is food," he said. "We take it where we can get it, and even from that village, going back."

We both thought of consequences. Could there be trouble? Would anybody know who we were, that we came from up here? I asked Dylan.

"Oh . . . probably not, if we stay on the fringes. With summertime coming we probably won't seem out of place among the tourists . . . other strange faces . . . kids on vacation. Probably."

Summer. Summer and I hadn't considered it. A summer coming unlike any summer of Bridget's before. Later I said, "I'm remembering the Notch."

Dylan was asleep, but thrashing.

After breakfast the next morning we didn't hurry off, because it would be impossible in one push to reach the village store during its open hours. Instead, we tidied up the camp the way you do any house before departing on a trip. When it came time to get the key and lock the house's front door, we barricaded our cabin doorway in case of furry thieves. We slung on the backpacks—empty except for some snacks and the rolled sleeping bags attached to the bottoms—and left our meadow behind.

It felt odd: the backpacks again, on a journey again, looking out for the enemy again. Unlike Dylan, I was on my first adventure back outside our private canyon, and as we reached the logjam across the canyon mouth, and wriggled through it, I cringed like a chipmunk in a bare field when hawks are circling overhead. Downriver we went, scouting . . .

searching for colors and motions that didn't belong.

"In the village," Dylan said, "we might be two kids coming from anywhere and going anywhere. But out here we can't afford to advertise our home territory."

We went through the river's marshy section, although now the ground was less spongy and the grass not so lush. Then, the ghost forest, the forest-fire trees. That cemetery hadn't changed, with the bodies still standing and falling bones piled around. More walking and we stopped to eat.

"Is this the condemned woman's last meal?" I joked, feebly, the food having problems squeezing down my throat.

Dylan tapped his boot encouragingly against mine. "You're a veteran," he flattered me. "An old pro, eh? You already know you can do it."

Brother, did I dread the Notch.

And so imagine my surprise (and chickenly relief) when we stood at the lip of the gorge and blinked down through the Notch: the rumble was there, the battering water, the spray, but also—on the sides—lower and wider ledges.

"Dylan, the river—"

"—has dropped. Look. We should have predicted that. Look. Chriiist. It'll be this winter, months, the rainy season, before the Notch does its job again, the way we want."

Dylan, of course, took my good news as a bad blow. Good news for him would have been if the ledges had washed out altogether, turning the granite walls slicker than glass. Underneath my relief I knew Dylan's disappointment made sense, as usual. Without saying so, we both recalled those footprints by our canyon. The puzzle was solved.

We crossed the Notch, carefully, because regardless of the wider ledges, to climb through that foam would give a combat marine the faints. At the fork in the river we spent the night. Tomorrow, hard to believe, we would see other humans besides Dylan and Bridget.

First we heard trucks in the distance, their loud exhaust pipes rapping to us over the river sounds . . . next, cars passing on the road when we got closer. We hiked up out of the canyon and near the top came across the local garbage dump: a fan of papers, rusty cars, boxes, bottles, cans, smells, all sliding down the canyon slope. Like two winos poking into alley trash cans, we scavenged through the treasure, not too proud, our trip a success without costing us a dime. We pried out of the mire three dirty but untorn wool blankets, several handy boards, and a stack of recent dry newspapers already tied in a bundle, setting the whole lot where we could load it on our return upriver. After that, we fixed on our best social respectability by dusting off clothes and combing hair again. Dylan said, "The main thing is, don't call attention to ourselves." Over the top we went, into civilization.

Immediately, we could tell that summer business had come to Trinity Village. The two gas stations busily filled up cars and pickups: plain cars and cars pulling trailers or boats, plain pickups and pickups with campers or pulling trailers or boats, sometimes all three. The bitty café had standing-room only, the lunch hour being at hand. And at the store, the beer-bellied proprietor was fastened to the cash register, keeping it ringing, his face pink/purple from the beer and the happy music of dollars.

Dylan and I wandered down the aisles, two country kids in a candy store, trying to decide which goodies to buy with our pennies. Chocolate? Bananas? Real bread? How about cheese? Yum. Butter? Strawberry jam? Just strawberries, a carton of

juicy strawberries? Hey, pork chops. Hot dogs? Beef patties?
Sugar-glazed ham, with spices? Yum: saliva time.

"Here we go," said Dylan. "Halibut. Or here, flounder."

"Very funny."

After practicality set in, we bought those foods that
wouldn't spoil, dehydrated foods and powders that would keep
in the mountains, the sort we had been using all along,
especially instant mixes—soups, baking mixes, puddings,
casserole gunk—and lots of dried milk. Trouble was, we now
had more food than money to pay for it.

Reluctantly, I began putting back some of the packages
when Dylan stopped me, saying, "We'll be needing all that."

"Sure," I said. "We could use the whole store, if we had the
cash."

Dylan removed his gold wristwatch.

"What's the deal?" I said, lowering my voice. For some
reason, we had caught the interest of other people in the store,
attracting sidelong peeks since we walked in, even though
they were decked out themselves in Bermuda shorts, straw
hats, slogan T-shirts . . . various kooky tourist garb. "Are
you thinking of swapping your watch? No."

"Why shouldn't I?" He polished it on his shirt. "We can't
eat a watch, and we tell time mostly by the sun."

"You'd never get it back, that's why. This isn't a pawn-
shop, you know. Don't give away your family watch."

"I'm not giving. I'm buying."

At the counter we spread out our money to show that we
were paying customers, or partly. We already had the
attention of the storekeeper, who viewed us top to bottom,
twitching his purple nose as if we hadn't bathed of late.

Dylan said, "We have a little situation here."

The storekeeper, having heard that tone before, stiffened

straight up. He was a tall old guy, a head taller than Dylan.

Dylan elaborated: "We find ourselves, see, a bit short—"

"No credit," the man snapped. "The policy is strictly no credit. Strictly no credit."

"Oh, we intend to pay," said Dylan smoothly. "I have this watch—"

"Watch? The policy is cash only. Strictly cash. Stores don't barter in watches and chickens no more, boy. Now buy what you want with what money you have."

"It's gold, eighteen-carat, including the band."

The man unbent, slightly. "Hand it here." It was a superb wristwatch, as anyone could tell, and he turned it thoughtfully front to back, commenting, "I . . . have myself . . . a good watch . . . already."

"Over two hundred and fifty dollars new," said Dylan.

No exaggeration, I happened to know.

The man squinted, tilting the back of the watch: "This your name—this D-y-l-a-n?"

"It is."

"Why you selling a gift watch from your parents? Huh?"

"Money. Like I said. We got caught short."

"From your own parents. Printed, or what you call—inscribed—right on the back." He shook his head.

Dylan's boots shuffled. "That proves how much we need to trade for that food."

"I'm suspecting," the storekeeper said, "that this watch is stolen property. Weren't you and the girl there in here a while back? Huh?"

With that, my pulse elevated a notch and I began marking the distance to the exit.

Dylan played the offended party. "The watch *is* mine, and,

no, we have not been in here before. In fact, we're from Canada, my cousin Helen and I, backpacking on vacation, traveling through your country. Yesterday, talk about *stolen,* we got roughed up and robbed. Our wallets. I'm lucky to have this money and my watch."

Clever, because now there could be no wallets to examine.

The storekeeper returned the wristwatch. "How much you short on the groceries?"

"Eleven dollars, only eleven, plus a few pennies. The rest is cash."

Shaking his head the wonderful man said, "For the watch all I can allow is half that, say six dollars."

"*Six?*"

"Six."

"Listen, you can see that watch is *gold.*" Dylan's voice scaled dramatically higher, and the tourists were wholeheartedly rubbernecking now.

"And I told you I already had a wristwatch."

"And you know that watch is worth an easy *fifty* dollars, let alone a measly *eleven.*" Dylan had a bear-chasing glitter in his eyes, his reddish beard bristled, and, good grief, I noticed he still wore his belt with the hatchet and hunting knife, like a gunslinger who forgot to unbuckle before riding into town. With us, it was habit for Dylan to wear his hatchet and knife. But he had said "Don't call attention to ourselves" and there he stood, Tarzan from Canada, armed, about to thump his chest and wail his battle cry.

"*Dylan,*" I said between clenched teeth, leaning against him and pinching him through his shirt until he winced. "Time to catch the train."

We paid, loaded the packages into our packs, carried the

eleven dollars' worth of extras back to be reshelved. The storekeeper looked like he might be disappointed about the watch.

"Wait for me by the canyon," Dylan muttered.

"Why?"

His face told me, Don't ask again, so I went and waited and didn't ask again.

When Dylan came from the store, toward me, he had his pack on, and his watch, his legs covering the ground in exceedingly long strides.

"Did you lift that extra food?" I said, not positive I cared to hear.

"Walk."

We walked, me matching his pace.

Behind us someone was calling. Over my shoulder I saw the proprietor, stepping out in front of his store.

"Don't turn around," said Dylan.

The storekeeper's diminished but penetrating words reached after us: "Hey, you two! Canada kids! I want to talk to you!"

No way.

Down in the canyon we grabbed our garbage and beat it. Meadow bound.

SEVEN

The Wild Children

i _____ As the weeks and the summer passed, our routine and our feet etched a tracery of paths across the meadow, from the cabin to the firepit to the creek to the deer trail leading down the canyon, and from the creek to the washing platform to the pond to the swimming hole to the deer trail leading up the canyon. Those paths cut a pattern —brown against faded green—as familiar to us as the lines on our palms. More so. Deer runs also wound their gradual ways up all the canyon and mountain slopes, carefully following the best grade. We accepted the advice and the trails. Our fifty-dollar boots received a fortune's worth of scuffing, poking, scratching, bumping, stubbing, thunking, splashing, and appreciation.

Since in the mountains we went to bed early, with the coming of dark, we woke up early at the other end, before sunrise, and sometimes Dylan left the cabin before dawn, if he had a first-light hunting spot to stake out. Coming from the blackboard-black cabin (folding up our blanket doorway), the meadow outside revealed itself in grey tones, although the muddled sky had no actual daylight yet. The sky slowly began bleaching out, and for a short while it disappeared into the nearly no-color of watery milk. But look down, stir the fire, look up again, and a blue sky was there. Hardly ever did we see pinks or other colors at dawn, because the sun had to be high in the clean air before it cleared the ridgetops and gave us our sunrise.

Every morning came a blue dawn, without clouds, and there never seemed to be much wind until midmorning. The trees surrounding us on the mountainsides stood at rest. Someday I would like to write a good poem describing this time, the stillest time of the day or night, with only a stray pop from the rekindled fire and the gurgles of the creek. Smoke rose straight enough to have been painted there with a ruler. We cooked breakfast and in the early air our food smells filled the meadow, and probably half the canyon. Off in dens and tunnels and hollow logs, noses must have twitched every morning. While we cooked and ate, the nippy dawn began lifting and brightness took its place.

After cleanup, Dylan went to hunt. He had a dozen snares set along the canyon to check or move, and besides his usual fishing methods he was testing nets made from a snarl of twine, reeds, and cloth, both throw nets and fixed nets. Not much luck so far. Whenever he went to the river, we arranged his schedule: where he would be, how long, when and how to search for him without being seen myself. While he was gone, I stuffed my pockets with plastic sacks and selected a deer trail, following it up the canyon's steep side and up to the sloping mountains, spying after roots or berries or tender plants. If the deer or the rabbits or the birds or *anything* ate it or chewed it, I collected it. And I found myself turning into a regular savage. If I came across a snake, I took a stick and killed it for the meat, coiling the body into one of the sacks. If I surprised a ground squirrel, I tried to kill it with the stone I kept ready in my hand. If I stumbled onto a fawn . . . well, I was under strict instructions from Dylan to club it or choke it to death. Veal, he said. At least, he said, tie it down so he could come and do the job. I didn't beat the bushes to find any fawns.

All the deer runs ended at the ridgetops, then traveled along the ridges, practically riding paths for horses, beaten flat and dusty. My favorite morning hours were spent walking those ridgetops, high in the heavens, with an airplane view. In every direction mountains piled together with other mountains, blending one into the next, on and on, into the blued and blurry distance. If I continued walking far enough westward there was a knoll where I could see down, down, down into the big river canyon. Often I parked myself on the knoll, under a solitary fir, just to gulp in all that panorama, or to watch the river below wrinkling, tossing white spots, glinting back the sun. Up here, on the ridgetops, was where the breezes first arrived. When my fir began stirring its arms, that was the sign for my return down to camp.

By noon it would be hot, and I mean sweating hot, the kind when you flop in the shade and still sweat. The breeze usually fizzled away, retreating to the ridges, gone from the meadow until late afternoon, and we panted and dreamed of ice cubes. I changed into a makeshift bikini outfit . . . very makeshift, never mind the sexy details. Dylan wore a pair of cut-offs. Finally we would go to the big pool, our swimming pool, and jump in—and get cooled off, fast. That mountain water always provided its own ice cubes on the most scorching summer day. We dunked, wet our hair, splashed each other, no doubt gave the trout granddaddies something to grumble about, and after we had a nice case of goosebumps crawled out, dripping, to enjoy a few delicious shivers. Within thirty minutes, back in again, riling the trout. In and out of the old swimming hole is how we spent the hot hours.

Later in the afternoon, and in the long twilight, we could resume our work. Dylan made his hunting rounds. "Stay downwind and keep your back to the sun," I would say, a hunter's joke we had between us that was more than a joke. He might flip back, "If you see bears, kill 'em for dinner" or "Remember that mountain-lion tail makes gourmet stew." That wasn't altogether funny, either. I busied myself in the meadow, adding rocks to our fishing piers out in the pond (so next spring's harvesting would be easier) or doing laundry at the platform on the creek, and, always, always, making arrangements for the evening meal. Meanwhile I listened for screaming rabbits caught in snares, to rush there and skin them before a fox or coyote or bobcat did. We had lost a couple.

With dusk, and Dylan's return, the temperature did an amazing switchabout, heat racing away through the canyons, causing the trees to sway and sigh, leaving behind the bite of mountain air. No bikini now. The fire was flaming and we considered those lost goose-down jackets. Weeks ago I had improvised a substitute jacket for myself by sewing together three wool shirts, two of mine and, on the outside, one of Dylan's. Dylan wore an extra shirt, and painstakingly he was saving, scraping, and curing all our animal skins, intending to trim and stitch them into a fur vest. After the fire died down and we had studied the stars in the cold, close sky, the sleeping bags and the cabin never failed to keep us snug.

At dawn, up again for more of the same, or nearly the same. Day after day. We got ourselves in *shape*—no fooling about it—whether we cared to or not. We could climb anywhere, crawling directly up or jolting down, without any sissified rest stops and without any sore muscles the next morning. Sometimes, when I accompanied Dylan to the river, we would even (like the rising wind) race back the last part, up along the creek, breathing hard maybe but not rasping and gasping.

Oh, and yes, for the first time in her life, paleface Bridget had what would be judged a ribbon-winning tan.

ii _____ It's depressing how much food it takes to keep the human body from being hungry. With no supermarkets, kitchen pantries, or refrigerators, you find out. Think about trying this one day: stroll off into the hills, go to sleep, wake up the next morning with an empty stomach. Now what? Now you search for something to put into your mouth or you have no breakfast. Now what? Now you search for something to put into your mouth or no lunch. Now what? Now you search for something to put into your mouth or no dinner. Now what? Now you go to sleep again, thinking up new places to search tomorrow. If once or twice you don't find that something to put into your mouth, what then? Then you stop searching—you scrabble. If you still don't find it, what then? Yeah, what then.

As our store-bought supplies dwindled, it was obvious that we needed to kill a large animal, a deer, for its meat and hide. Dylan said he knew how to dry the meat into jerky strips so we'd have a comfortable reserve laid away, instead of our stretching meals from rabbit to squirrel to trout to snake. Of course, how to lay hands on an owl-eyed, rabbit-eared, fox-nosed deer is a problem, but Dylan had a plan. Didn't he always?

The likeliest hunting for deer was where they came to feed most, down in the big canyon at the river's marshy area, which meant carrying our packs and sleeping bags and spending the night there, hidden in the thick brush off to the side. Along

one of the deer trails leading into that grassy pasture Dylan
had built a hunting blind. During the predawn we would
leave our cozy sleeping bags and grope in the murkiness to the
blind, where we had to lie flat without budging, waiting for
early light and for the deer to come down from their beds near
the ridges. A lasso at the end of our rope—slightly buried
—circled under the trail, while the other end traveled through
Dylan's hands and was knotted to a tree trunk. According to
the plan, my function in this cowboy event was to be the
horse—keeping the rope taut and the deer off its legs.

Twice we made the expedition to the river marsh, spending
the night. Twice, no deer used the trail. On the third trip a
deer came, either because the hunting blind had become
familiar, or because three is a magical number. Either way, a
deer most certainly came. I was half-dozing, my face pressed
into the crook of my arm, imagining all my other fellow
predators in the Trinities who that same dawn were stalking
some poor furry or feathery victim. My sympathy went to the
predators as much as the victims, even slinky weasels robbing
henhouses in the foothills, because if you don't eat, well,
you're a victim too. My sympathy also time-machined back to
my ancient ancestors, whoever they were, from wherever, who
for half a million years or so crouched in the underbrush
waiting for prey, or gathered seeds, somehow scraping
through each hungry day of those 500,000 years.

An elbow jab from Dylan, and I came up from my reverie to
see a buck with spike antlers stepping toward us in graceful,
nervous starts and stops, its moist black-tipped muzzle
bobbing to nibble young shoots, and to test for scent. It
showed a healthy grey coat ticked by white/tan/black hairs—it
had moved that close—and gorgeous dark eyes the size of
silver dollars. We tensed. The deer's neat little hooves tapped

daintily on . . . on . . . far enough . . . and with a mighty
lurch that bruised my cheek Dylan yanked the rope, causing
all hell to break loose.

The buck leaped straight up, turned in the air, landed and
kept turning, raising a whirlwind of dust and mowing down
brush, and our blind, where it discovered its flat-faced
predators. In panic, wheezing, it backed away the full length
of the rope, expecting the showdown charge from us. Okay.
The charge. We had this deer noosed around one rear hoof, all
right, but it was a sticky situation, with the other three hooves
able to flail and cut like chisels.

"Pull," said Dylan, and we pulled, but the deer refused to
trip off its feet and just hunched down against the rope, so
scared its wet muzzle began dripping loops of mucus.

"Jeez," Dylan grunted.

We all looked at each other, the deer and the two of us, the
food and the eaters of the food, everybody panting and
looking. I felt guilty, ill. Except at the same blasted instant I
felt hunger, even with my stomach unhungry, because caught
in front of us was meat equal to fifty rabbits or more. Meat.
Gentle eyes, liquid brown eyes, wanting to live, but meat.

I asked in a squeaky voice, "What now?"

Dylan stood up, causing the deer to tremble harder and
strain the rope tighter. "Let me find a club." He pried out a
limb that had been used in the blind.

"You can't kill it with that," I said.

"Stun it. So I can get close enough to work the knife." He
gripped the branch meaningfully and sidled toward the deer.

I warned him, "Be careful"—advice he didn't need yet I
had to say.

The deer, in its heart, had known this moment would
arrive, and it went into motion, lunging here and there,

kicking its dangerous hooves, striking at Dylan when he got into range. Dylan raised his club. No use, the deer would wheel away or bolt forward, scattering me right along with Dylan. A cornered animal is awfully strong, like a person gone crazy, which come to think of it could be almost the same thing. Dylan tried advancing from several different angles, but no deal.

After the dust settled I asked, "What now?" again, and while we talked the deer wobbled its eyes at us, listening to our foreign, outer-space noises. The next plan seemed too dangerous to me, with too much Dylan-style direct attack in it.

"Any other suggestions?" Dylan offered, willing to find an easier solution.

I had none, and the sun was already crossing the morning sky.

We began by twisting Dylan's club into the rope, so that having levered one end of the club behind the hitching-post tree, we both could pull around and around the tree and winch the deer directly to our boot tops. Away we went, rotating the branch around and around like hauling in an anchor, the deer hobbling on three legs, closer as the rope got shorter. When the deer was brought up short—its hooves within reach of us—we tied off the rope and converted from being sailors to being wolves. We split and circled the deer on two sides: as I distracted it from the front, Dylan slunk in from behind. I crouched no farther than a single yard from its head, waving my hands to hold its attention, peering into its beautiful wide eyes and feeling and even smelling its heated breath gasp into my own face. In Dylan's hand, rising, was the hunting knife, carefully whetted to a razor's edge. Arcing himself like a highjumper, Dylan leaped and came down full length on the deer's back, locking his legs around the belly and his free arm around its neck, toppling the deer with the blow, and it thrashed there on the ground, wild, straining to heave off the killer.

But the deer was no wilder than Dylan and Bridget. Battle dust clouded all about us. Dylan clung fast and I grabbed the spiked antlers on the flopping head—together we bent back and back the surprisingly long, slender neck, until it curved like a bow. *Bleat, bleat,* cried the deer. Quickly the knife slashed across the throat, popping the tight skin with a pitiless sound. PRRIP. Again Dylan raked with my father's knife, now forever *his* knife, jabbing harder to cut deeper, through tendons and buried arteries. Something pattered on my face and arms, in my hair, something sticky and moist. From the dust clouds was falling a red rain. I could taste it on my lips. Again Dylan plunged in the knife, losing his grip once on the slippery handle.

The head I was gripping weakened. My hands could feel its strength go, and then the deer simply gave up, or went into shock, or understood the need for struggle had passed, and it laid its head quite still, waiting for death. Dylan and I hung on and waited too. The ribs that had been straining, now subsided. The naked tongue slipped downward out of the mouth and twisted. The brown silver-dollar-sized eyes . . . Ah, you imagine the rest.

"You ever been baptized?" asked Dylan, kneeling upright and unkinking his muscles. "The pushed-under-water kind?"

"I've never been baptized, any kind."

"You have now. Look at your skin."

"Look at yourself." His color had changed to maroon, from waist to forehead. "That's nearly total immersion, don't the preachers call it?"

"Praise be, Sister Bridget, I've seen The Way."

"The way to slitting throats."

"The way to independence. Food is our independence."

"Then praise be to this deer," I said, bringing myself to touch it once more.

Dylan nodded, gently resting both his arms on the carcass, with affection apparently, the same arms that had just bled away its life. "Praise be to this deer," he echoed, using his real preacher's voice. "The Indians used to honor, even worship, the animals they killed in a hunt. They thanked the animals for giving the gift of life. The Indians never dared to rile the animal gods, for fear of getting punished by starvation."

"Moral: Never kill an animal without needing it."

"The gods would zap you for that one."

I did find it easier now to spread my hand against the deer's limp neck. "We needed you," I said.

Looking at my hand, flattened there against the deer, I became aware gradually of a difference inside me. I began digging in my mind and my mood to locate what the change was, exactly. Something about that hand, something about my red hand. What? I found the answer, and it surprised me. My hand was covered only with plain blood. Nothing else. You see, always before, whether skinning a squirrel or cleaning a bird or even a simple fish, the blood had been *the* blood. All blood, and especially blood right on my skin, had always gotten mixed up with horrible car accidents. But here I was soaked in the stuff—practically baptized in it, as Dylan said—and it was just deer's blood. Just plain blood. The difference now must have had to do with the deer itself, the dying, somehow. The bleeding deer had left me with that scene of its quiet body, its calm drift into the finish of living.

For that sight, the animal gods rate more thanks from me than for food.

And when Dylan related some Indian ceremony he had read about—joining spirits with the dead animal—we sampled it by smearing the deer's blood in three lines across our cheeks. The idea caught on and afterward, with other animals, we did that. I know how screwy it seems, how ghoulish, or juvenile, but honestly the blood ceremony made me feel better, like broadcasting to the world that Bridget wasn't running around snuffing out lives for the pure hell of it.

We cut off our deer's head and hoisted the body up by the hind legs, from a tree limb. We next discovered that gutting a deer is a heap taller task than cracking open a rabbit, which you can nearly do with your bare hands. After considerable slicing and yanking, out tumbled the innards, the bulging paunch and the coils of pungent, colorful intestines. Lesson number one: at all costs, don't puncture the intestines, unless you're planning to go on an instant diet. Out came the bladder—be alert there, is lesson number two. We scraped and clawed out the fragile pink lungs. And so forth. The whole affair, I expect, is like being in an autopsy room at a hospital or morgue. After a while, it's business as usual.

As best we could, we covered the pile of insides with a bigger pile of rocks. Before dark the coyotes would be digging. Since we had to carry the deer back to our meadow, we didn't skin it yet, or bother to wash ourselves at the river, but loaded up, Dylan balancing the carcass across his shoulders and drizzling a little trail of its blood from each end.

"Heavy?" I asked as he adjusted the weight.

He grunted yes. "But who cares. Think about what we

have, what the heavy is. Steaks tonight, grilled."

"Steaks in the morning. Steaks tomorrow night."

"Think about the buckskin we have here. Every step is a joy."

We started down toward the marsh to collect our gear, which I would carry along with the deer's head, already held by one spike in my fist and also dribbling blood. Dylan figured on skinning the head for a hunting decoy, another idea he gleaned from his Indian books. Say, that head by itself was *heavy,* making me constantly switch grips and even tuck it under my arm. A deer is one-third neck and head . . . check to see, next chance you get.

At the marsh pasture we trudged toward our sleeping spot, concentrating on our weighty freight, silently remembering the living deer—at least I was. Morning was becoming noon and the heat had arrived, and some flies.

Dylan said something.

We walked farther out across the open marsh grass and Dylan asked, "What?"

"What what," I said, shifting the deer's head again, shooing a fly off its drooping tongue.

"What what? Didn't you call to me?"

"No. Did you say something about these flies?"

We stopped, fast, because a voice somewhere was really calling, and we both heard it: "Hellooo!"

We pivoted for cover—except no cover.

"Hellooo! Hellooo there!"

I located the voice, and the men, in the shade of an alder by the river. As I told Dylan, they stepped into the sunshine, three of them, coming toward us, waving.

"Hellooo!" They carried rifles.

"Guns, Dylan."

"Hunters. Stupid, stupid, to let them find us in a clearing like this."

They were near enough for us to make out their faces, so they could make out ours, blood stripes and all.

"Pretend we don't hear," said Dylan, turning his back to them, "and walk normal. Forget the gear. *Come on,* up the canyon. Act normal."

We started upriver, walking at a fair pace, resisting looking around to see if the hunters were following. We crossed out of the marsh and had hopes.

"Hellooo! Wait! Wait!"

Closer than before.

The path was rougher now and we walked faster, but peeking back through the brush we saw that they were coming faster, too, and didn't intend to stay behind. Dylan broke into a jog, the deer bouncing across his shoulders. We would have left them flat, but darn if the hunters didn't begin jogging themselves, determined to find out what we two oddities were.

"Wait! Hey! Stop!" The voice rang less friendly, and more pinched for air.

Dylan and I were almost running now, both gulping hard, both stumbling under our loads and sweating under the sun. It struck me: we were the prey, just like the deer we were lugging, and they were the predators, what we had been that morning. *This* was the sick sensation of getting a noose around the leg. At that moment, because of my distraction, I lost my hold on the deer's bobbing head.

"Dylan!"

"Leave it—help me here!"

The head rolled in the dirt, and I had a final view of its brown eyes . . . filmed with sandy grit. I dashed to Dylan and we took the carcass between us, the front end over his shoulder, the back over mine, and we ran in single file —awkward and tripping each other, but we tried.

When the hunters came to the dropped head a wavering tune went up, somewhat like dogs striking a fresh scent, and their curiosity must have been roused another notch higher too because we could hear them plainer, closer, crashing through the brush. We came to a barren stretch and Dylan ripped out a curse. Sure enough, before we disappeared at the upper end, the hunters entered at the bottom. Everybody froze for an instant. One of the hunters actually positioned his rifle, probably from the sheer reflex of chasing things.

"Hello!" shrilled the same voice, very excited. "Do you two speak English? English? Speak?"

Later we would recall the voice asking that nonsensical question, and later still, even fathom it, but right then we turned without a word and skedaddled, racing in a desperate flounder. No luck. The deer was doing us in, and the hunters would soon be on us. No luck, no choice: we ditched the carcass, shot-putting the precious meat into a salmonberry clump. Without our load we vanished from those would-be hunters, up the river and into our side canyon before they so much as glimpsed us again. Hidden there we watched them eventually stagger into sight along the river, halt, search around, then mill around, rub their chins, relieve themselves, go back slowly down toward where we tossed the deer.

For the longest time we sat, without speaking, bowed over with tiredness and wearying thoughts. Dylan's face was dark from the thoughts, the shade, the dried blood. "Let's go to the meadow for a swim," I said. "It's hot." But that night we had a cold sleep without our goose-down bags, and a cold, cold night without our deer.

The following morning, scouting with extreme caution, we

reacquired the stashed sleeping bags and packs, and we came across the rope where I had dropped it in the marsh grass during the chase. We found everything except the deer.

Bitterly Dylan said, "And what do you suppose happened to it."

"Coyotes dragged it away?"

"The head, possibly. And the body they'd chew on, but coyotes could never tote it off, and wouldn't want to, anyhow."

"Mountain lion?"

He wouldn't consider it. He had his answer: stolen by the outsiders, who acted the way they always do. Could be, said Bridget.

Not many days after, we got ourselves spotted one more time, despite being careful. On a blistering afternoon we had gone to the river canyon to do some early-evening fishing. While waiting, we climbed a ridgeline, as we usually did nowadays, spying far up and down the river for intruders or movement of any kind. Safety first. Nothing seen, so we walked downhill to the canyon's lip and stood on a prominence, enjoying the vast space opening below and the start of a breeze curling toward the heights behind us. When we chanced to glance straight down, two men were gawking straight up, mouths visibly agape, standing by a little yellow tent pitched too close to the canyon wall for us to have noticed it, or them, from our lookout above.

Dylan toyed with a small boulder with his foot. "Shall I shove this over the edge?"

"How good is your aim?"

"If we were cannibals, I might. We could use the grub."

That was fact.

"Look at them stare," said Dylan, and he helped matters by

lifting his arms in a grand dramatic sweep. Praying to the sky gods, I guess.

"Let's sell tickets," I suggested, and it occurred to me that we probably could, as we posed there in our hot-weather attire, or more accurately, lack of attire. Trinity Alps Pornography, Inc.

iii _____ We didn't fish at the river that day, of course, and afterward things sort of dragged along, until the supplies shriveled away again and we resigned ourselves to one last go at the village. We would peddle Dylan's gold watch, or if we had to, borrow some food when nobody was looking. Lord, we hated trekking back there, to that place, but when we lost that deer of ours it seems our fate was sealed.

And, by and by, there we were, sneaking downriver again, sleeping at the fork and then poking through the dump. From the junk we pulled out some extra rope, and a pile of the newest, cleanest newspapers, which are nifty for starting fires, and for several other activities around camp.

Walking into the village we were plenty nervous. Not much action stirred on the street, and Dylan remarked, "The tourists are gone." That was our first sure evidence that summer had officially gone too, because we had lost count of the weeks and months.

"It's somber," I said, although the day was warm and the sky blue. "I don't like the feel."

At the nearest gas station Dylan brought out his watch and gave a spiel. "What's it worth to you?" he asked the man, in conclusion. "Make me an offer, any offer." The man scarcely turned his eyes on the watch, but remained the way he had been since we showed up at his gas pumps, hands limp at his sides, looking at Dylan then at me, Dylan then me, Dylan then me. Dylan swished the watch at face level: "How about it?"

"Maybe he was retarded," I speculated, as we went queasily toward the trailers and cabins.

"This whole village seems retarded to me."

I knew what he meant, and it was more than a wisecrack. A sneaky transformation had come over us. These buildings, for instance, were all wrong, were *not normal*. Buildings, any buildings, somehow just didn't sit right to my frame of view. And these people here didn't sit right. No. Their movements, and sounds, and their colors and odors too, weren't normal. Normal had become another life—trees, creeks, mountains, meadows, Dylan—like life on another planet. It scared me, finding other people so alien. Or we were the aliens.

Dylan knocked on wooden cabin doors and metal trailer doors, but either kind, the stares were the same, and nobody appeared to hear much of his advertisement about the gold wristwatch. We moved on to the crackerbox café, where a couple of truckers and a couple of old retired-logger types sat on the battered stools at the counter, transfixed by our entrance and letting their coffee get cold.

Unnerving.

Outside, we chewed our fingernails, searching for some spot where they might understand English a bit better, semislinking down the bare street. "There's the other gas station," I said, without any real hope or enthusiasm.

"Psst, hey," said Dylan, low-voiced, "take a peek behind us, *slow*ly."

Behind us, bunched by the café, was a gaggle of followers: the service-station man, two husband-and-wife teams from the trailers, most of the café's patrons, some rubbernecking new-comers.

"Psst," said Dylan, "peek over at the store."

We had kept away from the store. I was supposed to go there without Dylan, later, when we got the money. But our friend the storekeeper, tall and baldish, had now planted himself out on his porch, craning a neck in our direction.

"Dylan, are they all looking at you and me?"

"Let's find out. Walk."

We curled back in a return route, and the people also curled, following at a safe distance, like iron filings separated from a magnet by glass.

Unnerving. What, did we belong in a zoo? We stopped at the canyon's edge and held our ground, because after our long trip it would be brutal not to sell the watch and get food. The people stood their own ground, examining us and gossiping, while we sprawled in the shade, sucked blades of grass, and acted as peaceable as two stray but harmless puppies. Perhaps we could wear them down and win them over, we thought. And sell a wristwatch.

A county sheriff's car came wheeling down the center of the street, zooming too fast to be on any routine visit. Somebody had made a little call on our behalf. The car skidded to an excited halt. In the canyon we remembered to sling on our packs, with the newspapers already tucked inside.

Alongside the river that evening, while making camp and brooding about food, I saw a fresh picture of ourselves, brought on by those stares in the village and by the deduction that if those people weren't normal to us, we weren't normal to them. I saw Dylan, opposite me. His gleaming copper beard, although hacked short around the jawline and chin, had impressively thickened, reminding me of General Sherman from a Civil War photograph. The hair on his head, still uncut, fell to his shoulders Indian style, held in place by a generous rabbit-fur headband. My own hair was longer than ever, with its own headband—fancy squirrel's fur, three inches wide. From all those campfires, woodsmoke had saturated our hair, impossible to scrub out, and while we didn't notice it anymore, to everybody else we must have reeked at twenty paces. And our clothes also undoubtedly smelled of smoke, besides being a crazy quiltwork of patches from fixing the continual small rips.

Yet more than our garb made us different. That I saw. Studying Dylan and comparing him with the villagers, I couldn't exactly isolate what it was at first. His eyes seemed fierce—the whites rolled and flared—even as he relaxed there by me. Finally, I realized the fierceness came from the jarring contrast between his darker skin and lighter eyes,.except this was no case of a simple suntan. We had *weathered.* The hot days, the cold nights, the water, the wind had branded us as outdoor critters, unconnected to houses and village streets. We had turned the tints and textures of bark, soil, leaves. The identifying mark had been stamped directly on our hide: different.

The finisher hit me back at our meadow, when I browsed through the stack of newspapers one midday and found an item headed WILD YOUTHS REPORTED IN MOUNTAINS:

> The mountains and forests of northern
> California continue to provide the setting
> for reports of mysterious inhabitants, in

the tradition of the famous Sasquatch, or Big Foot. However, the latest sightings concern not that ten-foot-tall monster but wild teenage children, according to the Redding Police Department, where a three-man hunting party filed a report earlier this week. The men stated that while in the North Fork region, near the Trinity Alps Primitive Area, they surprised a "young male and female, Caucasian in origin but completely savage in appearance and behavior."

A description of the pair—viewed from as close as 100 feet, it was claimed—included facial tattooing or paint markings, waist-length hair, a mixture of native and store clothing, the latter seeming to be old discards.

In addition, the clothes were said to be blood-stained, as the two were carrying the fresh body and severed head of a deer. No weapons were visible.

According to the men, all of whom are city employees from San Jose, the pair did not seem to understand English or to be used to the sounds of spoken language, and did not themselves speak. The two also seemed frightened of the men, running away at "remarkable speed" though carrying the adult-sized deer carcass.

"They acted just like untamed creatures," the report quotes.

Police spokesmen offered no speculations,
or any comments on the accuracy of the
report.

I showed the newspaper to Dylan. "My god, isn't that us?"
Dylan read, and reread.
"Well?"
"It's us."
We pawed through later issues of the paper and came across
a follow-up story, captioned with the question FERAL CHIL-
DREN? It reviewed the earlier report, which was now
"supported and expanded" by the observations of two campers
hiking in the "identical location." The campers had seen the
"nearly naked" young couple standing atop a "perilous"
canyon wall, balancing like "mountain goats," "apparently
performing some ritual to demonstrate courage." One "possible explanation" for these "young primitives," said the
newspaper, "should their existence be fully confirmed," was
the theory that they had been "abandoned when small, and
somehow had grown up in a natural or wild condition, similar
to unwanted household pets that are dumped in the remote
countryside."
No other news flashes on Dylan and Bridget, at least in the
papers we had at the meadow.
Those were enough, thank you, to flabbergast me twofold. I
mean, we bury ourselves here in the Trinities and believe it or
not we end up in the lousy newspapers. "Half of California
knows we're, quote, Nearly Naked," I told Dylan, since we
nearly were at that moment, it being one of the autumn's last
summer-hot days. I expected Dylan to be purple with worry,
but instead he was squinting calmly at the sky. "Dylan, is that
a Parable-Time face?"

"Parable. History. Both. Those newspaper pieces remind me of some California history: the last wild American Indian and what happened to him. Ishi. Do you know about it?"

I did, a little. "He was uncovered in this century."

"1911. That means he was still hiding out twenty-five years after Geronimo's Apaches were captured."

"And then they took him to San Francisco and he was studied there and at the university in Berkeley."

"Our old neighborhood."

"Once I saw the Ishi collection at the Cal campus. You've seen it more than once—good guess?"

"True."

"Lay the entire story on me." I knew he wanted to.

Dylan settled himself. "Look in that direction. His tribe lived almost directly across the Sacramento Valley from us, in the Lassen foothills. They were hunters, fishers, gatherers. Like us."

"Sounds familiar, all right."

"Yeah. They did that for centuries, probably for thousands of years, before the Spanish came, and the music stopped. Smallpox, TB, measles, flu—half the California Indians dead in a decade. Ishi's people did better than most, up in their hills, because the land was god-awful steep and choked with manzanita brush and poison oak. Worthless. Then the Forty-niners arrived, then our pioneers, and California joined the Union. The real squeeze started for gold and more ground, even into scrub country. Mining silted up the rivers and screwed up the fishing. Gunshots spooked the deer. Grazing took over the foothill pastures. Hill Indians were rounded up and forced to migrate. Most died off. Ishi's people fought back some, about the only California Indians that did, along with the Modocs. They raided livestock to eat. They killed a few ranchers."

"Ouch."

"The end. Those hill Indians in easy reach were erased. It's figured maybe two thousand of them got it one certain year, a year when Ishi would have been alive, very young. Extermination. Afterwards the only Indians left living in the hills came from Ishi's local group, tucked away in a remote patch back between two creeks. Somehow, Bridget, they hung on for fifty more years, counting Ishi himself—until 1911."

"How many Indians?"

"At first enough to survive, raise new generations, if they could find the food. But they couldn't, not with bows and arrows. They had to raid livestock again, and get shot at again, get killed, and worse, get followed to their homes."

I knew how the story turned out, and I was cringing. "More massacres," I said.

"Professional Indian posses you might call them, sometimes using dogs, went into the hills and caught the Indians in their camps, gunning down complete families, complete villages. Zap, zap, target practice. Great kicks, killing real human beings. Finally only a small village was left, under a rock overhang, and one day four ranch workers trapped the Indians there and banged away, at the babies and all. When that finished, about fifteen of Ishi's tribe still lived and hid in the hills. Each life now was extra-precious, because, you see, they were the total population of a whole nation, which is what they considered themselves, a separate nation. Any new loss, in particular losing any young members who could bear children, would be a double blow. And before long some did get shot or captured, so the rest pulled back and vanished into the farthest thickets, just disappeared, good as ghosts. Times must have been hard, holed up that way, trying to stay alive. Ishi grew out of boyhood. Others died. The ranchers thought no more Indians existed. For forty years—starting from when Ishi was a boy—there must have been fewer than ten of them. In the last years only four."

"Besides Ishi, I remember, one was his mother."

"And one an old crippled man, and the other a woman about Ishi's age. Four hungry mouths and only one hunter —Ishi, who was middle-aged by the end."

"How did they get found?"

"By fluke. A surveyor's party stumbled into the camp. Only Ishi's mother was there, because she couldn't walk. The surveyor's party took every tool and every scrap of the food supply, for damn *souvenirs,* Bridget. But when they came back the next day, Ishi had already moved his mother and they caught a glimpse of the younger woman helping the old man escape. Those two had some sort of accident, and Ishi never saw them again, nobody ever did. His sick mother, with her bad legs, couldn't have lasted very long, right? Food stolen. Winter coming. Snow. No shelter."

"That left Ishi."

"Think of it, Bridget. To know you walk the hills alone, to know you end your nation, the last of your kind, and for three more years to travel the trails that your people crossed for centuries, and to watch the seasons, Bridget, to keep on without another human soul and not give in or crack."

"Oh, Dylan, how sad. No other voices, no other faces, only memories, and sad memories. Oh, sweet heaven, how sad."

"For three more years he held together, always on the move, afraid to start a fire, but staying tough somehow, until he had no place to hide and starvation drove him down from his hills all in a daze. He expected to get killed."

"Instead he got headlines."

"And the role of a carnival freak. Step right up and see the last authentic wild American Indian. Make us some genuine Stone Age arrows, Ishi. Living in a museum, a museum, for Christ's sake. From the open hills to the inside of a museum."

"He wasn't happy there?"

"Well, he was alive there. With everything gone, and nowhere else to go, he might as well be alive there. But happy? The last loser in the middle of the winners?"

Dylan's recitation was over. It took an interval of several minutes for the raw message of the parable to settle in on me: We were Ishi. Our newspaper stories were Ishi's. The Spanish intruders, the greedy Forty-niners, the ambitious pioneers, the pushers, the shovers, the grabbers, the bigots, the killers of babies, all still swarmed on the move, outside our mountains, and we were the last of our nation. What's more, Dylan *relished* being what the newspapers called us—wild. At last he could officially be the enemy, on the Indians' side. Ishi's spirit, arise and fight.

Did Dylan really believe that parable?

Spooky things happened, as if Dylan had whispered his Ishi story into everybody's ears and coached them on what parts to play. Scouting along the river canyon, for example, a little buzzing sound lazed by us, followed by another noise, more distant, a sharp, short crack. Again: bzzzzzzzz, *crack*.

"What?"

"Crouch," said Dylan, leading the way into the nearest trees.

Far downstream the small figure of a man broke loose from the surrounding shapes of rocks and made itself clear, heading toward us.

"Why, that fool," I managed in a tiny voice, appalled, "that nearsighted fool. He was shooting at us."

"He was. But he's not nearsighted."

I glanced at Dylan, at his grim face, at his narrowed eyes boring into the approaching hunter. Actually, I could imagine that face waiting in ambush, prepared to strike. I said, "Are you telling me the man could make out who we were, and tried to kill us anyway? Dylan?"

"He's a man with a gun," said Dylan, which didn't quite answer my question but which didn't quite not answer it either. Getting shot at is kind of its own answer, poor eyesight or not.

The man might as well have had bad eyes, because we Indians had no trouble disappearing from him and his rifle.

All this was new and on my mind, when one morning the big blow fell. Up atop the ridgeline I sat at my favorite lookout, under the old fir on the knoll, enjoying the view. Dylan as usual lurked someplace in the river canyon below me, scrounging food. Such a pleasant morning it was, too—warm but not hot, with white cumulus clouds etched into a metallic blue sky. Nice. Except movement down in the canyon caught my attention, and I counted one, two, three, four, five, six, seven, eight, nine, ten men coming into sight, walking along the river in an almost military file. And when they got nearer I saw that the first four, the leaders, did in fact have uniforms on, although over the distance I couldn't tell what type. Rangers? Forest Service? Sheriff's deputies? Of course I had no inkling of what brought them out here, but I shivered in the sunshine, knowing that by now Dylan had stashed himself away—or I hoped he had—and was watching the men pass.

They didn't pass. They made a right turn from the river and headed up our own creek, toward our own canyon. Then the trees blocked my line of vision.

I as good as jumped off the ridgetop, scooting and sliding straight down the mountain slope, not going back to the meadow because I had to spot those men again and see if they had climbed through the logjam, and I had to warn Dylan, if possible. Twice I traveled on the seat of my pants, without intending to, so that I arrived at the creek bruised but in record time. I hurried downstream, until suddenly I knelt, holding my breath, listening. Footsteps were coming *up-*stream, faster than mine.

I rushed to hide—too late—and then Dylan and I startled a year off each other's life. "Are they coming?" I asked.

His eyes were bright. "Hurry. Back to the meadow."

"But did they cross the logs?"

"I saw them, yes, yes. Run."

Our race back to camp wasn't for fun, like earlier times, and we ran it at full stride, no exaggeration. In the meadow we continued at high speed, not even talking. Dylan leveled the canopy over the firepit with a flying kick. While I gathered the cooking gear and stuffed food, clothes, everything important, into the packs, and lashed on the sleeping bags, Dylan tumbled our cabin down, scattering it and our whole homestead camp in a whirlwind attempt at camouflage. Inside thirty minutes the work of many days was mashed flat.

"No!" I cried to Dylan, when he started for the fish pond and our dam on the creek. That would be too much, to lose the water and those fish.

Like two fleeing gypsies, we hitched on the bloated packs, heaped over with all our earthly possessions. We quickly skirted the fish pond and passed the swimming hole, up the canyon, without a stop to say farewell to our wonderful old meadow.

Where were we going? On and on up the canyon, the only escape route practical with us toting these wobbly piles of tarps, ropes, blankets, even newspapers. Where did the canyon lead? Never before had we been to its end, and possibly it didn't lead anywhere, deadending at a headwall and catching us in a box. But on we went, scraping our loads between boulders and branches, hurrying along the deer trail, bumping into trees, until after several hard hours we had reached unexplored territory. Behind us, we supposed, came the ten mystery men: the pursuit team, the rescue team, the surveyor's party. Take your pick. The point was, you understand now, whoever they were made no difference, because, whoever, they would do us harm.

The canyon steepened, the creek nosedived underground into two big mushy springs, the deer trail quit. End of the road, folks. In front swooped up a nasty rise of slick rock, rope-climbing country. Better find a hole to hide in, I told Dylan, or double back. Dylan shed his pack, wanting first to scan the scene. He zipped up over the rocks, more monkey than man, trying for enough height to check out the canyon behind us, scrambling higher, wedging inside a crack, so deep into the crack he disappeared.

He stayed disappeared. I waited. No Dylan. Help me, it had finally happened—an accident—and as I almost shouted his name, his long hair blew from the crack, and it jiggled a wild dance as Dylan avalanched down to tell me about his discovery and our escape. Secret Creek.

EIGHT

School at Secret Creek

i _____ How can I explain to you what this new place meant to us. How? Easy, I think, because (brace yourself) after one little day, and after scouting the new canyon, Dylan honest-to-heaven laughed. Standing alongside our very first campfire there, he looked up, past those wickedly steep cliffs into the fading daylight sky, and smiled, then _laughed_. And I was amazed, seeing such a strange sight on such a familiar face. But he laughed more than once in the next weeks, always at Secret Creek, only at Secret Creek.

We named the canyon that, Secret Creek, for the best of reasons. The canyon was tucked away like a hidden island in the air, a sunken island even, rising high up yet sunk deep down at the same time, with the sole passageways inside being through the slit we had accidently discovered or by mountain climbing over the cliffs. And twisting along the floor of Secret Creek was the actual secret creek, popping up from nowhere, splashing for a half-mile in a series of pools, and disappearing underground again. An astonishing fact: the pools were full of fish. How did the fish ever get planted there? Our best guess was that the secret creek once connected with our old creek, before shifts in the earth lifted them apart, eons ago. We also believed that this water passing by our feet, after it vanished, oozed out at those springs in the big canyon below, meaning we touched and drank the same water that would eventually fill our beloved trout farm.

So you can see what a secret place we had found, and how safe we felt, and why Dylan at long last relaxed about Indian-hunting posses. The narrow canyon snaked along for no more than a mile, advancing upward into rockier terrain with bald spots of granite showing among the firs, and finally on up to a treeless rim far above our heads. We were wrapped inside a miniature world, hidden away from outside civilization like in the story of Shangri-La. What a super journey we had traveled, from the sardine-can-crammed East Bay to this home up in the heavens, this private paradise saved just for the two of us. That's how we began to consider it. We were putting down footprints where no human creature had walked before. Success! We had worked ourselves backward to point zero, Total Escape, exactly what Bridget and Dylan had sworn and planned to do.

In the next few days we explored the crannies and crooks of Secret Creek, and discovered the other main reason for laughing. Near the upper end of the canyon (only two bends below where the creek emerged inside a slimy bowl of moss) the right-side cliff sloped back and then steepened again into a bulging overhang. It appeared that an ancient rock slide had come spilling from a weak spot here in the wall. We climbed the slide by squeezing between the granite hunks or walking directly over the loose talus, going up a rock ladder. After reaching the overhang, we expected to bump noses against flat stone, but no. Instead there waited an inviting level platform, and behind this platform, surprise, a dim hollow in the mountain.

Our tongues tangled over the same hope.

"Suppose—" I said.

"I think—" Dylan said.

Our feet tangled in the scurry to look inside.

Luckily, we didn't trip into the waiting arms of a bottled-up bear, although we found the bones and bits of fur from somebody's past lunches. Our dilating pupils saw more and more that tickled us. It was four times roomier here than in the cabin, with enough head space for standing, and no dampness, no wind, and easy security.

"Home Sugarsweet Home," proclaimed Dylan, and the words thumped from stone back to our ears with a cozily trapped sound—secret words in a secret cave in a secret canyon.

Naturally we moved in all our gear and went to work, being domestic again. The platform under the overhang made a perfect patio and observation deck, where we ate and where, lord knows, we sat for hours gazing out over Secret Creek, talking, talking, talking. At the back of the patio we built our firepit, just at the cave entrance, so that the sleeping quarters got heated while we cooked meals yet the smoke could exit without choking us to death. It rose, leaving its soot on the overhang, and by feathering against the rock, faded outside minus any tattle-tale signal.

Inside, the cave was almost as level as the platform but it required some heavy cleaning out—everything from boulders down to pieces of gravel crud. We used what rubble we could to build the firepit and a tighter doorway. The rest went over the edge, to rejoin their brethren from ages ago. To roll the largest three or four boulders was a feat, very athletic, accompanied by grunting and self-doubt. Catching my breath afterward, I sang, "It's so nice to have a man around the cave. . . ." Dylan, who was leaning back resting at that moment, turned his eyes on me, over me, then looked off. "I like your muscles, too," he said, with no special up or down, or loud or soft, to his voice. But I caught a special meaning, I thought. Secret Creek was bringing more than one kind of change to us.

We collected straight and forked branches, did some whittling, and put in shelves and clothing racks. We lugged in the usual log tables and log benches, after peeling off the bark for a smooth, furniture finish. Freshly peeled logs, incidentally, also make a first-rate incense or room freshener, should you one day ever find yourself setting up household in a national forest. Incense cedar—mmmm. Anyway, the entire cave was first-rate too before a week ended. Floors had been swept and mopped. Every pot and pan was in a cupboard, every sock in a drawer, each toothbrush in a holder—even if the holders and the drawers and the cupboard all looked more like sticks tied together. The blankets and sleeping bags were in place, cushioned and insulated from the stone floor by mattresses of dry grass wrapped inside plastic sheets. A corner was reserved for storing and repairing the hunting equipment. Another corner would hold our food supply. And the door into the cave was fixed so that it could be practically buttoned shut with the tarp.

Later we added the fancy touches, such as a bin on the patio for dry firewood and paper, and a half-ring of slate slabs around the firepit for heat reflectors, and for bed warmers if necessary. All this made the patio very comfortable and our favorite area. As I said before, we sat there a lot, talking, observing below the motions of our creek, our trees, our everything. Being up in the air was a good feeling as well as a good view. Only the red-tailed hawks could lord it over us, and they did.

Dylan was downright taken with those redtails. To him they

were more than the prettiness of their dreamy patterns flown against the skyscape, and if he believed in reincarnation he would have chosen to be a red-tailed hawk in his next life. "Imagine spending an afternoon inside a cloud," he mused. "Not like in an airplane, but with no part of your body, not one square inch, touching anything solid."

The hawks maintained a regular flight station over the canyon, soaring along its ridge updrafts, or spiraling in the afternoon thermals, floating higher and higher on a warm fountain of air until they were black dots, lost against the sun. No reason for a hawk to circle that high, other than the fun of it. Sometimes they came swooping right in front of our cave, swiveling their regal heads to size up the new cliff dwellers. Those cold eyes could drop my thermostat to freezing. Dylan learned to imitate their sky-piercing *keeeee,* a cry designed, I think, to petrify the minds and bodies of earthbound Bugs Bunnies and Mickey Mice.

ii _____ They were good days, and we seemed to be living our version of Genesis, strolling alone through the celebrated garden, all of it shiny and unused, exactly what it should be except no fruit grew on the trees. Adam and Eve even saw each other without fig leaves on, and shame they knew not.

Dylan won't like my telling this.

Truth is, that did happen, the fig leaves were off, and truth will be what you get, my friend. One noon, by coincidence, we turned up undressed at the same point in time and space. Only one pool at Secret Creek was suitable for deep bathing and we hadn't yet worked out a schedule. Bingo, surprise. And what could we do? It would have been wrong to flounder around, and cover up, or be flustered, or even talk about it. That we understood. We had been through much too much together to be coy, including the many nights we had stripped in the dark and slept inches apart. Besides, the mountains would have laughed, so to speak, at our blushes. We would have spoiled Secret Creek. So we went ahead and skinny-dipped together, letting it be no different from swimming together in the past, when our swimsuits after all had been plenty abbreviated. So it was no different from the past. For flesh-and-blood Bridget and Dylan, it amounted to no difference.

Baloney. That night Dylan and I crawled into the same sleeping bag, a first for us. Now Dylan *really* won't like my telling this.

Strange, we never said a word on the subject. We had a usual evening meal, spoke the typical conversations, did the normal chores, sat admiring a fat moon that climbed and put a coat of white enamel on the platform. I suppose, actually, we were thinking of the pool at noon, and of our nights together, and of the possibilities. When we finally stood up, our fingers joined. We squeezed through the doorway, side-by-side, and not wanting to separate this closeness kept on squeezing, into the nearest sleeping bag, Dylan's.

Miss Bennett, our teacher from back in second grade, had never dreamed of this when she smiled and said, "Look at those two kids, always perched together, a pair of little doves." Dylan took off our shirts. I was bare underneath, bras being a nuisance when you're roughing it in the mountains.

Two full-grown people in a sleeping bag means you both seem to have one body, and no place to put your arms except around each other, and no sensible place to put your faces except very close. That's what we did. Enough silver moonlight passed through the door to illuminate our faces. Pressed together, we felt instead of talked—felt our single body, our body heat, our feelings.

After a while Dylan said, faintly, "Hello." His breath and his lips, almost on top of mine, spun my head like a strong jolt of wine.

"Hello," I said. No fooling, hello, this was an introduction between us, to something new, or to something old but admitted for the first time, after a lot of simmering below the surface. The brother-sister days between us were over, thank god.

Dylan said again, "Hello."

"Hello." I moved my lips, hardly making sound, our mouths so near we breathed inside each other's breathing. It was a tantalizing nonkiss, almost kissing and breathing at once, and I poised for the final subatomic fraction of space to be crossed, my pulse rate blown totally out of order. Was Dylan's heart hammering too?

His answer came through his eyes. They unveiled in the moonlight, and at last I saw past: at last, at last, there was a glimpse beyond that blank shell and into the unprotected Dylan Lander. We looked, and it felt closer even than our bodies touching.

"Bridget," he whispered, unblinking, "we may be up in the mountains, but you're the queen of all California."

The words rolled shivering into, under, and along my skin. This was no shot of wine, but pure stoned pleasure that had me now. Fingers were in my hair, combing and stroking —Dylan's fingers—the fingers that had always belonged there. I had to start inhaling faster, to keep up with my heartbeats. So did Dylan. In all our years together we had never once kissed each other and now I waited for the kiss—and more. The moonlight waited. . . .

Sorry, friend. Here is where the juicy X-rated part should come, but it doesn't. Send this to *Ripley's Believe It or Not.*

While the moonlight kept on, Dylan stopped. Pulling one of his arms off me, he gave a small gasp and rolled his head back.

Right away I asked, "What's wrong?"

He didn't reply until his breathing settled down toward normal, and that took a few minutes. I couldn't see his eyes because he was looking up at the cave's ceiling.

"Bridget, you know what happens if you get pregnant."

I said I did. And of course I appreciated his watching out for me, which he was. I just wanted my kiss from him at least. I knew my biology, and kisses don't carry any sperm. But it soon came to light that he had more than the biological consequences on his mind. After reviewing the birds-and-the-bees routine, Dylan said, "We'd be forced to go back, then, you better believe. Straight back to the East Bay, two teenagers in trouble and begging for help. God."

"Oh," I said.

"We'd be trapped there then for good. No more Secret Creek for us."

"Yeah." Whatever the hell happened to my first kiss from Dylan?

"Give me prison instead, if I ever leave here."

He went on like that. I got the message. We talked some more, about other topics. Finally, he craned sideways, looking at me once again, and his words trailed into stillness. He sighed. Crinkling his face, he reached up two fingers and pushed shut his eyelids, the way they do to dead people.

"I wonder," he said, "if you would kindly slip back into your own sleeping bag."

"Tempted?" I asked him, lightly, when really I wanted him to spill out his heart to me.

"Well, you've added on some different parts in recent years. Don't blame me."

"You mean you notice such things?"

"You're very noticeable. Now come on, Bridget, please. Hurry. I won't be able to sleep tonight as it is."

I slid out, and into my nearby bag, but I wasn't altogether satisfied that Dylan's passion for Bridget should be ruled by practicality, or even the best of intentions. Afterward, I wondered whether I made a mistake, and many a time I ask myself that yet. Maybe I should have stayed in his sleeping bag, kissed him, kicked off more clothes, and seduced him—risks and everything—into some kind of future. Even pregnant, it would still be the two of us staying together. Or could any of our futures work for Dylan? Because, you see, I suspected that he was worried about more than any sex stuff, or my getting pregnant, and about more than being forced back to the city. This bright moonlit night I had my first deep suspicions: Dylan must be afraid of me for another reason, scared blue around the gills.

Transitions were coming to Secret Creek. One morning, before dawn, the sounds of wind brought me awake. I heard them coming up the canyon, flurrying, like thousands of rushing little footsteps. I listened to the sounds and . . . was that wind? I fumbled into my jeans and jacket, creeping past Dylan out to our platform.

Outside it was as dark, nearly, as the cave. I sat on the log bench. The night in front of me, around me, hummed with rustlings, patters. The entire canyon lullabied, from wall to wall. A slipping over stone started, gurgles, then *splat-splat-*

splat bouncing along the outer edge of our patio.

"Rain?" asked Dylan, drowsy, when I returned.

"Raining. No sprinkle, this one."

His muffled voice made a remark. Something like, "It had to begin."

And the California wet season had begun, with more rains during the next weeks, including a two-day storm that made the creek dance a jig. Smoky grey clouds would slide in from the coast, until the sky was filmed solid and the grey got greyer, drooping, lower. If clouds can be called the sky, sometimes we stood with our heads in the sky when the wet foggy clouds rolled right over and down Secret Creek.

Rain meant that time was changing as well as the weather. We had lost the handle on the exact month, let alone the date or the day of the week, and can you imagine how odd it is not knowing if the day should fit you like a weary Wednesday, or a free Saturday, or a Sunday before school? (By now school had surely launched its new year.) Whenever our birthdays happened to arrive, we wouldn't recognize them, or Christmas Day, either, or when to hide eggs, light sparklers, keep clear of black cats, or eat turkey. This ignorance had a good side, however, because we never felt ourselves being pushed through the old Monday–Sunday schedule. Without the rules, we couldn't play the game. In the Trinities, each day was that day only, not known by a name, like "Tuesday," but by what the day did itself or by what it did to us. "The day we killed the second deer." "The day of the lightning storm." "When you bruised your arm." "The last full moon."

Even minus a calendar we could tell that time was on the move. Check and you saw it. Mornings gave a discourteous nip now, and one morning white shadows nestled on the north side of boulders. The sun's path, meanwhile, had moved into the southward sky, and by the creek the alders and willows showed a sickly yellow. These signs said that summer had moved into autumn and they foretold other movement ahead. To winter, and snow.

Our own appearances, by the way, had changed with the other changing scenery. I sewed a heavy lining into my triple-layer shirt/coat, and on chilly mornings I wiggled into an extra pair of pants. I saw myself resembling a shoplifter who walks out of a clothing store wearing every garment she has just stolen. Unflattering to the figure, sure, but it keeps the cold away. My long hair, which for convenience I had often been braiding, I loosened and wrapped around my throat, as a muffler. The headband was lowered on the sides to serve double-duty as earmuffs. Dylan did the same with his headband. His hair fell too short to be a muffler, but his dense beard, with a (romantic, I thought) mustache, sheltered his face. And by now Dylan had completed his fur vest, a wild, shaggy mosaic made from a half-dozen different kinds of beast. He was a walking zoo, or anyway a walking taxidermy shop. His vest broadened him more than ever, like he wore football shoulder pads—some Cro-Magnon middle linebacker. He had also, for the worst-weather days, stitched leftover pieces of fur into leggings, an aggregation of shades and shapes that he tied off with buckskin whipcords at his ankles and knees. Fabulous. I felt sort of dizzy, he looked so rugged and dashing to me. But instead of throwing myself at him again I fell back on teasing, saying that his costume resurrected a bunch of buried movies.

"You're a Viking on his way to discover Vinland. Kirk Douglas."

"Agreed," said Dylan.

"You're a Teuton, a yard wide, bushy hair and all, bellowing in a Wagner opera, without the horns on your head."

"Not bad," said Dylan.

"You're some Goth dressed up in a woolly mammoth suit, off to sack Rome. Victor Mature."

"Okay, except he always played a Roman and wore a toga, not skins, unless they tossed him into the Colosseum to fight."

But in a few days the vest and the leggings didn't seem unusual on him. No more movies. Really, what Dylan and I wore had nothing to do with costumes. Like the other animals around us, we had grown longer fur, making ready, and like them now we waited.

iii _____ Dylan had sufficient hides for his vest because we learned much (we _had_ to) at Secret Creek. "Going to school at Secret Creek," we termed it. Lesson number one was finding the answers to the food struggle—we quickly ate our reserve supply—and we did achieve a breakthrough, thank goodness. Starvation will spoil every pretty sunset, believe me.

First, we became very effective at using the snares, especially by combining them with bait. Almost each day produced a catch of some kind, a rabbit or squirrel swinging off the ground, meat to be plucked and dropped into the shopping cart. But the biggest winner was our deer hunting. After considerable experimenting we improved far beyond the cowboy-lasso method, developing a snare from twisted strands of piano wire that would work without our being there to trip it. Instead of hobbling hooves it was set to strangle necks, like the small snares, and that job it performed with vicious success, as we found out one morning while making rounds along the stations of the trap line.

Dylan stopped on the trail, pointing. "It's sprung," he said, without excitement since this had happened before. "See, the trigger is up."

I didn't expect anything, myself.

We jumped when we went bumping into the body. No one cheered with joy, we were so stunned to find a whole dead deer, ours for the taking. And it was a dead deer, no mistake, because you know what a wire snare does. A circle of dirt had been battered puffy by frenzied hooves. Every lurch to escape had only made tighter and more certain the capture: in a deer noose, panic is the hangman. The wire had sliced through the skin and buried itself jugular-deep out of view, making even odds whether the deer bled to death or strangled. Its swollen tongue poked straight up, from trying to lick in a last morsel of air. The eyes told everything and nothing, at once, as they stared like any living eyes, yet didn't see.

We felt guilty about not paying the price for this deer, not being there to watch those eyes die. But it was food, food, food. We daubed ourselves with blood stripes—the three across each cheek—anxious to show respect and gratitude. Bless those animal gods.

Flop, off came the head with Dylan's knife, the wire loop having already simplified the task. Dylan raised his eyebrows.

"What?" I asked.

"I hate to say what I'm thinking."

"What is it?"

He rolled the wire snare between his fingers, repeating his "Hate to say," then ducked his own head inside the loop and pulled it firmly around his neck, denting the flesh. Up went his eyebrows again. "Can you *picture* some man, a hiker from the village, strolling into this?"

I could. "Take that off. Off, Dylan."

Our imaginations aside, we did wonder if such an accident could likely happen, because we also set the deer snares beyond Secret Creek, in areas where outsiders traveled. Begrudgingly we made quick forays out of our snug paradise, into the river canyon and its side canyons, in order not to wipe out Secret Creek's thin deer herd. During winter, our hunting would be restricted to these nearer regions. So because we set snares at all points, my recommendation to everybody is beware of any path that narrows, where you find yourself bending to shove through a brushy hole, ducking your head, and you notice an arched branch, and you step over two parallel logs, automatically stretching forward your neck. . . .

At the cave we worked late that day, and the next, butchering the deer into lean strips for smoke curing and for drying into jerky. The trick to surviving over the long haul is to preserve meat after you catch it. While jerked venison may imitate a hunk of scrap iron (requiring healthy teeth and lots of saliva to convert it back into chewable food) and while it does smell a little potent, just consider the relief of loading your pantry with meat for those days ahead. How bitter if any of that deer had spoiled and needed burying—our future dinners being dumped into the ground. As for me, I welcomed a touch of rank aroma in the cave at night. Knowing there's food in the house makes for sound sleeping.

Dylan spent hours on the hide: scraping it, washing it, kneading it like bread (to keep it supple), rubbing in ashes, finally folding it away to cure. His next leggings would be pure buckskin, not hybrids. Possibly by spring we could bring out a totally new line of Secret Creek special fashions.

To vary the menu and balance the diet we still fished, both inside Secret Creek canyon and out. The fish we usually ate fresh. And we roamed far, gathering any object approximating a berry or a nut. With these we stored bulbs and other tubers, pods, seeds, even certain barks. We piled an imposing hoard into the cave.

"Remember that fable about the good little ant who worked hard and saved up for winter?" we told each other. "Yeah, and wasn't the grasshopper sorry later he had goofed off?"

This was quite a novelty for us, you know, feeling comfortable about having enough to eat, enough shelter, and safety enough from being caught. A safe stomach and a safe neck. Secret Creek's school had taught us our first lesson very well. It looked like independence at last.

Lesson one at school being successful allowed for lesson two—known otherwise as the Great Debate—since now that we had success we also had the spare time to sit and debate what to do with ourselves. Funny business, success.

Bridget: "A year from today, I'm wondering, will we be sitting here, just like this?"

Dylan: "Here, at least."

Bridget: "And the year after, I wonder, and the year after that?"

Dylan: "The deer will. The redtails will."

Bridget: "But they were born here. They've never been anyplace else."

Dylan: "Lucky them."

Bridget: "Now, Dylan, you're avoiding the issue again."

Dylan: "Now, Bridget."

We would sit on our platform, usually in the evenings, unraveling those hours' worth of conversation I mentioned before, giving the fire an occasional poke. Cozy colors flickered on the stone walls. Outside our lighted patio hung the surrounding black space—bitty us, big it. The shorter the daylight hours the longer our campfire talks, and the more interesting. After eating and the usual tidy-up jobs, we warmed at the fire—relaxing muscles—and jabbered on until we were yawning as much as talking. Besides being our only substitute for books, newspapers, magazines, broadsides, radio, television, films, concerts, and lectures, our talking together wasn't merely to be sociable or to fill idle hours. You remember who we were, where we were, and you remember that in addition to our new jerky, lots else, from the past, required chewing and digesting. To begin, the simpler stuff.

Dylan: "What, do you suppose, would you have been studying in school today?"

Bridget: "Today . . . I studied moss. Edible Mosses, Intermediate, I'd title the course."

Dylan: "No, what *would* you have. That is, if today's not a Saturday or Sunday."

Bridget: "Ah. Regular school, not Secret Creek school. Let me think. There would be more English, I know. Probably more Algebra. Some electives. Creative Writing. P.E. —volleyball, say. Why?"

Dylan: "It boggles the mind. Look at our difference . . . that turned into this, or this into that."

Bridget: "Different except for the P.E. Here we have P.E. eight hours a day. Already we're university graduates in physical fitness."

Dylan: "But do you realize how much has changed for us? Imagine sitting in a classroom, looking out a window at . . . anything. The sun. A tree. Put a window across the front of our platform here."

Bridget: "Let me ask a question."

Dylan: "I hear a serious tone. Go on."

Bridget: "Will we ever need any of it in the future—the regular school?"

Dylan: "Do you mean should we be back *there,* memorizing Spanish verbs, taking tests, raising our hands, college prepping? Bridget, you're a lady and a scholar."

Bridget: "Not that. Only, would we ever need those things, I meant."

Dylan: "For?"

Bridget: "Well—"

Dylan: "Well?"

Bridget: "For college you would."

Dylan: "Yep, for college. Now tell me what I do with a diploma in the Trinities."

Bridget: "In the Trinities or not. Might we just need to *know,* have the information, some knowledge, some . . ."

Dylan: ". . . piece of civilization? Cities build up that idea as being important. Here we have only ourselves to build."

Bridget: "That sounds grand, but where would we be right now if you hadn't studied survival manuals from the good old civilized public library. Dead?"

Dylan: "Since we weren't born and raised at Secret Creek, we had to learn the second-hand way, until Secret Creek could teach us best. And it has, true?"

Bridget: "Jesus, are you telling me, Dylan, no more *books* for us?"

Dylan: "Well. No public libraries, no public anything for us criminals, unless you find one down here by the rock slide."

Even hardened criminals have to sleep, and end debates. Suspend the debates, more accurately, because the arguments, questions, answers, rebuttals, and (tentative) summations were all alive and lively the next day. For example, we speculated on what Mrs. Pace, our own minishrink, thought about us. "Two marks in the loss column," we agreed. And the gossip among our former classmates?

"Teenage couple elopes," I suggested, would be one nice interpretation. I omitted a more cynical variation on the same general theme.

Dylan didn't. "Pregnant teenage couple elopes," he said.

"How about 'Whatever happened to those two, What'shisname and What'shername?'" I said, proving, a tad late, my own hard nose. "'You know, the two who were so loused up last spring.'"

Dylan approved.

I pushed on: "Or how about nothing. No gossip. Out of sight, out of mind."

"I hope so. And that's what we ought to do—forget every silly soul of them. Let them go worry about their cafeteria prom."

Dylan, let me remind you, can be stern.

Our discussions eventually reached the less simple topics, after wearing through the top layers and into the center of things. What about Dylan's parents, for instance, and Charlene? How did we fit into their lives now? Were we shadows to them, or substance?

"They have their routines, without us," Dylan claimed, "just the way we have ours without them. In fact, hauling our bodies here to the mountains helped unclutter their lives, which they'll come to appreciate someday. We were nuisances, don't forget. Troublesome. Sacks of weight."

I said, "Come on. A responsibility isn't always a nuisance."

"Sure it is. Hand-in-hand."

"Negative on that, negative."

"You were a nuisance to your aunt. Deny it."

"A bother, okay, but I'll bet she still has the search out for her Bridget, her nuisance. I'll bet that whenever the telephone rings in Santa Barbara she's sitting next to it, heart pitter-pattering, hoping."

A snort from the cynic. "Why, she feels obligated. And she's guilty as the devil about botching her guardianship. Maybe, see, somebody will accuse her of selling your house and running you off. She worries. Same with my parents —they'll keep searching, too, for a decent period. My disappearance is another ego problem, another red-faced flop for the two of them . . . messing up on parenthood this time. A busted marriage and now this. What will people say? So my parents worry, worry. Think how much easier everybody's life will be without us."

In the firepit, the tag ends of our wood shifted and fell with a last flare onto pulsing coals. It was late enough for the thick coalbed to stay alive until morning light and breakfast.

Dylan glanced over, investigating my silence.

"All these months," I said, "and you haven't eased up on your folks one bit."

He clucked his tongue: *click-cluck.* "They don't need me to forgive them. Hell, they don't even need me. My mother has her men friends to take care of her. And the old man is—god knows where, busy with his own show. Look, we're shot as a family, flat finished, and we're better off out of each other's hair."

I said, "Then they're not thinking about you really, only being embarrassed. Is that it? Nothing else?"

"And feeling sorry, like I said."

"Nothing else?"

"Twinges, possibly."

"Twinges of what?"

Dylan turned back to read the coals, his rigid profile and glimmering beard traced by the glow. "Who knows what."

"You're their only kid, Dylan."

With a patient nod, he acknowledged my remark. "And the wrong kid."

"What does that mean?"

"I have my theories."

"Tell me."

"All right." Tilting his head, he looked over straight as a sword at me, expressionless as ever, calm, too calm. "When I was growing up, I always thought we were happy, like most other families, and we did the things most families do, so to me it all seemed fine. I got my Christmas presents. I had my birthday parties—you came to those. I went camping with my dad. I got this wristwatch. But, later, thinking back on it, I saw that something must have been wrong, some part missing, that a young child wouldn't have the sense to notice. You know? For example, they never told me why I was their only kid. Why no brother or sister? Why was one enough, or one too many? Did your folks ever explain that to you?"

"Medical. My mother couldn't have more babies."

"Mine never dropped a hint. And now I've made some deductions. I think they got married because of me, you follow? I was an accident, a back-seat slip-up, and they went ahead, got married, tried to stick it out at least until I was older, but it didn't work. They were trying to make the best of a bad deal, and I was the bad deal, you might say. Anyway, at last everybody is free."

"Dylan—it's crazy—why dream this up? Why make yourself the guilty party?"

"No, no, I have my theories," he repeated.

I sat there speechless at his brooding. I ached to help him, soften him, somehow. How?

Bedtime. Good night, good night, sweet prince, my dear Dylan. Tomorrow will bring more talking.

Talk and dig though we did, the great nugget of the Great Debate stayed mostly underground. Label it the "when return, if return" subject. Now that we had accomplished Dylan's goal of total self-reliance here at Secret Creek, I sent out feelers to learn how long we would be practicing it, and what lay ahead for us. He was hazy, unfailingly.

Take one stormy afternoon when we holed up on our platform, stoking the fire, watching rain splatter and whack against the cliff. It was thundering, too, big booms firing from the peak tips, ricocheting down Secret Creek in a quick string of THUMP-THUMP-THUMP-BUMP. A perfect setting.

Coldness, I spoke of first. I asked Dylan to meditate on how cold it would sink here this winter.

"Very cold," meditated Dylan aloud, dropping (deliberately?) an extra log on a blaze already too warm.

"Wood shortage" were words with an ugly ring, I advised.

He pointed below at an entire forest of firewood, in various stages from standing to conveniently flat on the ground. "Only temporarily wet," he added.

BABOOM. THUMP-THUMP-THUMP-BUMP.

"Nice," smiled Dylan. He has a fondness for storms, if I haven't mentioned that before. For a party, order him thunder and yowling winds. His tanned face, creased with pale streaks near the eyes from squinting outdoors, squinted now at the rain putting a sheen on boulders and pockmarking the creek.

I enjoy ripping rainstorms myself, but living in snow would

be a first for me, and Dylan. Would it snow here anything like
it rained?

"Kind of," he said, idly.

"Kind of?"

"In deep winter, I reckon."

"That could mean being snowed in."

"Kind of, for a while, but we won't be sealed off for, like,
weeks."

I then reminded him of the Donner Party. Every California
schoolkid has vivid technicolor-textbook memories of the
Donner Party, eighty-nine foolhardy, westward-ho pioneers
caught in the winter mountains, eating horses, shoe leather,
each other. Pull off Interstate 80 someday to see the
monument and a museum. Moral: Fail big enough, you can
end up famous.

"Wrong mountain range—" began Dylan.

"I know it happened over in the Sierras," I interrupted,
"but the lesson is still the same." Kind of.

"Bridget, survey our home." He waved his hand overhead at
our domed shelter, dry for centuries, and back at our
windproof cave, with its sleeping bags, blankets, and heaped
corners of foodstuffs. "Why fret?" His curving, rust-peppered
mustache twitched upward at the ends. "What are you
nervous about?"

Truth is, I may have been edgy, but there was too much
mountain maid in me, too much deer and rabbit blood under
my fingernails, not to believe we would manage. Really, you
know, my questions only tried to sneak around Dylan and get
him thinking about what we should do with ourselves,
whether this winter or the next or the next. We were young,
for god's sake, with our long lifetimes still ahead. And now
that our brother-sister team had turned into something more

interesting, where was it going to take us? I needed to think myself, and what *did* I think, for that matter, and what if my thoughts would be different from Dylan's thoughts—what on earth would we do then. Dylan?

I grew blunter, more clever: "We're squared away here at Secret Creek for . . . years to come."

Agreement from Dylan.

"We can provide all we need . . . right here . . . for ages."

A nod.

"Indefinitely, in fact."

A nod, and suspicion.

"Indefinitely. Absolutely indefinitely."

No answer.

"Absolutely indefinitely?" I asked.

"Okay—absolutely. What is this?"

"Our canes, I suppose, we can make from any tree limb. No problem there. But would we go collect our Social Security checks when we're 65, and Medicare?"

I thought I had him. But he just split into his widest, white-toothed grin, looking like a twelve-year-old boy wearing a beard. He said through the white teeth, "Fortunately that decision can wait until we qualify."

"Now listen, Dylan."

"Now Bridget."

"Now Dasher, now Dancer, now Prancer and Vixen. You *know* what I mean, Dylan."

"And you know what I mean, Vixen Bridget."

"You're stinking stubborn, I know."

"Accusing me of that sin again?"

The Great Debate, on occasions, carried past our campfire hours and lingered on in the dark, from our sleeping bags inside the cave. Spoken by invisible bodies, echoing against the granite walls, these words were always direct.

I asked him, "Have you ever considered what would happen if one of us got a real smash, or sick? Very sick."

"Yes I have."

"Acute appendicitis, say. Burst appendix, in the middle of the night. Or hemorrhaging."

"Collapsed lung. Food poisoning."

"Right, that type of thing—badly sick. What'll we do if one of us gets badly sick, Dylan?"

"Badly die probably."

Correct answers have such a soothing brevity about them. Good night.

In the blackness another night.

"Dylan?"

"Mm."

"Actually. Actually, how long can we live here?"

"As long as we need to, or want to."

"Still, just on and on?"

"On and on."

NINE

Secret Creek Speaks

i——————————————A redtail drifted across the morning sky. At the upper end of Secret Creek a cheerful scallop of early sunshine was edging down inside our canyon. No wind, and the white firs and ponderosa and sugar pines stood tall in their groups, prepared as ever for the new day. Below us our creek took its gentle left turn, bent back again, burbled over a bed of pebbles—and into its first frothy pool. Some small birds flittered there, drinking or feeding.

Dylan sat out on the patio's lip, dangling his legs while sorting lines, poles, bait, flies, for a fishing run downstream. He started a casual, conversational singing, with enough coolness lingering in the air to form faint smoke puffs around the lyrics.

> "Mr. Rabbit, Mr. Rabbit,
> your ears are mighty long.
> *Yes, bless God, been put on wrong.*
> *Ev'ry little soul gonna shine, shine,*
> *ev'ry little soul gonna shine along.*
>
> "Mr. Rabbit, Mr. Rabbit,
> your eyes are mighty red.
> *Yes, bless God, I'm almost dead.*

> *Ev'ry little soul gonna shine, shine,*
> *ev'ry little soul gonna shine along."*

Since the words of the old folk song didn't suit the upbeat morning very well, Dylan rewrote a few verses, keeping limber his quick-wit talents.

> "Mr. Rabbit, Mr. Rabbit,
> your ears are mighty long.
> *Yes, bless God, hadda listen to this song.*
> *Ev'ry little soul gonna shine, shine,*
> *ev'ry little soul gonna shine along.*
>
> "Mr. Rabbit, Mr. Rabbit,
> your eyes are mighty red.
> *Yes, bless God, been keepin'*
> *you and Bridget fed."*

While listening at the campfire I cleaned, then sterilized, our breakfast ware, boiling some water taken from our faithful plastic jug. Lifted from this boiling water, the stinging-hot pans and cups, knives and forks dried fast by their own heat. Experience tells. The whole business of breakfast took only minutes for us, one simple pattern among a slew of patterns.

Patterns, routines, repetitions—our days were measured off by the steady pulse of these rhythms. In the murky first hour after waking, we would lash shut the door and speed out of Secret Creek to the river canyon, using an eye-opening trail up the cliffs. Although this new trail was almost straight up, and almost as scary as climbing the Notch, it too got to be a routine and it saved us hours by letting us cut cross-country to the river. If we caught much game in the snares, there we stayed, chewing some jerky strips before skinning and butchering and burying. Then we would loaf or doze in the underbrush, maybe try a little hidden fishing, always on guard, and come home in the dusk. When the snares were empty or had only a Mr. Rabbit or two—like this morning —we returned to our cave immediately, cleaned the game, cooked a regular breakfast, observed the sun rising above the canyon, and spent a leisurely day fishing and puttering around Secret Creek. Our evenings you know about.

We had ourselves in proper order, with animal skins nicely curing, a hillock of firewood already cut to size, new footstools for the hearth, and an improved diet. Lately we had been saving the extra animal fat, which Dylan pounded into the jerky, converting it to pemmican, a tastier and healthier product, he claimed. To prevent scurvy (landlubbers also can get it) Dylan added tea to our menu—brewed from evergreen needles. Lots of vitamin C and it'll clear out the sinuses. Fish we tried to include every other day. Time to go fishing.

We ambled not walked down Secret Creek, the slight downgrade lifting our boots for us. Been here before, World, before and before. Step over this root . . . jump on this flat boulder . . . duck this limb, cross, weave . . . been here before. Born and bred in the brier patch.

Many of our friends remained with us despite the fading season. A mountain quail legged it out of sight into a thicket, a squadron of band-tailed pigeons whooshed overhead, veering off and upward in impressive air-show formation. I saw moving against a tree trunk the white-and-turquoise smear of a nuthatch, and scratching through leaf litter a crowd of Oregon juncos. I heard, downstream, the insolent *yack-yack-yack-yack* of a jay cursing somebody.

Dylan was casting a store-bought trout fly, embellished by him with a few deer hairs, while I fished with insect eggs, grubs, or whatever crawly things I found under rotten wood. The more they flipped and twisted on the hook, the better they were for bait. Our score so far: me, 2 meaty sparklers; Dylan, 0. After my second catch, Dylan switched to live bait, reluctant to put away his personal creation, saying, "Anything that snazzy ought to work."

I handed him a bug. "Have you forgotten? Beauty is not in the eye of the poleholder."

"Beauty is not in the eye of the poleholder. Very good." He nodded, in compliment. "Very good. She's read her Shakespeare. And a millipede by any other name would taste as sweet?"

Casting, we let the current float our lines by boulders, into shady spots, pools, all the likely areas. No hurry. No rush. Our quota this morning was set at four—conservation of the fishery—and it would be filled soon enough.

Our sky blossomed above our Secret Creek, robust blue, rippled with wispy cirrus clouds. (A delicious name for an ice cream: Blueberry-Cirrus Ripple.) Sunlight penetrated to the creek, crosshatching a design of shade and shimmer, making the water suddenly livelier, more vocal. We paused, took a cold after-breakfast drink—sucking it directly from the creek—and also took in from around us the smells of wetness, of damp ground, and the slither-music of wetness in motion.

Dylan hooked a solid fish, a fighter. Three down and one to go. We calculated just the pool where number four could be found—our bathing hole, left unfished for days now. Weaving along the stream's edge, between clusters of alders, willows, and mossy boulders, we came to the stepping-stone ford we had built and went across, chattering about who would get the day's last catch. We looked at the end of a choppy riffle down the creek and saw our pool, and over at a nearby thicket we saw, poking out, a pair of human legs.

ii _____ We went rigid. Too late. Our loud words had already carried through the air, the man was sitting up, his bewildered eyes found us. Contact.

In time, still sitting, the man raised a hand in greeting.

What would you do? One fine morning, let's say, you woke up, went downstairs in your locked house, and Behold: a stranger in your kitchen, sitting easy, waves you a welcome. You wouldn't run away from inside your own home, and neither did we. We advanced on the stranger, not speaking, not waving back, almost stomping our boots at each step. Dylan actually was panting, from being so angry and taken aback, so strung out with shock. And his reaction was contagious. The more adrenalin that pumped into him, the louder my own breathing got.

With a smile the stranger began to rise, but noticing everything about us—our faces and our clothes—he decided against it and sank carefully at our feet as we arrived. He was a slender little man, shorter than me, who wouldn't have been imposing even standing up on a log. Dylan towered over him like a slab of Secret Creek granite. Furry granite, I should put it, because he had on his vest.

The man continued smiling up at us, and wow, was it freaky to see another person that close, with teeth and lips and eyes and skin that weren't Dylan's, in fact were contrary to Dylan's. He was slim, as I said, wiry compared to husky Dylan, with hands no bigger than mine and a jaw tapering to a neat, nearly female chin. His eyes and eyebrows were a similar shade of brunette. He wore a kelly-green stocking cap and a green twill jumpsuit affair, amazingly tidy and store-bought next to our ravels, patches, furs, feathers, bloodstain shadows. I guessed his age to be mid-fifties. Beside him lay a string of our trout.

He a-hemmed, clearing his throat. "Well, well, howdy," he offered. "Hello there, friends."

Forgive me, but a new voice blasting out in Secret Creek made me squirm, the equivalent of having, pardon me, sewer muck tracked across a white virgin carpet. I couldn't stop my hostility. It happened, the way leaves tumble in a gust. Action, reaction.

Dylan, alongside, wrapped his hand around the hatchet handle at his belt. When his knuckles turned ghostly—ready for a move—it then occurred to me: Should I be afraid for us, or *of* us? Dylan could crumple this guy's skull with one sweep, and a dead body would dissolve here, undiscovered, in any crevice under a heap of stones.

"I'm Curly," said the man. "At least that's what people call me, Curly. It made sense, once, but now I reckon it's closer to nonsense." He popped off his stocking cap, revealing a mostly bald head. "I'm still Curly, but not curly anymore, as you can see," he said. The cap snuggled back into place.

We had nothing to say. Curly must have been one very puzzled fellow, and nervously he eyed Dylan's hatchet hand. Partly, I think, Dylan and I *couldn't* talk because to give this man our words would have acknowledged he was really there, and granted him some sort of permission to be at Secret Creek talking to us. If we ignored him, this Curly might sooner or later evaporate and his dead fish reappear alive in our creek where they belonged. Possibly he didn't exist. Possibly we were hallucinating, and you don't want to be heard talking to your hallucinations.

No telling what we would have done—just keep staring at him and ignoring him into nonexistence or bash him there—when instead Curly claimed our attention with an odd remark. In another attempt at conversation he said, gesturing at our private bathing hole, "This here has always been a fine spot."

I blurted, "Always?"—suddenly imagining an unknown onlooker during all my past baths.

"Yes, ma'am, this hole is always good for three or four fat ones. See?" He pointed toward his trout.

"Are you saying"—Dylan's hollow voice had a tremor to it—"that you were here at—here once before?"

"Oh, you betcha, sir." Relieved to hear from us, Curly got more comfortable and did some mental arithmetic. "Let me—mum-mum-hum. Twelfth year, this is. Twelve years running I've been here to fish, sometimes in the spring for a week, sometimes in the fall for a week, one or the other. Once a year, for twelve years." He seemed a little surprised himself. "Twelve."

"Impossible," said Dylan. "There's no sign anywhere in the canyon."

"I left no sign," said Curly. "Anybody who litters this place ought to be hanged, right? Imagine finding a beer can here, or a gum wrapper."

"You arrived this morning?" I asked him.

"Just arrived, ma'am."

"And from down the canyon?"

"I only know one way in, by climbing through that crack from down below. You know it? It opens up about—"

"How did you find that?" Dylan interrupted, more accusation than question.

Curly chuckled a bit. "You mean how did an old geezer like me ever make that climb?"

Dylan didn't chuckle. "I mean how did you find it."

"Well . . . by chance." He reflected, completely serious now because it was obviously completely serious to us, and because he was remembering for himself. "'Course I was twelve years younger then, more what you call athletic, and maybe more adventuresome. I had been fishing up the main river, having a fair-enough time, when I felt the bug bite—the bug, you know, that gives you a fever to do something a little crazy. I got this craving to go a-wandering off, the farther off the better. I wanted to be lost. So I started walking without thinking where especially, just enjoying myself. When I ran out of room to walk, the bug fever told me to climb and look at the view. I climbed smack into this place, and I looked, all right, and stayed here for two extra days. I had good feelings. And I knew then that I'd be coming back each year, you betcha. Twelve years . . . and still the same feelings. Let me make a little confession to you folks—some years I never wet a hook. Oh, I brought along the pole and the other gear, but they never got unpacked, and instead I did lots of lazy-boning and lying down, the way you caught me a while ago. Too busy being lazy to go fishing. Anyhow, there are other things here worth hooking besides fish, things you need to lie down for, you agree?" He smiled—shyness, not humor. "Here's another confession. I never once told anybody about this canyon, not even my wife, my own family. Hard to believe? Selfish, I suppose. It was one secret I wouldn't give up. Listen, I used to pretend I was the first and only person ever to plant foot here, kind of played a game."

"You're quite a talker," muttered Dylan. We sat, fast, both of us under a crushing weight. Maybe we had camped inside Curly's locked house, rather than the reverse. His great secret and our Secret Creek—the same—and added together they canceled: zero secret among us three.

"Sorry for jawing," Curly apologized. "And how did you folks find your way inside?"

"The same," I said.

"The same bug bite?"

"No, the same crack from below." No need to publicize our other routes. "The same, by accident."

"And you been here long?"

That cut too close.

He said, "I can see you have, so no reason for me to be nosey. Well, I envy you, having the seasons to watch here, having more than seven days out of a year. Lordy, even one day more than seven I'd envy." His brown eyes blinked, like coming awake on a sleepy morning. "But people would be waiting. They'd expect me back, and I want them to expect me back, you know? My second vacation week I always spend with my family. Always from here," he looked at the cliffs, then at us, "to there."

"We don't have anyone expecting," I said, and Dylan scowled at me for silence.

"You don't?" asked Curly, surprised at my certainty. "No one, ma'am?"

"Nobody," I said.

He absorbed that, before remarking, "Sometimes, I found out, you do without knowing it."

"*Nobody*," barked Dylan. "You can't hear her?"

Curly fell quiet again, examining Dylan and me. "Pardon," he said, "I did hear her. Nobody. And that means nobody for you, too, does it, sir?" I always meant to ask Curly if he had been in the military, or what, with his "ma'am-ing" and "sir-ing" spread so thick. It seemed upside down for an older person to call me "ma'am," when I hardly dressed like a ma'am, and didn't feel an inch like one. Yet, whatever his motive, his politeness had a charm to it.

"That does mean me," answered Dylan, "but don't express any regrets. Having nobody has advantages over having somebody. It's the somebodies who can chew you apart, *sir,* while the nobodies never bring a moment's harm."

"Lordy, that's the truth," Curly said. "And a wonderful choice of words. But, let me think, excuse me, isn't there a problem with your idea?" Dylan elevated his eyebrows, inviting Curly to continue, and Curly said, "Well, the nobodies never brought any harm, but shucks they never brought anything else, either."

"Like?" Dylan asked.

"The good things that people bring."

"Like?"

"Oh, the affection—"

"Hold it." Dylan snapped his fingers, which he could do as loud as a pistol shot. Plainly he had worked himself up into an arguing temper. "Don't read us the propaganda sheet, whoever you are. We've been there before. Tell us about some of those *good things* as real as what we have here in this canyon. Not words, not fuzzy junk, no might-have-been's or could-be's, *things.*"

"Ah-ha. This canyon . . . you say." Curly concentrated briefly. "Now, sir, I'm reminded of my great-grandmother, who was born and raised in Connecticut, and all her family and relatives the same. She got married at sixteen or seventeen or thereabouts, the way they did in those times, and soon after the wedding her husband, my great-grandfather, determined to set himself pioneering out west. Off he went scouting ahead. Whenever he crossed some state and came to a likely spot, he wrote back to my great-grandmother in Connecticut, giving the usual details, about the soil, the timber, the water, the weather. She always returned just one answer, never changing it, and I've read them myself because my great-grandfather saved her letters and passed the bundle on when he died to my grandfather, and my grandfather to my father. The handwriting is that old-time spidery kind from inkwell pens."

An interlude developed.

I said, "And her answer? That she always sent?"

"Her answer," said an impatient Dylan, "was that none of the new places sounded any better than dear old Connecticut. The grass only seems to be greener on the other side of the continent. That's the moral, isn't it? Our first homes are our best homes."

Curly shook his stocking-capped head. "No, her answer wasn't that. She never wrote a word about Connecticut or against leaving her home. And she never asked a word about the prairie in Nebraska or the mountains in Colorado. In her letters she just asked a question, the same question: *Hiram, can we raise children there?*" He picked up a dry willow stick and broke it into five pieces. Then he lined the five pieces in a neat row. "They did later have five youngsters in Colorado. Five living. The way I see it, sir, my great-grandmother knew there was at least one *thing* that no location on this earth can guarantee on its own. Say, what do you suppose she would have said to raising children here, or even trying? No thanks?" He turned in my direction—for agreement, an answer? I had no answer. But it was still a question I could wonder about. Hiram, can we raise children at Secret Creek?

"Now go on," said Dylan, looking irked to have met up with another quick-draw storyteller.

"Sir?"

"Go to the next part."

"After they raised their family?"

"*How* they raised them. What your great-great and grand-grand did with them, or to each other. Having babies is simple stuff—in Colorado or in Connecticut—compared to the next part. Get on to it."

Curly squirmed some. "You're a wise fellow," he said.

Dylan pressed him: "Then what really happened next wasn't so nice." He was dueling with Curly, I could tell, Great Debating with him. Incredible. Here we sat, at Secret Creek, gunning and debating with a man named Curly.

"They've been buried ages ago . . . and who can tell." Curly moved his trout away from the spreading midmorning sunlight. "They were people. There must have been the usual ups and downs. But because of those children and their own children, I'm here, and I thank them." Curly glanced up, puckering his pointy features into sharper points. "I believe they were mostly happy with each other."

After a medium wait, Dylan spat between his boots, his first spit in many, many weeks. We all watched the dribble beading with dirt. Instead of the spit soaking in the ground, the dirt drew up into the spit.

Curly stirred his row of five sticks and rearranged the pieces into a rough circle. In an undertone he said, "I went through a bad time once, speaking of kids and being happy—or unhappy, that is." He wagged his green stocking cap, apologetically. "Here I go again, jawing, pushing my personal history on you folks when it's probably not wanted. Anyhow —to keep it short—I got a divorce years ago."

"Oh?" asked Dylan, nudging it just enough into an actual question. He harbored an irresistible interest in the topic of divorce.

"She hurt me. She did something a wife should never do to a husband. After that, we tore at each other for a while, you can bet. I can hear us like it happened yesterday. Lordy. It makes me blush."

I had a dickens of an itch to ask Curly what his wife did that a wife should never do, but it seemed safer to get Dylan's opinion later. "That bad?" I asked instead.

"I'm afraid that wasn't the worst, ma'am. I went on to make a mistake, a mistake bigger than hers, and afterwards I finally learned what I did wrong. I had let it be easier for me to hate her than to forgive her. Know what I mean? Of course my hating her gave me considerable comfort, for a spell, but I ended up with nothing—no wife, no kid. Even my hate pulled out and left. One day I looked around . . . and nothing."

"You married again," I said. "You talked about a family."

"I do have a family, a good one."

"But if you had stayed with the first wife—"

"—I wouldn't have this family now." Curly nodded at me. "My first wife and I might have parted anyway, all right. But not by hating each other off the face of the earth. Get this: I couldn't for my very own life tell you whether she's alive or dead, or the whereabouts of my first child, a son, or what he looks like." Curly turned to Dylan. "I wouldn't recognize him passing me on the street, or if he was you, sitting there."

At that notion, we took a moment to listen to the creek splash into the bathing hole, go almost silent, splash out again.

"Admit it," said Dylan, blunt, the way he can be. "You're

better off without them, and for sure those two, wherever, are better off without you and your trying to prop up and hold together a bad deal."

Curly fine-tuned his circle of sticks. "Better off . . . without seeing my son?"

Dylan rubbed himself under his fur vest, giving a familiar skyward stare. He stroked his mustache ends. "This reminds me of the Diefenbacher case, a man found dead in his house. It was in the local papers. A mad episode." He said to me, "Remember it, Helen?"

No comment. I recognized a Parable Time being loaded up in the pistol when I heard one.

"What was it?" asked innocent Curly.

"Apparently"—Dylan settled himself—"this Diefenbacher man bought into a brand-new subdivision, an expensive kind with Spanish architecture, tile roofs, curved streets, real classy, and I guess he had saved his entire life for this, and was so excited that he talked somebody into letting him move in before the subdivision was officially open. Great. Meantime, it gets discovered that the subdivision's water supply is contaminated—really putrid. Naturally they delay the opening, but no one stops to think that poor Diefenbacher is already living in his home of the future."

"Lordy," said Curly.

"That water had to stink coming out from his faucet, yet he drank the cruddy gunk, because the autopsy showed he did. Why drink it? He must have told himself: 'Now, Diefenbacher, this is a new house, your own home, so water must be supposed to stink this way.' *Aarg*—how could he have forced the poison down? He did. And next, the power company shut off its electricity to the subdivision, but Diefenbacher kept in his house. He lived at least several days, according to the doctors. Try to imagine what went on in there during those days or nights. Here is Diefenbacher in the dark, with a few candles lit, eating rotten food, drinking putrid water. Here he is, stomach cramps, shakes, swallowing and killing himself, and afterwards everyone asks how he could ever do such a thing. Well, I know why. Because he was sticking it out, making the best of a bad deal. Whatever his life was, it was his, and better to stay in the house than to leave and end up with nothing at all. Besides, he probably got used to it after a while. Like your Colorado family, he was mostly happy before he died, in a puddle of puke."

End of parable. The creek rang much louder than it had before—somebody had turned up the volume.

Curly was the first to bestir himself, unbending a stiff leg, scratching above his ears, where remnants of that once-famous curly hair fringed his scalp. "Thinking back about my years of living," he said slowly, "I can't say a lot for certain. Nope. But I can say this. You must forgive the people you love for not being what you want them to be, and even for not being what they should be. Because, you know, the whole business of living is never what you want it to be or what it should be. As he steadied his dark eyes at us, his voice dropped, gentle, hard to hear. "And I found that blaming other people is blaming yourself, that hating other people is hating yourself. It ends the same."

For the space of a few heartbeats, I could feel us loosen toward Curly, a confidential mood that might have led to telling him our true story. But Dylan stiffened. He got to his feet, and the swollen way he held himself made Curly and me stand too.

Dylan's words were every bit as hard as he looked. "Don't play parent here," he said, "always giving the same advice:

'Learn to live with less' and 'Bitter must come with the sweet.'
Except you don't know what the bejesus to say when it's all
bitter and no sweet." In two big strides he was square against
Curly, talking down at the kelly-green stocking cap. "I want
to ask something. Do you intend to stay?" It was only a rude
question, not a threat exactly.

"I'm going to leave," Curly said mildly and immediately, as
if he'd had his answer before the question ever came.

"When?"

"Now. You won't catch me messing in what you folks have
here in the canyon."

He had started away when Dylan stopped him. And this
time Dylan did threaten.

"A warning," said Dylan, in a vibrating bass. "Don't.
Don't-you-report-about-us." His eyes flattened into a dull,
venomous grey.

Curly shook his head. "I wouldn't do that."

"You have no idea how much I mean the warning."

"I think I do. Remember, this place is my secret, too."

"No rescuing tricks. We don't need help. We are absolutely
able on our own here, understand?"

Curly glanced at me, so I seconded Dylan: "We can handle
anything."

"Yes, ma'am," he said. "I can sure see"—he reviewed
Dylan's animal vest—"you two are able, no doubting that,
sir."

Dylan was about to lay more muscle on him but Curly
hadn't finished. "Let me swear a promise to you both," he
said, "because I understand what the worry is." He made a
significant pause, to stress the occasion. "I promise not to say a
word about finding anybody in this canyon. You'll be safe by
me. And let me give another promise. When I come back next

spring, if I meet you here, in the canyon, I'll about-face and leave again. Just signal from a distance—we won't even need to talk. I'll understand." He dipped his head. "My best to you. Goodby."

Gathering his fishing rod, he was off downstream.

We forgot to say our goodby and Curly forgot his string of fish, unless he forgot on purpose. Then we watched the green jumpsuit and green stocking cap diminish, saw Curly stop, locate and put on his pack, and finally vanish around a bend. Dylan began mumbling.

"What?" I asked.

"I have to make certain he leaves our territory. Otherwise I'll fret all night." And Dylan glided after him like a trailing mountain lion. Territorial imperative.

That night Dylan was tossing and turning in his sleeping bag, although he had seen Curly climb down from Secret Creek and even had shadowed him part way to the river. In the cave we continued the debate brought in from around the campfire: Would Curly report us? Dylan fussed that he would, combing Curly's promise closer than a Wall Street lawyer combs for tax loopholes, and predicting that a vow not to "say" any word meant you could still write it out on paper.

"Really now, Dylan," I sighed at him through the dark. "You heard him say that we'd be safe."

"Yes, ma'am," Dylan mimicked, "yes, sir," caroming the words off the cave walls. "You fell for that ma'am/sir, did you, Bridget? And for those sappy stories, I suppose, about those divorces and lost kids and Colorado pioneer women? All hogwash, all lies, lies."

"Like you tell, Mr. Diefenhammer?"

"Diefenbacher."

"The man will keep his promise, Dylan," I said, repetition number ten of that claim since our evening meal.

"How do you *know?*"

"His face when he promised."

"Crap." But in a minute he added, "You think so?" because he wished like blazes for me to be right.

I did think so. "Say," I realized aloud, before sliding into sleep, "we could have asked him what month and day it is."

TEN

An Indian Gets Captured

i_____ The day that the unexpected happened was another golden morning, full of sunshine. This made the third consecutive day of good sun since the meeting with Curly, and Dylan labeled it autumn's swan song, or a last jig before paying the fiddler, take your choice. Mind you, hot it was not, and not terribly warm either, but when the sun comes up bright in a clear sky it makes you think warm. I wore only a shirt on that morning, with my coat left up on the hillside together with our fishing gear.

We were at the river canyon having great luck. A tender yearling had completed its brief life inside one of our deer snares, and now the carcass was near the river where we could better finish the butchering. Guts and head had already been buried in the brush, at the spot of the snare, while the hide we had just sliced and tugged off in a solid, usable piece. It helps to have lots of water when you skin and cut an animal. After saving the hide, the next move was to quarter the carcass so we could tote the chunks down those steep cliffs into Secret Creek.

Dylan went back up the hillside to fetch some cloth and our fishing line, for wrapping the meat. I stayed behind—on watch, of course. Of course on watch. The supreme rule outside of Secret Creek was not "Look for food" but "Look for *them."* People. We had practiced three birdcalls and two hand signals as various warnings, in case of an emergency. Bridget completely understood the supreme rule.

But Bridget was also dreamy nowadays, prone of late to gaps, spaces, sudden blanks.

I sat on a river-rubbed boulder, already dazed by fiery circlets of sunlight dancing along the water—on and off and up and back—like a hypnotist's swinging silver pocket watch, like hundreds of them. River sounds, too, swung back and forth, over and over and over. Elbows went on knees, my head bent forward, down, the numbing vapor from raw deer flesh lifted in an invisible cloud around me, and I plunged into a deluxe reverie.

Curly came to my mind, first, with his green stocking cap, its green fluff ball bobbing at the tip. I saw him striding down Secret Creek canyon and I tried to visualize him back with his family, in his house, talking with his kids, his wife. What did his wife look like? I pictured her (get this) as Charlene. No special reason, unless Charlene had been out of my thoughts and her turn to get in again was overdue, or unless thinking of Curly, and Curly's ideas, made me guilty about ignoring my own aunt.

How would Curly explain her? What story would he tell about her, because, he would claim, Charlene must have a story, an explanation, for her fussy, unmarried ways. She had been hurt once, he might say, made afraid of taking any chances. So sick, say, as a child, she believed herself dying, and she swore never again to hold anything close because she might die and lose it. Or a true love, say, gone from her ages ago yet not gone from her memories and never to be replaced by another man. Or Charlene made timid by my very mother, say, who always sparkled more, always shone brighter, than her sister. Or, say, both my mother and Charlene in love with my father. Charlene loses. Lord (or lordy), there's a thought.

Could be. Curly did start you considering all the could-be's. But the most probable story, and the best one anyway, was the least complicated. In this story Charlene is really the Charlene I already knew: just fluttery, fussy, earnestly earnest, just happier not being married. In short, Charlene. My important addition to her list of qualities, however, and the one that Curly would have already found, is that Charlene, unlike Rhett Butler, still did give a damn about Miss Bridget. As Curly might put it, Charlene was a pain in the neck, but not in the heart, where it counted.

When Charlene sang out "Rise and shine, Bridget, early bird catches the worm," did it matter so much that I was the worm and not the robin and she should have said instead "Sleep in, Bridget, relax"? Didn't the old bumbler intend to do her best by me, even in selling my house? Intentions must count for something. Charlene's corn-pone platitudes and Dylan's parables had that in common, if nothing else—the wish to help me out.

And for our Mrs. Pace a story could be found, if one pondered it. How would you care to listen Monday through Friday to a string of sulky adolescents, a crowd of misfits, including dumb-ass pill-poppers, smart-ass truants, suicidal uglies, flunk-outs, and sure, castaways from broken homes and—the pinnacle? the pits?—brand-new orphans who run off. The Pacemaker no doubt had her own problems and if she yawned in the face of some teenager's travail, we can understand. She's human, right, Curly? And Charlene is. And us, right, Curly? I am. I can forgive. I think I can even forgive myself for not dying with my mother and father.

Yet Dylan . . . is he like us? Dylan would understand Mrs.

Pace, down to her last yawn, but would he believe in forgiving her? Most important, would he ever forgive his own family?

Ask him now. He was back from up the hill. I heard boots on gravel and saw legs beside me.

No Dylan. Instead, I raised my daydreaming head to find myself neatly surrounded by six men wearing packs, the classic scene of the careless Indian caught in the open. I gaped at their pale city faces. They gaped at wild Bridget with butcher blood up to her elbows. I goggled at those strange close bodies, at those strange clothes, and smelled an unfamiliar and not altogether pleasant scent. They goggled and they probably smelled . . . whatever I was.

Friend, I was terrified, no bull. After all our running and hiding, I had done a dumb thing and the worst had happened. Believe it: if they had rushed in to club me, I'd have felt no surprise. With luck, I could dash through the circle and escape—I had the speed over them, I bet—but my bones locked tight on me, the traitors. And I should have copied Dylan's greased tongue: "Hi, fellas, great morning, huh? Hiking out? If you come across my dad around the bend, tell him to hurry because I'm tired of sitting by this mess. Isn't this blood awful? I can't wait to get back home and stay in the shower for three weeks." Except no tongue would work, not Dylan's or mine either. The savage was voiceless.

Our mutual fascination, and silence, lasted until it grew into too heavy a burden to hold up. One of the men, wearing a hunter's safety vest which was colored fluorescent chartreuse to show up a mile away, spoke out: "How did you kill this thing?"

Not only did I fail to answer, but my eyes avoided the deer, admitting nothing, registering nothing. The fellow repeated his question, louder, and I repeated my blank face and now all their eyeballs did triple duty in scurrying over me, searching for clues, wondering about the headband, a redtail's satin-sheened wing feather tied dangling from the band (a luck charm), some whipcords of buckskin in a sash at my waist, those repair patches sprinkled over my pants, and my darkened skin.

A different man moved closer, tall, lanky, with gold-rimmed sunglasses of the airplane pilot's variety. "Miss?" he said. "Miss, can you hear me? Pardon?"

"She's not hearing it, Matthew," came an opinion.

Matthew with his glasses kneeled down right before me and positioned his eyes in front of mine. "Miss, can you hear me talking?"

His eyes were ocean-water grey, similar to Dylan's, I recall.

The chartreuse one said, a little pained, "What the hell is this?"

"No deal, Matthew, something's wrong," came the opinion again, from a man that politeness would call chubby.

Matthew puzzled for a minute, trying to read my history in my eyes, before he resorted to sign language, pointing to his mouth, flapping his fingers like lips in speech. "Talk?" Shaking his head he pointed at my mouth. "No talk? You no talk?" He poked a finger inside his mouth, and wagging his blondish head and raising his blonder eyebrows, formed with his lips a big silent NO?

Neither a ripple nor a glimmer emitted from deadpan me. No. Me NO talk.

"Why she's *deaf,* you guys," exclaimed a voice from behind me, with a touch of pity.

The chubby one disagreed immediately, in high-pitched, scratchy upper-C tones. "I know a deaf person," he said, "a cousin of my wife's, and a deaf person that old would be signaling with her hands or at least with her face, and probably would say a few words to us, because they can make sounds. I can most times understand the cousin when she goes slow."

"This is weird," said the chartreuse one, ungraciously. "I tell you, weird. Look at her—come up here close—see? You never saw anyone like her before."

He was shushed by two or three of the others. "Don't say that in front of her," cautioned a man who turned out to be the palest and mildest of the lot, and the thinnest. "We don't know what may have happened to her up here, Russ, or if she needs some sort of help." He reminded me of what an ideal minister should look and sound like, an Episcopalian minister, for example, although I overheard later that he did something at a Wells Fargo bank.

But Chartreuse Russ didn't shush too well. Stubbornly he said, "Nothing's getting through to her in the first place, absolutely nothing. Well, is it? And go on and tell me I'm not right about how odd she looks."

No backtalk there from anybody, and their ring of six tightened around me to study better just what they did have. Sitting without my coat, in only a rolled-up shirt, I still could feel my spine and forehead sprout sweat. What next, Bridget?

"What's your thinking, Matthew," asked Chubby in his skinny voice, "search her?"

Since "search her" can become "strip her," I was considerably relieved when Matthew gave a firm negative. "Besides, the pockets are all gone from her pants," he said, an accurate observation.

Then the minister remembered: "Where did the other one go?"

The staring swerved from me to him.

"The big furry one."

"What?"

"Big. Furry-like. Or lots of hair." My so-called minister cleared his throat, a nervous *hum* and an embarrassed *haw,* asking himself, possibly, if he had been seeing strange visions. "Furry, like a bear standing up, sort of. Up on the slope behind us there. Didn't anyone else . . . ?"

Fortunately for the minister's sanity in the years ahead, Matthew had also seen Bridget's mate.

"What the hell is this?" demanded the chartreuse-breasted Russ.

When everybody turned to scan the canyonside, I felt tempted, too, because I knew Dylan's exact location. Naturally I didn't, and naturally in any case there would be no bear and no Dylan (for sure) to spot.

"Okay, what was it?" they questioned Matthew, who had already returned his attention to me.

"*He* not *it.*"

Chubby said, "Wait. He? You mean *hers?*"

"I suppose."

You got it, guys—mine. Bridget, Dylan, us.

"Human, all right," seconded the minister.

From over my shoulder was asked, "How about that fur you saw then?"

"She was waiting for him," said Matthew, a trifle impatiently, "whoever he is, whatever he's wearing. They were dressing out this deer when we showed up. But he won't come back with us here, is my guess, or he would have before now."

"He's up there watching us, this very minute, isn't he," the minister realized, slack-jawed.

That caused a stir, some uneasy turning of heads, and triggered a muscle in Chartreuse's vocal cords. "What the hell is this?"—more a complaint this time.

"You already asked that," said Matthew, apparently the owner of some common sense, and humor to boot.

"So what's the answer?" Timid, this chartreuse one wasn't. "Who are these two and what are they doing here together and where do they live for chrissake? And what'll we do with this girl now that we discovered her?"

A few hardy late-autumn flies were finding our deer meat, which thanks to Bridget was not in sanitary wrappers and on its safe way to safe Secret Creek. That deer belonged to us, and our stomachs, not to the flies for a wasted killing. Its dried blood not only caked in the hairs along my arms, but made the usual rose-brown ritual stripes across my cheeks, crinkling the skin.

"I feel," decided Wayne, my minister, "that this girl might need special help. Medical. Uh, perhaps even"—significant roll of his eyes—"psy-cho-logical testing. We can't just leave her in the mountains like this. We have to check into her, for her own safety, you see. It's our responsibility—"

"Wayne is right," interrupted Chubby. "We need to check this out, find why she doesn't speak the language, find out things."

"Does everybody agree," Matthew asked, taking count, "she should come back with us, willing or not?" When everybody did, he too agreed, counting himself in, sinking me and disappointing me, because for some reason I had been depending on him to lay the others low with a mighty civil liberties speech and turn me loose. I had a desperate hunch he would. But he only added his own interpretation of Bridget's condition: amnesia. She may have, he ventured, "suffered some powerful shock" and now she was "like sleepwalking in order not to remember what happened."

That appealed to the minister, who then wondered what the "shock" could have been.

"A dozen possibilities," said Matthew. "Kidnapped? By the other one?"

On that jolly note, they formed a bodyguard around me, raised me to my feet, and began herding Bridget away. I figured they would carry me—handle me—if I went limp, so better to zombie along with them. All six arranged themselves into a close escort: the minister-banker called Wayne, Chubby the balloon man (shape, not sales), Russ of the chartreuse vest, biblical Matthew, who could easily pose for an American Airlines ad, and the two voices from behind my back—both those men, it chanced, wearing fluffy goose-down jackets identical in kind and color to our stolen pair. I labeled the last two men Goose-Down One and Goose-Down Two.

"What about the deer meat?"

"The other one will pick it up—leave it for him."

"Say, would he follow us, do you think?"

"You reckon?"

"Far?"

No one knew, and I wasn't telling.

"Does she want to wash off that blood?"

"She's not much used to washing, I'd guess."

"Give her an opportunity."

Matthew led me to the river, but I preferred not to bend and wash. Let them get a good eyeful and noseful of deer blood on a Trinity Indian. Matthew leaned his head next to my empty sleepwalker's face. Speaking quietly, almost privately, he said,

"I have a daughter about your age." He sounded apologetic, as if we had a secret between us and he had been caught breaking it. "Your parents must miss you . . . want to see you. I know. At least they need to talk with you."

I hadn't answered before, and I didn't answer now, especially that. And the entire trip downriver I spoke not one word, like a proper captured Indian. It occurred to me I might live a hundred years in the white man's world and never hear my voice again.

ii _____ We clomped downstream in the custom of true greenhorns, turning stretches of gravel debris into pure racket, barging snap-crackle through thickets when a comfortable game trail waited twenty mere yards away. It embarrassed me, frankly. I almost heard snickers coming from inside the brush and from the shadows of trees, wherever we passed. The jays never bothered to announce us, because why mention the obvious.

I learned that the men had begun their journey up north, but despite it being downgrade the men suffered some with their packs, which were full enough to supply a Mt. Everest expedition and were topped off by family-sized tents, no doubt de-mothballed from basements back home. They took pauses for lots of load shifting, muscle rubs, sitting. Don't blame me if I never once sat or rested. I admit to the pleasure of rubbing it in: tireless girl watches grown men get pooped.

When we went into motion, they convoyed me in the famous stagecoach tradition—two men in front riding point, two alongside riding shotgun and sandwiching the gold (Bridget), and two behind guarding the rear from attack. Chubby/Chartreuse Russ formed one pair, the minister/

Goose-Down One another, and Matthew/Goose-Down Two the third. Since each set on occasion traded its position in the convoy, I got educated by all three.

Aside from troubles with their heavy packs, the group was in light spirits and pleased with itself. They had the definite earmarks of a successful safari (to jump from stagecoaches to Africa) with bubbles of excitement rising to the surface. They were bringing back, undamaged, a rare Mountain Patched Bridgeticus for the zoo. The main reason the pairs rotated positions, I suspect, was to allow equal turns walking beside this Bridget animal and equal chances to examine her. They came, they examined, they talked.

The minister (also known as Wayne) and Goose-Down One (a.k.a. "Pud") made a cute couple, and if a few cells had gone in a few other directions early in one of their lives they could have been destined for fifty years of harmonious matrimony together. First the minister sermonized, after which his partner would nod appreciation or ask a half-fried question, after which the minister was pleased to preachify again. Round and round it went.

Flanking me, Goose-Down One listened while the minister, on my opposite side, spoke. "Think for a minute of what we have here," the minister said, turning his thin face edge-on toward me. Obviously he no longer saw any need to protect me from overhearing cruel revelations—if this girl might be refusing to hear, she therefore will not *over*hear. "We have here a hidden tragedy of some kind or another, Pud."

Goose-Down One acknowledged the point.

"It's buried right inside her, and I'm sorry to say we can't reach in and pull it out for her. Only she can do that."

"Only she can do that."

"And she might never . . . that's the sad part of it. It could be too late—just too deep or too big to handle."

"It could be. One of those it could be."

"Think a minute—" The minister actually stopped short, putting us off stride. "What, Pud, *what* caused this?"

We all thought as we fell back into step.

"I can imagine the case, I'm afraid," said the minister. "I'm afraid so. Born illegitimate. The mother drags her daughter along through a string of boyfriends, then into a botched-up marriage. Everything's stacked against the kid. The husband beats the wife, and the daughter watches. Next he starts to hit the daughter. Then it happens, Pud."

Our footsteps rattled during the suspense. Goose-Down One asked, "Then it happens?"

"Whatever breaks her."

"Whatever breaks her."

"It must be awful. He murders the mother. Or he does something to the girl almost as painful."

"Almost murders her?"

"No, no, you know what I mean—sexual. And so she runs away, out of her mind. She goes to a strange town, maybe even ours, Pud, Santa Rosa. She needs a friend. She's only a child, Pud. And who finds her? Someone finds her, all right, but who would bring her way out here to grow up into— I know who. Some loony as cracked as the Mad Hatter. This poor girl. What will become of her, Pud?"

The minister's voice went wobbling out of control, so I believe he meant what he said, and felt it. Somehow he reminded me of both my aunt and the Pacemaker. He was soppy, à la Charlene, but solid of heart, like her. He was a pushy do-gooder, à la Mrs. Pace, but at least, like her, not a do-badder.

Goose-Down One had a comment to make, and he made it.

"I wonder if the big one back there, fur and such, the one you spotted, has a family connection with the Big Foot from the papers, that Sasquatch monster thing."

The minister and Goose-Down One were replaced by Chartreuse Russ and squeak-pitched Chubby (a.k.a. Lennie). Chubby had his very own Bridgeticus theory fully prepared —laid out and notarized. No idle mind for him on this trip. He called, in a cagy voice about to burst with good news, "Russ, hey. Better comb your hair and polish your shoes."

Old Chartreuse was watching me—sticking close as a tick. "Why?"

"Because I expect we'll be in the newspapers by tomorrow, and in the schoolbooks by next year."

"How so?"

"Remember when we found her you said to us, *You never saw anyone like her before.* Remember?"

"Sure. And it's the truth."

"Wait, now." Chubby all aglow, pressed in, the better to deliver his good news, speaking directly across my face. "You said it right that first time but we didn't know *why* it was right. We never saw anyone like her before because nobody like her exists nowadays. Nobody."

"You mean—?"

"I mean this girl is some throwback, some freakish throwback, an undiscovered Indian. No joshing now, a wild Indian. My wife took anthropology classes and I read enough myself, count on it, to fit the pieces together. How it ever could happen is amazing. A group of Indians might have retreated up here into the mountains to keep away from the Spaniards. A tiny group like that could learn to live here. Mountaintop life. Always on the slip. Over the centuries maybe a few glimpses of one, from a distance, but too far away for anyone to suspect the facts. Okay? The new generations born up here are pure Indian again—language, customs, everything, the complete works—and they learn what the anthropologists call a 'code of concealment.' Probably it gets built into their religion, like: if the Blue-eyes see you, your spirit loses its path to eternal paradise. Only some bad years come, with too many Blue-eyes interfering with the hunting. There's hard weather, not much food, and no more babies. The last pair alive starts taking chances, stealing clothes and a little grub, hunting in the valleys . . . in the open . . . in the daylight. And then, Russ, then one morning *we* nab the female. After centuries, one morning *we* stroll by and bump into the discovery, lucky us. Next *we* copyright *our* story —title it *Rendezvous with Yesterday,* I already got it planned— and peddle it for real bucks to the newspapers, and TV, magazines, a publisher, movies even. If we stick together, hold our ground, it's worth goooold.''

Chartreuse Russ had a practical bent. He asked what became of the parents of these last of the wild Indians.

''Dead,'' Chubby said, discouraged by such slowness from his comrade. ''Look, the girl doesn't know a word of English, right? And if she signals to us or recognizes us she breaks the taboo. Her store clothes? She had to pick them up from sheds and clotheslines and dump heaps, to keep warm, but notice how the native trappings mix in.'' Chubby urged his voice from its normal high to higher still. ''And think about how they killed that deer without a gun. Hell, look at her skin and those *Indian markings on her face.*''

But Chartreuse Russ wouldn't rise above lukewarm for this latterday-Ishi business. He had already latched his personal attention back on me, anyway, and hardly needed the advice about looking at Bridget. Understand, Chartreuse's boredom with Chubby's claims wasn't from disagreeing with them so much, no. With his practical mind, Chartreuse just brewed his own brand of enthusiasm. When he looked at me, whatever he plainly saw, I plainly was. Too bad for me, since he liked what he saw.

"Lennie," he said, "I do see her skin."

"Well, then."

"Nice."

"Huh?"

With a rakish maneuver of his eyebrows—Sheik of Araby —Chartreuse made clear what "nice" meant.

"Oh," said Chubby, "yeah."

"You don't think she is?"

"Sure. Sure she is." Chubby was suffering decompression bends from this rapid veer in the conversation's atmospheric pressure.

"Nice eyes."

"Yeah."

"Beautiful hair. You think?"

"Right."

"Right. And she can sure fill out a pair of pants."

Meantime, I was struggling not to crawl inside the nearest hollow tree or to attempt some hipless, unisex walk which would show that the sleepwalker had her ears open.

And Chartreuse Russ had more presents in his chartreuse sack of fluorescent compliments. My hands, my shoulders, my lips were all very nice. In summary, it would be "a helluva waste to leave her buried in these hills."

That was Chubby's same feeling, from an anthropological viewpoint.

"The female shape evolved to be admired by men," said

Chartreuse, "and it's natural to enjoy looking at a girl who turned out . . . who turned out the way evolution intended she should."

"Well, right."

Miss Evolution toed the line, in her natural glory.

"She may not be clean, Lennie"—chuckle—"but we can always buy soap and water cheap."

Clever.

After a spell Chartreuse Russ remarked, half to himself, his humor gone, "Notice she's wearing nothing under the shirt. You can tell."

Chubby had noticed. "Indians didn't," he explained.

They lost their front-row seats, for the while, to the photogenic Matthew and his marching mate Goose-Down Two (a.k.a. Wynn or maybe Flynn). Matthew seemed to have fallen into an untalkative mood, leaving the conversational load to Goose-Down Two, who was the neighborly, service-club sort who got restless in a social vacuum. The farther we went, and the less successful the dialogue, the more he chattered. But he had an honest, please-like-me smile and ditto his timid brown eyes, which could belong to a friendly lapdog. Whatever he sold in his office back in town—insurance, was it?—I'd trust him to sell without baring any fangs.

Goose-Down Two was in the process of reviewing their schedule—how tonight would be the final night of camping out before they hit the highway later tomorrow. On schedule. As planned. Esther (his wife?) would be waiting at the village with the station wagon and probably a six-pack of cold beer. As planned. "We did fine," he said.

Matthew agreed.

"Great fun, too, incredible scenery," said Goose-Down

Two. In about a week his film slides would be ready, three rolls' worth, and then the club and everybody could see proof of their trip—in color. "We'll remember this, I bet, for years to come," he said. "Of course, who could have known about finding the girl? *That* we didn't plan for."

Matthew agreed.

Goose-Down Two sighed, clucking his tongue. "Matthew, I got a little eager with the camera at the first. Dadgummit. There's not one shot left to take a picture of her, not one, can you believe?"

Matthew believed.

"Can we all cram inside the station wagon tomorrow? It makes . . . eight of us, you know, with Esther. Now hold it. Where the devil do we take her tomorrow, when we get back. Somebody's house, you think? Matthew, we both have daughters about that age, but is it legal to do that, I wonder, you know? Maybe no? Should she go straight to the police station then?"

Matthew believed not.

Goose-Down Two agreed. "I'd hate to see her locked up or something, if we have any other choice. Regardless of Lennie's cousin or his wife's, or whoever, I still claim she might be deaf and dumb. She could even have been abandoned here when she was only a child, because some parents can't manage situations like that, with handicapped children."

Matthew had doubts.

"I'll tell you what we got to consider," said Goose-Down Two, ominously, "and deep down, really, I feel this is the answer. I have this suspicion when I look at her face, Matthew. It's her blankness. She just might be one of those brain-damaged people. It would unravel a lot of the mystery about her, and the other one, the one you saw."

No response from Matthew, taking lanky-legged strides and not noticing Goose-Down Two, or me.

"Matthew. Things on your mind?"

The different tone registered, and he did look over. "I guess so. Sorry."

"The girl?"

"In a way."

But he offered no more, leaving me hanging, curious, along with Goose-Down Two.

iii _____ I heard the Notch before they did, although they heard it soon enough, to judge by their quaking knees.

"What the hell . . ." said Chartreuse Russ.

Another turn in the canyon and the gorge presented itself, the same towering walls, with river flush against rock, same whirlpools, same thrashing whitewater, foam, same echoed roar. The Notch was running a heavier flow again, but not yet like in the spring or during a storm, and the lower ledge still stood above water, free for a trail.

End of the stagecoach ride. All six men bunched up, a flock of nervous sheep afraid they might get sheared or, worse, might float away in a mutton stew. They held a conference to re-readjust packs and discuss strategy. One said, You go here and I'll go there. Another said, We'll go there and you go here. Another said, He'll go here and they'll go here. Another said, I'll carry this, you carry that, and when you go here he'll go there and I'll go there while they go here.

A long nervous chorus of that went on before we started across. The minister, pale under the best of conditions, now had faded into transparency—candlelight would shine through him. Matthew's face matched his own blonde hair. When we reached the ledge and creamy spume was spraying up with the surges of the current, splattering our clothes and greasing the path, Chartreuse began cussing a chartreuse streak, but the rapids smothered most of his words. Chubby seemed to be saying, "*Yeeeeeeee.*"

Everybody acted surprised when we made it to the other side alive, and as we resumed the hike, Goose-Down Two said, aside, to Matthew, "She didn't bat an eye, the whole time."

Downriver again, stagecoach again, and the afternoon shuffled off into shadows and a lavender sky. At the river's fork—the old fork—the men built a fire along the bank and unloaded for their last night in the wilderness. With center poles and guy-ropes and metal stakes, the big camping tents were tugged, tipped erect, and pounded into life by hatchets ringing against the steel stakes. Bustle was the enjoyment of the hour. Wood was being chopped, and stones were lugged up to circle the fire, and a cooking grate made an appearance, receiving a fresh layer of crackling tinfoil. From the crammed packs came cans and cartons and boxes and bottles and tins and bags of food.

"A farewell banquet," was the general cry. "Cook it, don't carry it. Eat everything but tomorrow's breakfast. Hoorah."

Pots began to bubble, pans to simmer, and then smells laced the twilight air—a mixture of memories unfamiliar at first and almost without names. Just a moment. Yes, biscuits. Yes, beef—beef stew with seasoning—salt, pepper, garlic. Potatoes. Gravy. Noodles. Cheese. Eggs—a cheese omelet. Pork and beans. Corn. Soup—chicken, and cream of mushroom. Crackers, mixed. Chewy dates. Applesauce, with nutmeg sprinkles. Cookies, mixed. Candy, including chocolate bars. Tea, coffee, milk, orange drink.

I prayed for the dusk to hide my weakness, because I couldn't hold back my anxious saliva and the telltale swallowing. Jerky and pemmican may fill your belly, but not your imagination. Regardless, and although I hadn't eaten since breakfast, when they set a loaded tray down by me I didn't budge. Wasn't it still disloyal to eat the enemy's food?

"The girl's not eating," advised somebody, stirring up a response.

"What? She has to."

"Say, would she starve herself to death, the way captured wild animals can do?"

"Let's be careful. She must be hungry."

One by one, over the next minutes, the men managed to pass alongside and drop tempting tidbits on my tray. Even Chartreuse did. The aroma had me in a semicoma of faintheadedness. The minister knelt and delivered a sermon on the virtues of each individual morsel on the tray. He withdrew, hopeful. Did my enemies have to be so courteous with their torture?

But when the sky faded to a true night sky, and the dishes were being cleaned by firelight, my tempting tidbits remained untouched, cold. The minister was elected to escort the unconverted, unfed sinner to her tent, and he gave his head a sad wag with every step. As we arrived, Matthew exited. "All comfy in there?" the minister called after him. Then he patted and fussed with the tent flap, the very image of a (bony) mom lovingly fluffing a daughter's pillow, not unlike what my own mother had done. He was working up a sweet-dreams speech, I think, but let it go. "You get yourself a good rest tonight," he said instead, brightening his face and his tone, never quite losing faith—a rightful minister—that I might hear him.

Inside, alone, I smelled the hot food before I could see it.

And I must have been one of those fidgety wild animals, after all, because in the privacy of my dark cage, where nobody could watch me and where I could even avoid watching my own weak self, I ate. Gobbled. Slavered. It tasted as good as every smell had promised.

A bulky sleeping bag waited atop an air mattress, and stretching out on it reminded me of once being in a sailboat at sea, when my father still sailed as a hobby. Roll left—slap, slosh, dip, bob—roll right. My eyes made their best adjustment to the near-blackness and followed, on the tent wall, faint firelight designs. In the background, from around that fire, came snippets of songs, boasts, teases, bursts of laughter, the party sounds of men celebrating a game well played, their vacation and their feat well done.

Listening to them was like putting my life in reverse, and reliving the sounds of a family. Whoever out there owned this tent had kept his kids in here before, right where I was, during their summer camping. Those kids must have had fun in here. Family fun. This tent must have seen some good times, just the way I saw good times, back then. I heard, outside, the happy voices of the men. Outside voices from the outside world. Blurred by distance, and the tent, they seemed to be my father's voice, my father's voice when I overheard him talking in a nearby room. And why shouldn't they? The men were about my father's age. Father's voice, fathers' voices.

But, closer, much closer to the tent, there broke in two voices I recognized—Matthew talking to Chartreuse Russ. Although their voices were being held down, no more than whispers, they weren't soft.

"Instructions"—Chartreuse Russ was saying—"from who?"

"Me, to you. And I'll be checking."

"Wait a holy minute, what did you think I was doing here?"

"I think everything. I've seen you staring at her."

"Just what the hell do you mean?"

"I mean everything I say. Stay clear until morning."

"What the hell is—"

"Cut it."

Footsteps moved away. Other footsteps followed.

Quiet once more, with the only voices being the distant ones, garbled mainly, from the campfire. My unexpected visitors gone, I went back to waiting alone. I listened to the voices and the quiet, both. The mountain quietness was like sitting with an old gentle friend. We didn't need words to understand each other. But the voices were older than any old friend could be, and told me about my human self, whether or not I even wanted to listen. Chartreuse and the dopeheads had voices, just as much as Curly and Matthew did, and I did. We all had voices and we all needed other people, otherwise we couldn't be heard.

I found myself obeying an instinct, and I called forth my mother and father in my mind, to question them about these men and about what I should do. They came, standing in front of me, clear as could be. It had been a while and I searched them over. They seemed unchanged. Their child, Bridget, asked for help. Help me, one more time.

No. They just stood and stood—unable to speak, unable to hear. I was saddened into seeing that I had brought back only memories, not living images who could be a real part of my real life. My parents had their memories to give, with their past examples of themselves—which I treasured—but nothing beyond that. For any help today and for any tomorrow I had to ask Bridget, or Dylan, and I wondered if Dylan would have answers other than his One Big Answer, which was to wear his suit of armor, or whether he could ever risk pain again, for anybody.

So I listened around me, waiting, hearing voices and quiet, voices and quiet, hearing what was unusual and usual for me, blended.

Later, the campfire deserted, when I had only the quiet to hear, the soft *sssst* of a razory knife sliced down the rear wall. The nice tent took a nasty slit, like in the rescues you've seen in those cowboys vs. Indians films, except we were the Indians, escaping from the palefaces' teepee, and that's a switch.

World, Hello

i——————————————— There was part of a moon out.
In front of me Dylan crossed in and out of night shadows,
submerging and emerging, quick yet with no clumsy haste or
noise. I stuck close behind his shaggy vest, a jitteriness
fingering my spine, expecting a sudden shout, a rush of
chasing feet.

But the wild creatures were already away from the cage,
melting into the forest, and city slickers keep lousy guard and
sleep hard. When someone did give the alarm, though, and
they did wake, would they take after us? Could be, for a ways,
a mile or less. Probably they wouldn't bother much. Let the
Indians go, because you can't catch an Indian at night anyhow.
Tomorrow send out the helicopters and the National Guard
—the cavalry back at the fort—and have them do the
catching, if they can. Besides, Mrs. Goose-Down Two would
be waiting in her station wagon, and never let a Mrs. or cold
beer wait too long, the rules read.

So Chubby would mutter, "By god, those *Indians*," and kiss
farewell his fortune and fame.

The owner of the ripped tent would return it—sutured but
scarred—to his basement.

The minister would leave a prayer behind for lost Bridget,
wishing her to get found, someday.

Matthew would—what? I'd like to have known that answer. Whatever his feelings or thoughts, he would end up leaving along with the others, since they all lived out *there,* not in here, and they had their own daughters and sons at home.

Well, we were on our way back, too: not back home strictly, just back, up into those black mountains ahead that filled the dim sky. There we could hide, get swallowed by steep canyons and by the long green miles of trees, make secret paths between granite boulders, and one more time be Dylan's Ishi. Marching through the night I felt on me, in me, both the happy pull of escaping, and the unhappy push of a Trail of Tears. Pulling at me from the mountains came silent shouts of freedom, urging me to leave every complication, every burden, behind, and instead to cruise these canyons with Dylan and kick up my heels. "Come on!" the beckoning mountains shouted. "Hurry! Get away! You and Dylan, free, Indians, f-o-r-e-v-e-r! You and Dylan! You and *Dylan!*" But this pulling was at the same time a pushing, a hand forced against my back, a shove that hurt like sadness, making me want to slow down or even turn around on the trail, because I was pointed in the wrong direction. No use yanking out my compass, either. No compass needle could show the way for me this time.

And here we were again in another middle of the night, and another middle of a crisis. Why did so much heavy stuff seem to happen at night, starting with last March 26th? Think about it. Bad news came that night. We sneaked away from our homes at night. Our shaky passage up the Sacramento Valley—culverts included—we managed only because of night, and the same here, now, in the Trinities. What was this habit we had for night and flight? Dear darkness. Would darkness always have to be our special friend?

At the river's fork, we passed the identical spot where once we had stood with our new backpacks and wondered whether left or right mattered in the mountains. And again we stopped, but not because we were undecided about which branch to pick.

Dylan turned and his face asked, You okay?

I nodded. Yes, okay. What else could I tell him, my Dylan, who never failed to do his best to make me okay.

The two streams swooshed together, bumped, wrestled for a hundred feet before mingling into one indistinguishable flow. It made a pretty scene, day or night.

Dylan seemed to say, Remember this, remember when?

I nodded. Remember. If this girl can remember her second grade with you, Dylan, she certainly won't forget anything that happened with you later. I remember, Dylan. But now, what about now?

We followed the old remembered route, our old road into the deep mountains. It must have been midnight or after, and the full cold had settled down, so we walked a stiff pace to stay warm. Sweating has its uses.

Upstream we went, along the river, bending, turning with it. When we moved through brush and lost sight of the water, we could still hear its lisping sounds, talking to us, keeping us straight, and when we broke into the clear, the river would wave to us in the moonlight, its surface rippling like silver skin. After a while our legs began to pump and we knew the grade was getting steeper. The river got louder, running faster, rumbling over rocks, while the moon spotlighted the thrashing of whitewater rapids. We were strong. No Sunday hikers were going to match strides with us Indians. So long, Matthew, and assorted crew, say hello to your daughters and sons for us.

The more we walked, the more landmarks kept showing up in the night, looming into focus right before our noses. There came the Notch, an angry river punching against the cliffs and flashing its teeth in the moonlight—scary once, simple now for two mountain goats, even in the dark.

There came the forest-fire trees—which could pass for a woodland of telephone poles—and there came the spot where we had first been short enough on food to try eating a plant named miner's lettuce. (I'd say "miner's spinach" would be nearer the mark.) There came the big meadow, the arena for killing our first deer. On his way down to liberate me (yesterday? ten yesterdays ago?) Dylan had stashed here our latest deer, the butchered one that Matthew and crew had stumbled upon. I still wore the deer's blood, and Dylan did, and now we slung the meat over our shoulders. Nothing had changed.

There came the side canyon with the logjam across the front, creek water spilling through the wood, the same smaller canyon that had beckoned to us as a path to nowhere in particular and therefore was a better place to be. So we turned up there again, to lose ourselves again. Nothing had changed for us. Our lives were a circle, inside a circle of Trinity Mountains. The moon remained bright overhead, although the stars were gone, erased from sight by the beginnings of dawn. Another morning, Bridget.

"Look," said Dylan, motioning to the far end of the logjam as we climbed over it. A bobcat sat there, observing, altogether unperturbed. Did it recognize fellow beasts? Dylan tried a version of bobcat talk, and the bobcat blinked. "It says welcome back," Dylan interpreted. "Says it'd like a chaw of our deer, please."

I was becoming a little sick to my stomach, I discovered,

maybe from that deer meat, which was approaching the ripe side. But maybe not, because I had smelled lots worse before without it bothering me. Possibly my stomach was hearing about something that my head didn't know yet.

Going up our old canyon, every shape and step was familiar. Rocks and trees and the ground can be like buildings and signs in your city neighborhood—you don't actually need to see them or read them any longer to know what they mean.

The sky picked up blue and more blue. Dylan, I could see, was warming with the rising sun, and he began to walk so fast that I complained. I wasn't especially tuckered out, but my crazy legs for some reason suddenly wanted to go limp on me. Dylan gestured at each pool where we had fished in the creek, at the places where we had gathered firewood, and where we had run races up from the river, at a bluebird, a tiny wren, a stray pair of quail, of course at a lone, circling redtail. When the sun at last shoved itself above the mountain ridge, we had reached the little meadow and the remains of our first fortress in the wilderness. The cabin was down and scattered just as we had done it when on the fly that frantic day, the pieces now camouflaged some more by extra fallen leaves and twigs. The hatchery pond was the same. Balancing on the same rock piers, Dylan unwound his fishing line to catch breakfast. I gathered the usual dry moss, roots, branches. The same flint. The same firepit, untouched. But rising with the curls of campfire smoke was a difference.

After we had eaten the trout, while we were lying on the grass and resting in the sunshine, I heard myself tell Dylan that I was going back down the next morning, out of the mountains.

A fox sparrow gave a fancy trill.

"I mean it," my voice said. "I'm going back home. When the house gets sold, if it isn't already, I'll go with my aunt to Santa Barbara."

Dylan leaned up on the grass.

"Dylan."

"What? I was drowsing."

"I mean it, Dylan."

"Home. Did you say home?"

"Back."

"But you are home."

"I'm not. Where home is for sure, for me, who knows, but not here."

"Secret Creek is."

"No." I shook my head—kept shaking it. "No, Dylan, no."

"Did you say Santa Barbara?"

"Santa Barbara. Charlene's Santa Barbara."

Dylan analyzed me for a minute, sizing me up, trying to decide how serious this mutiny was, or if I had just opened a new chapter (raising the stakes) in our game of teases and threats. But the place and the timing were all wrong for games, and he asked slowly, "Do you mean it?"

"I do," my voice said.

"Do you *mean* it?"

"I do, I—"

"*Bridget?*" Dylan felt our difference now, this difference in our old meadow, and his face went white, taking a smack. I don't like to have my own face shocked with bad news that way—I hate it—and by god here I had done it to Dylan.

His saying "*Bridget?*" in that horrified tone made me quake, a guilty quake, like being a blasphemer inside a church. I admit being sort of surprised myself to hear Bridget speaking those blasphemous words to Dylan—about Santa Barbara —but then not so surprised, either. My sinking, weakening stomach and legs had known what was coming. The more I walked up the river, closer and closer to this canyon, the more they had known. And sitting in that dark tent down at the fork, listening to the men's voices, I had known. And listening to Dylan's picture of the future, during our Great Debates, I had known. And listening to Curly, I must have known. And earlier yet? Being who I am, very much my parents' daughter, probably I should have always known.

So I repeated, both surprised and unsurprised at my voice, "I mean it, I do."

Dylan analyzed me again, one of his jaw muscles popping, and said, "Those men, what did they say to you?"

"The men?" I asked a little dumbly, recognizing the message of that jaw muscle.

"Those six men, those six clowns in tennis shoes leading you away. That's it, must be. They fed you some bull and you bought it."

"No."

"It must be. I'm not stupid. The day before, you were Bridget, and now, the day after, listen to you. Did they say, 'Come back to the city lights, honey, no decent girl would live out here, in a cave, with a caveman'? Or, 'You have a whole future ahead of you, dear Young Thing, don't waste another precious day of it in these lonely mountains'? Am I close?"

"They said some stuff, but not very much to me."

"Why not?"

"Because I said nothing to them."

"Nothing? Not a word?"

"Zero. They thought I was crazy or retarded."

Dylan began puzzling, aloud. "What then. Something. What were they like?"

"The usual: a few decent, a few not, a few in between."

"So let me think. So we tear you out of their tent." To illustrate, Dylan tore out a vicious handful of meadow grass. "And we spend the night and the morning pushing ourselves up to our mountains. We sit down, catch our breath, look around and—why, lookee here!—we made a mistake. We walked *up*hill all that time instead of *down*. Or did *I* make the mistake, because, really, you wanted to be left in their tent?"

That Dylan, he could slice with more than one type of knife, and never before, in our entire lives, had he spoken to me with such anger. I said, "You know better. They were grabbing me off someplace as a prisoner, not letting me go on my own."

"So now. Bridget is going to find her own way three hundred and fifty miles . . . through forest and freeway, and get back home, if it's still her home, otherwise onward she traipses another three hundred and fifty miles."

Some cuts can be too sharp, even from Dylan, and I returned a cut in self-defense: "Mr. Boy Scout, are you the only pathfinder in the West? You bet I can get back. Bridget can get herself where she wants, when she wants." That was reasonably true (not whistling-in-the-mountains brave talk) and true mostly thanks to Dylan, although I didn't mention it to him. He already knew.

Dylan was hurt, and mad, but sarcasm never had been his style with me, and he sank backward on the meadow again, lowering his voice, talking to himself almost. "I'll be easy with you and you with me. Bridget, I know you can get back."

That sound of his! Oh, I identified that voice, although

many weeks had passed since I last heard it, many months. It was the dream-distance voice of Dylan, and I'll take him mad instead anytime, because he was locking himself away, alone, into his transparent shell. If that shell went shut I might still see Dylan inside, but never touch him.

I sat up tense, scared of things crumbling apart, when I hadn't even asked my most important question yet, my only question.

Up he leaned on an elbow, our eyes meeting.

"I'll go with you down to the Notch," he answered.

"I meant the whole trip. Come with me to the East Bay, or Santa Barbara. I want us to be together. You know—you've always said—we have to be together."

We looked at each other, but it was more than looking. Impossible to describe. Dylan came unlocked again, with his eyes wide, wide open for me, letting me in, and we, you could put it, kissed with our eyes. Never had we seen into each other this far before, or seemed so near, not even that night we were tucked inside one sleeping bag, faces touching, under the big moon.

Dylan said, nearly a groan, and hard to make out, "Stay here."

"What?"

"Stay right here, with me. Don't go. Never go. Please."

My eyes closed, crippled for an instant, and when I opened them his had shut, and his kept shut, tight, as if Dylan were asleep.

ii _____ Both of us did doze in the sun for a couple of hours. We were worn down from no sleep during the night, and from other strains that had more to do with tired minds than tired muscles. Sleep can be a good place to hole up and hide for a while.

When we stirred ourselves from the meadow bed, the holing up was over, and we automatically went into our Great Debate, realizing that it finally needed a winner, that a vote and a decision would have to come by day's end. This time it counted for real, not another practice argument or another evening of entertainment around the fire. The prize could be the ultimate jackpot: winning your favorite human being.

We were sitting by the pond. Dylan pointed casually at the water, but I saw his actual point, his message. (Who knows Dylan's mind better than Bridget does?) Look at the pond meant look at everything in the mountains, see what you would be missing, giving up, losing.

"Is this going to be Parable Time?" I asked him.

He shook his head and just pointed again. No parable required.

I understood that message, of course, and for a minute examined the afternoon sunlight as it slanted through to the pond's pebbled bottom without any surface glare. "Nothing that clean or clear about Santa Barbara," I said.

Dylan let the pond and the sunlight do his talking.

"Because there are people in Santa Barbara, aren't there," I went on, "and only mountain creek bottoms can be mountain creek bottoms, all clean and simple. People are muddy and complicated. But are we creek bottoms or people? Dylan, we belong with the people."

"The muddy people."

"Our muddy people."

"Mud is mud, even when it's your own mud." Dylan gave up on the pond and switched to me. "Put yourself with your aunt. Think ahead to next week, next month, next year. What do you see? Any difference from living with her last spring?"

A fair question. The honest and likely answer: "She'll be an old hen clucking and fussing over her dear chick. I'll be her little Dear again, her little girl again."

"Tell me."

"All right. I see . . . the two of us alone in her house in a dull, sleepy section of Santa Barbara. Dull, at least, if you're not there. Every evening Charlene talks about my folks, especially my mother. This dumps a load of depression on me each night and I carry it to bed. Every morning she tells Bridget what to eat for breakfast, how to dress for school, when to do homework, what college to attend, and never to stare at men."

"You're staring."

"Some guys I can't resist."

Dylan found a small flat stone, for water skipping. "Bridget, why go—from this—to her?"

"Because something occurred to me about Charlene."

"Oh?"

How could I explain to Dylan about my exploring reasons and excuses for Charlene being Charlene, when he had turned altogether sour on excuses of any sort? He only wanted heroes and heroines, not compromises or "sensible" explanations, not reruns of his *father and mother*. A bubble of panic formed inside me. Wouldn't it, really, be impossible to win the Great Debate? The world could never become what Dylan needed it to be. I said, "Something occurred to me about her, something obvious, but I never took it seriously before." Forward, into Dylan's silence I plunged: "Whatever Charlene did, she did to help me, not hurt me. She did her best. So if her best isn't very good? Can I expect her to do better than her best? That's what occurred to me: Can I complain if she did her hundred percent? Could *I* do more than *my* best, and what if somebody didn't think my best was so hot—say, if Charlene didn't? We take the best we can get. It must even itself out, get equalized, like some mathematical equation. Besides, Charlene is my mother's sister and my only family. She's probably still worrying about me. Not probably—she is. Maybe I feel sorry for her."

Dylan chucked his stone across the pond—five skips. "Your aunt. That's nice," he remarked, "very nice, a sense of duty. The catch is, it's fake. I can do without it, a fake family, a fake duty, and you could too. Come on, tell me, who changed your mind?"

"No one."

"Curly?"

"Curly made me think more."

"Not those men yesterday?"

"They reminded me that not all people are fanged monsters—just some. But no one changed my mind except me. Listen, you're right, nothing back there'll be any different, not Charlene, not the whole thing. The difference is that I can live in it now, without turning off the good with the bad."

Dylan, naturally, was appalled. "That's called fooling yourself."

"Why am I fooling myself but you aren't?"

Dylan picked out a thin pebble, working a firm grip around it with his finger. "Six or more hops and I win?"

"No bet." I bent and drank the cool water, my forehead damp, my panic bubble expanding inside.

"Bridget, you just said that nothing's actually different in the world. Okay. That I understand, but the rest I don't." He tossed the pebble. Six hops. "Remember . . . we cut out of that world once when it beat on us. We made a certain renunciation pact one day in a hamburger place. You remember. Why, Bridget, go back where we got beat on before?"

Lord above, that was Dylan, wasn't it? When Dylan swore an oath in April, he had the nerve still to mean it when spring had long gone, had been gone for centuries. Old elephant brain. Never forget, and particularly never, never forget a hurt and an oath against a hurt. I love that sonofagun for being stubborn, I do. Even when I disagree with him, and break the crazy oaths myself, I want Dylan and anybody else like Dylan to be around me, to have some things I can depend on.

But how in heaven can you reason with an elephant brain, a rememberer of hamburger-hut oaths? Along with my rising panic came desperation. I was plain afraid, and I had to break through, jar him into another view of the two of us. "Dylan," I said, pleading, "you don't, you can't, leave the world. Jesus, not the *world*. Wherever you go, the old world she trots right alongside, and let's not fool ourselves." I took a wincing breath before getting cruel. "Renunciation pact? Let's don't be kids."

"Is that what staying here means," he said, squinting at me, "being kids?"

No time for retreat now. "We can't mope around here, feeling sorry for ourselves, the rest of our years and years. What are we, self-pity freaks? What do we need, a fix of self-pity every morning to float us through the day?"

"Mope?"

"Pout, if that suits better."

"Pout? Pout? Are we talking about no dessert after dinner, or no trip to the skating rink? Is that what upset us and sent us here?"

"No, but we act like it was. We act the way kids do when

they throw a pout and threaten to run away from home. Face it, you want to punish your mother and father. You want them to think *Whatever did we do to Dylan? Why did we drive him away? Forgive us Dylan for being so bad, so bad to you our wonderful child.*"

Dylan said, "Let me consider that," and he thought awhile. He said, "Yeah. If they felt punished, I might enjoy it. Sure. But, Bridget, that's a bigger *if* than you can ever realize." He combed four fingers through the tangles of his hair, thick whorls the color of tarnished copper that clustered at his nape.

My panic bubble halted, began to shrink, leaving me room to swallow, and I wondered, I hoped: Had I done it? Was Dylan unbending? Was this his first tiny step on his way back with me? "They do care about you," I said, pushing to make the tiny step a longer one, "and they worry. They must. Give them another chance. Be honest, don't you miss them, Dylan? You hardly ever take off their wristwatch."

But he only asked, "We act like kids, you said?"

"When we fool ourselves, fantasize."

"What is this? What is this fantasy and make-believe and kids business? It *happened* to us, Miss Bridget . . . or should I say Miss Pacemaker."

"Easy."

"Well, it happened. And you were the one who wanted never to forget. Or have you forgotten why we were at that table, choking down hamburgers, swearing vows? Have you?"

That was it, exactly. I told Dylan the thoughts I'd had last night in that tent at the river fork, how I could re-create an encyclopedia of details—my father's eyes peering down, like wise brown moons, my mother's laugh that always swished her hair—but how I had lost them, forgotten them, as being alive. They were memories, not flesh. I still felt every same feeling, the same love, a daughter's love, and the same loneliness, painful as a swallow of scalding water, but I had forgotten the life where their bodies could appear, could love me back, hold me, and make loneliness leave. I had forgotten, and I only remembered the dead. "My father, my mother," I said, "it won't matter . . . whether . . . I stand on the mowed grass over their two metal boxes or whether I stand in this meadow. There or here, it's finished." Bridget had at last salted away her own toughness. I heard words coming from me, ones without cracks or wavers, words bumping down a flight of stairs: "They can't come back, can't come back, can't come."

Dylan said, without expression, "Mine could have, but wouldn't. That's what this diddly world is—things that could be, should be, but aren't. Bridget, listen to me. The world out there, not here, is the fantasy place, full of kids. Look at how they treat each other." His fingers went from combing tangles to stroking temples, and his head bowed. "Strange. You were the lucky one, Bridget."

"Me?" My bubble was swelling again.

"It's a way to put it, lucky. Maybe your folks were killed before they had a chance to . . . I mean, while they were still what they should have been for you, before anything got spoiled. Now your good memory of them can be sealed up, *click,* all of you safe, money in the bank."

My jaw must have fallen open, because he added a helpful illustration: "Like a hero who dies in battle, see, who gets to be remembered only as a hero, forever after." I shut my mouth, tasting some truth behind that notion, but too little or too bitter a truth for me, unless toughness ever ages completely to hardness, which I hope mine never does. But I did learn a big truth: what Dylan's parents had done to him bruised deeper than even what my folks had done to me. Dead is dead and happens once. Alive happens each day. My dear, dearest Dylan, for him it must be like having a highway patrolman knock on your door March 26th of every year, year after year, and announce, very unexpectedly, that a Buick Electra—license RMJ 638—was zapped into a heap.

I spoke as gently as possible, tapping him on the knee so he raised his head. "You know, we're not Indians or redtails."

He inhaled a prolonged, patient breath. "We're not, but then we are."

"It's our imagining it, that makes *everybody* else the bad guys, the hunters, and us the hunted."

"No."

"Are we hawks and Indians, really?"

"Don't pretend to be simple-minded. The point is, our lives are Indian lives, or anyway what their lives were like once, when they tried to be free."

"Dylan, even Ishi came down from his hills."

"When they starved him."

"He needed people, just the same."

"Needed his killers? He needed food."

"Hey, Indians are people, aren't they, from the human race? Guess what, Indians botched up sometimes, too, with their wars and so forth, besides being decent other times, or lonely. What could Ishi do after what happened had happened, be an Indian but not a human Indian? And us, we are what we are and what happened also happened. Come on . . . let's put a period mark after it, end it, and head back together, the two of us."

Dylan slung a handful of pebbles into the pond, splashing out a circle of waves, and I swear he began to puff up until he seemed half-standing instead of sitting. His bulky vest shook like a furry earthquake, with its rectangles of rabbit, raccoon, squirrel, and a spot each of fox and possum. Maroon dots flared onto his cheeks, spreading until his face was all one splotch. "What I don't like, I leave," Dylan said, choking red-hot on the words. "When something makes me shake and vomit in the middle of the night, I leave it. Fathers hating mothers and mothers hating fathers, I leave." His head jerked backward —hair bouncing with the jolt—and frightening the birds in the meadow, and paralyzing me, he exploded: "I leeeve!" His wild eyes, wheeling, snatched at mine, and holy grief he did remind me of a hawk, ready to swoop and squeeze its talons. "Whatever stinks, I'm through smelling, and I won't smell. What's ugly, I won't see. I run. But where? Only two places, only two. I run away to the inside of my head, farther and farther inside the more I stay back there, or I run away to here. Don't you think here is saner?"

My debater's knees wobbled, putty at the joints, and I wanted to reach over and pull us together—whether to mother him or to wife him I can't say, both probably. When I did reach, so did he, and we fumbled and held hands. We could have been two tired swimmers grabbing a hold, keeping each other afloat in mile-deep water. "Who are you," I asked him, awed, my voice small in the silenced meadow, "Dylan on the Cross? The world won't be perfect so you elect yourself—nail yourself—to suffer and bleed."

While we held hands, his face regained its healthy, unsplotched tan. Finally he said, "You sound like Curly."

By now I was ground down by this debating, wrung dry. As far as I cared, the Great Debate could evaporate, disappear, blow away, and never reshape itself again. I just wanted my bubble of panic to disappear along with that debating, and for Dylan and Bridget to stay hand-in-hand, like this, and get on about their lives. But really I knew we were falling into a terrible, sickening stalemate. My panic wouldn't be blown away by a lucky breeze. I juiced myself up for another effort—more talk—and I told Dylan that I had a story to give him, my own Parable Time, one that would have Curly's approval wherever he might be.

I began: "There was this young man who went for a walk at night into the woods, or he dreamed it, but either way he believed what he saw. Apparently, he discovered Satan living in the woods, and he overheard that Satan was throwing a midnight party. Being curious, the young man hung around to see what an actual sinner looked like and what sorts of sinners would show up. Well, talk about getting an eyeful. What a parade. There was his favorite teacher, Miss Nice from second grade, greeting Satan with a leer and a pinch on the bottom. There was Uncle Herman, setting a goat on fire for fun. There were his father and mother, kicking and cursing each other. There was *everybody*. There was . . . his very own wife, married only a few months before. At that the young man blacked out, and when he found himself back at home the next morning, or when he woke from his dream, whichever, he was a different young man. The sight of his parents made him sick. His wife made him sick. And because he believed everybody was a sinner, and he despised everybody, he had no choice but to be sick of himself."

Dylan turned my hand over, stroking the back of it thoughtfully. "You always were a good student, Bridget," he said, "with such a good memory. I think we read that story during our freshman year English, right? Hawthorne's version anyway." He continued to stroke my hand, repeating once "Our freshman year . . ." He stroked, meanwhile peering down at my skin like concentrating into a mirror of flesh, and pretty soon his caressing fingers moved from my hand up along the forearm, to my shoulder. "There's one hitch in your parable," he murmured, "that makes it wrong for me." Both his arms circled out, wrapped me inside a tight embrace, pressing me against the gentle fur of his vest, with my face tucked into the hollow between his neck and chin. "One person I will never despise. I'll never despise her."

His voice pierced me—as much as any hawk's talons. I wanted to ask the question oozing out from my puncture wounds: What *does* Bridget mean to you, then? The opposite of despise, the opposite of hate?

I was through with the debating and arguing. And no more parables and stories. Enough. It was time to say what mattered. It was time to say what I had always longed to say, ever since back in grade school, but never quite could. Directly into the warmth of Dylan's neck, by his ear, I told him that I *loved* him.

When Dylan didn't answer immediately, my bubble of panic burst, but for the wrong reason. His pause (so short, so loud) showed me that it was too late for panic, too late, that he wouldn't say "I love you, Bridget" and stick with me. I knew he did love me—I felt his hug clutching even tighter at me—and I believe he would gladly have admitted it aloud a year earlier, or thereabouts. Just too late, Bridget. Injected now into Dylan's survival instincts was a new rule: DANGER. LOVING IS HAZARDOUS TO YOUR HEALTH.

"I think about Secret Creek," Dylan said, explaining himself, "and rain falling down through the firs, and sun falling down on bare rock, and about everything else you can see around us right here. It's better than me, Bridget, and better than whatever's waiting for me back *home*, unless you go back there. Don't make it hard for me. I can feel you making me weak, damn you."

"Come with me, damn you."

We both smiled—sort of.

iii _____ Afternoons don't amount to much in the mountains when autumn is on its last stumpy legs. Already the pond had turned blank with shadows, the pebbles and sand hidden underneath, and birds had flown to treetops, soaking up the final minutes of sun. A border of sunlight slid up the trees, went higher to only the trees on the eastern ridges, went beyond the ridges to only the highest mountains, alpenglow, and finally beyond alpenglow to only the clouds. The canyon gathered together darker and darker shades of twilight, cool then cold.

With our blankets and sleeping bags up at Secret Creek, for protection we built a windscreen of branches, and inside we piled an all-night mound of firewood. In case of any spotter planes we propped a shield canopy, extra dense, over the fire. Meanwhile, we just talked about the business of setting up camp, and the differences between this time and the first times, last spring, at this same spot. When we finished it was night, and we stoked the fire and ate another meal of trout, cooked on green-willow spits. Elsewhere across America, no doubt, light bulbs and televisions had been snapped on and the night was young, but here we obeyed the cycle of the sun, which told us to sleep now and rise with the light.

We lay down by the fire and although I was plenty tired my eyelids refused to drop. I wanted to get through again to Dylan but didn't know what to say. Hadn't I said it all? And there curled Dylan, next to me, a half-roll away, less than an arm's reach. Did he want to talk? Sure.

From the dark around us . . . familiar night sounds. Mice skittering through leaves. Melancholy owls, hooting patiently inside the black hoods of trees, waiting for the mice. The short, high bark of a fox. An answer from across the canyon. Deer—those slight, slight rustling steps—coming to the meadow to feed. Raccoons probing the edge of the pond, splashing. Far away, the sharp yapping of coyotes, running and frolicking along a ridgetop. No insects—too cold. But a breeze rubbed over acres and acres of evergreen foliage. And many voices of water: silken, rolling sounds, trickling bell sounds, lapping and slurping sounds on rock, gurgles, murmurs, whispers, almost speech.

Not almost—the sounds *were* speech. If you should ever wonder why you grew large ears, leave your bright house some night and go get yourself surrounded by quiet and a few trees and bushes. Sit down and be still. You'll *hear*. The language can be scary or strange in the beginning, until you go to school, the way Dylan and I did, and you discover its dictionary of special meanings.

The way Dylan and I did. Do. Did. Do. I looked, and he seemed to be asleep. Are we past or present tense, Dylan?

Our campfire flames burned low, depositing a heap of charcoal logs as glowing and intense as hot steel ingots. The logs shone clear through, burning from the inside and outside both, and colors wavered, pulsed: flickers of electric blue, flashes of pale yellow, orange, pomegranate red. Patterns and shapes appeared, disappeared, reappeared. Enchanting, and it never failed to relax me with a mental massage. I felt safer right now, under the open sky, than I would back between walls and under a roof, with engine sounds groaning by outside, me there, Dylan here. He had this mountain language and I would have to relearn the old one of the city.

I tried to visualize a night, or a day, or talk, or touch, without Bridget and Dylan together doing them. I couldn't, not yet. We were each other's constant habit. Would I find any handy replacement to fill Dylan's vacancy? Sorry, no handy Dylans. You could search the entire haystack for the needle without finding another one like him. I leaned up on an elbow, to see my in-the-flesh Dylan, to see the person who had taught me survival, and not only Trinity Mountains survival but how to stay alive after dead parents. It would be so easy to reach out (this instant, while I had the chance) to shake him awake. I could say, "Trust me. I won't ever hurt you, Dylan." And if I did wake him, and if he held me, telling me about *us*, about love, without being his cautious Dylan self, and if and if . . .

If that happened, then I might perfectly well be going up to Secret Creek with him in the morning. Except it wouldn't happen. What an upside-down mess we were, when you considered us for a second. Here was Dylan, with his super yearning for independence, who had to buy it by giving up the one person he still wanted to depend on. And here was Bridget, practicing her so-called common sense, who in order to rejoin people had to leave behind the one person she cared about most.

I slept, waking once in the wee hours. The campfire had reduced itself to a big nest of embers, a circle of light in the night, mirroring the moon overhead. Sounds were fewer. Peaceful. Peaceful, and I was drowsy, yet the slumbering center of my consciousness suddenly gave a lurch, fastening onto shivery questions: Would I ever see Secret Creek for even a last time? Was it the finish of sleeping like this, waking like this? Dark trees, dark water, embers, moon, open sky, wild mountains, wild Bridget—never again? Should I shake myself completely awake, and stare and stare, memorizing every outline, every nighttime shade?

No need. It had already been memorized directly into Bridget's blood, weeks and weeks ago, and it would flow inside there, for keeps.

Cold trout and a handful of hazelnuts for breakfast. Campfire ashes covered with stones, like a hurried grave site. On the trail before sunrise, back down the way we had come up yesterday, back down out of our meadow, along the tumbling creek, over and around boulders, winding between the tall tree trunks. Full-fledged morning arrived. A dallying flock of golden-crowned sparrows flitted in the underbrush and sang. A chipmunk shrilled a warning, thrashing its tail. Dylan could have shrilled a reply—it was one of his better imitations—but he kept silent, and neither of us said much the whole trip. At the canyon's mouth, where the creek went spilling through the log barricade, no bobcat waited to signal goodby.

Going down the main canyon, by the river, we walked slower and slower. We studied white towers of cumulus clouds stacking up in the northwest, which might amount to rain later in the day. An invisible, soundless jet chalked a contrail across a blueboard square of sky: nowhere on earth, even Secret Creek, can you escape from those skywritings. We edged around the bends, in case there were fishermen or searchers ahead. We scrutinized mountain-lion tracks. We knelt to drink four, five times more often than usual. We sampled some

pinewood chewing sap. We poked in an abandoned burrow.
Fox.

But poke or sample, regardless, there in front of us
eventually stood the last bend before the Notch, and then the
Notch, full of splash and rumble. We crossed the lower ledge,
getting wet from the spray, and went on past the gorge, below
the whitewater, to a less noisy area. We had reached the end of
the line.

Dylan checked the clouds. "You'll be outdoors for a day or
so yet," he said, removing his fur vest, "and it could rain.
Probably will. Here."

"My shirt's wool."

"Take it."

"I can't take your vest, Dylan."

"Please, take it. I have everything myself back at Secret
Creek—the blankets, both sleeping bags, all the shirts, extra
hides. Here."

"But I can't. I look like I belong in a sideshow already, and
if I wore that into town, cripes, I'd be selling seats." My actual
reason: the idea of having Dylan's Trinity vest caged in a
bedroom closet someplace was too much to handle.

Dylan agreed. The vest went back on and his wristwatch
came off. "Hock this, or sell it, and hope you get whatever you
need for clothes or a bus ticket." He shoved the gold watch
into my hand. "The nearest bus might be Weaverville."

I told him my plan was to keep underground until
Redding, at least, because if they found me near the
mountains they'd suspect his location.

He said, in protest, "Redding? Why, that's a bitch of a
trek. We covered it by truck."

"I'll walk at nights."

"The police will just want to get my whereabouts out of you anyhow, wherever you turn up."

"I won't give it."

"You, lie?"

"No. Won't give it."

"Withholding information is against the law."

"Too bad. Sue me. Hang me."

Dylan chewed at his lower lip, thinking. "You won't have a bite on you once that chunk of venison goes. What about food?"

"I'll pick it, dig it, catch it, steal it. Same as always."

"Well, ain't she something. Okay. Except no hitchhiking."

"I remember last time."

"Pretty girls shouldn't hitchhike. Promise?"

"Promise, but you worry about me too much. This Indian can get there."

We looked at the sky again, at the clouds—now congealed into a solid horizon. Drifting in our direction, the clouds spelled the last of our recent sunshine treat, acting the part of a handy symbol about the two of us, the Trinity tribe.

"You'll get there," said Dylan. "I just worry because I'm selfish. You're not any old Bridget, you know. You're *mine*."

I understood absolutely.

Dylan asked, wistfully, addressing the sky mostly, "Why are we doing this?"

"I was about to ask you that," I answered. "We can't help it, or we wouldn't, Dylan, we wouldn't."

"Let me say one thing. I feel jealous. You have the guts to go where I'm scared stiff to set a foot. There's the final proof that my worrying over you makes no sense." He straightened himself, formally. "If the world starts chewing you up again, I'll be in a certain cave: same mountains, same address, your same empty sleeping bag. They'll never snare me."

"No," I said, "not you."

"Damn no."

"And . . . if you leave the mountains, Dylan, for a while—"

"I'll look in the Santa Barbara phone book, under Beautiful Indian Princess."

I tried some words.

"Bridget, hey."

It may have been close, but close doesn't count in crying, and I didn't, not quite.

After we had walked in opposite directions for a few minutes, I turned and saw him climbing through the Notch. From the distance, he appeared to be a genuine aborigine, with his warrior's hair and the animal furs, his easy strides, boulder hopping. What a shock he would give any stranger who saw him. The last of the white Indians. Now, on his return to Secret Creek, he dwindled from me, a smaller and smaller shape crossing against the huge granite wall—not turning around himself to look or wave. I waited to see if he would turn. But no. I believe he traveled through the afternoon and night, up the river, into the side canyon, up to the meadow—gathering the deer meat—on up and out of the side canyon, up Secret Creek and to the cave, before he once glanced back or rested.

"Dylan," I said aloud, although it was not possible for him to hear me, gone even beyond my sight, "someday bring the mountains down to the towns."

World, do the sad times ever end?

ABOUT THE AUTHOR

———————————— Dennis J. Reader was born in Santa Cruz, California, in 1939. He attended various California schools, receiving an M.A. in English/Creative Writing from San Francisco State College and a Ph.D. in Literature from the University of California, San Diego. His teaching experience has ranged from the third grade to graduate-school literature courses, with almost a decade spent as a university professor. He has served as an editor on both academic and literary journals, and his writing credits include scholarly articles and book-length publications, as well as poetry and short fiction in many periodicals. *Coming Back Alive* is his first work for younger readers.

Mr. Reader lives in the Santa Cruz Mountains of California near Watsonville, with his wife, three children (ages four, seven, and eleven), a D-4 Cat tractor, and an apple orchard in need of radical surgery.